Something Reckless

Also by Jess Michaels

Fiction

EVERYTHING FORBIDDEN
PARLOR GAMES ANTHOLOGY

Something Reckless

JESS MICHAELS

red

AVON

An Imprint of HarperCollinsPublishers

SOMETHING RECKLESS. Copyright © 2008 by Jesse Petersen. All rights reserved. Printed in the United States of America. No part of this book may be used or reproduced in any manner whatsoever without written permission except in the case of brief quotations embodied in critical articles and reviews. For information address HarperCollins Publishers, 10 East 53rd Street, New York, NY 10022.

HarperCollins books may be purchased for educational, business, or sales promotional use. For information please write: Special Markets Department, HarperCollins Publishers, 10 East 53rd Street, New York, NY 10022.

FIRST EDITION

Designed by Diahann Sturge

Library of Congress Cataloging-in-Publication Data.
Michaels, Jess.
    Something reckless / Jess Michaels.—1st ed.
        p. cm.
    ISBN 978-0-06-128397-0
    I. Title.
    PS3613.I34435S66 2008
    813' .6—dc22   2007047965
08 09 10 11 12 OV/RRD 10 9 8 7 6 5 4 3 2 1

This book is for every reader who has ever taken the time out of their day to tell me what they thought. I appreciate every comment.

And for Michael, my champion and best friend.

One

1819

"The woman must be stopped."

Jeremy Vaughn, the Duke of Kilgrath, looked up from his snifter of port with a frown as he watched his friend Anthony Wharton storm around the private room at Worthington's Club.

"What woman?" he asked before he took a long puff of his cigar.

David Forster, the Marquis of Chartsford glared at him. "Great God, Kilgrath, what do you mean *what woman*? We're talking about Penelope Norman."

Anthony nodded his head, his scowl deepening. "Exactly. The woman is a deuced menace."

Jeremy shrugged, grinding out the remains of his cigar in a sterling silver ashtray as he pictured Lady Norman. With her lithe frame, long, flowing blond hair, and turquoise eyes, Penelope wasn't exactly the kind of woman a man of his appetites could ignore. And even if he could, her recent crusade against the sensual excess of the men of the Upper Ten Thousand was making her the current talk of the *ton*.

Still, he could hardly believe she was worth all this ruckus. He came to Worthington's and met with his friends in order to avoid this kind of gossipy foolishness.

"How much effect can one woman truly have?" he asked mildly.

The other five men in the room all stared at him. These were his best friends. All men of means, aside from Ryan Crawford, whose father had cut him off years before. And all were men of appetites. They enjoyed every advantage their names and wealth afforded them. Especially ones that involved women.

They called themselves "the Nevers," a silly name coined by Jeremy's younger brother, Christopher, after a drunken night when the group of them had all vowed never to change or falter or love.

So far, only Jeremy's brother had gone against that vow. Christopher had married six months before, and was the only one absent from their meeting tonight. Jeremy winced at the thought.

Finally, Anthony gave an outraged snort. "How much effect? Are you bloody daft? The woman stole my mistress."

Jeremy bit back a laugh, but only because he knew the subject was a sore one with his friend.

"Come, Wharton," Ryan Crawford said as he leaned back into a leather chair. "That is exaggerating it a bit. You act as though

Lady Norman swooped in and kidnapped Fiona. Fi went of her own volition."

Nathan Ridgemont, the Earl of Dunfield, tipped his head back with a laugh. "Perhaps she thought this Penelope could satisfy her more."

Jeremy would have taken a moment to enjoy the spectacular image such a statement put into his mind, but he couldn't. Anthony lunged at Dunfield with a curse, and the room erupted in shouts as various friends grabbed for the scrapping pair. Jeremy caught Anthony by the arms and pulled him back as his friend struggled.

"Wharton," he growled. "Come on, you know Dunfield is only being an ass."

"And you aren't the only one who has suffered," Chartsford pouted when Anthony stopped fighting to be free and some semblance of calm returned to the assembly. "My wife, who was always so pliable and didn't give a damn where I went or who I went with, is now haranguing me night and day and demanding I give up my mistress. And all because of that wretched woman."

Jeremy released Anthony slowly and backed away. Wharton had become the closest thing he had to a best friend ever since Christopher abandoned him for the pleasures of hearth and home. Jeremy had a hard time reconciling this angry, red-faced man with the normally carefree gentleman he called a friend. Truly, Penelope Norman was more than just a mere annoyance for Wharton. She had come to represent the other man's deepest humiliation.

"What do you suggest we do about her?" Viscount John Lockwood asked from the corner where he had been sitting quietly, watching the entire exchange. He was the only one who had made no move to interfere with the fight.

Chartsford and Anthony exchanged a look that made clear what *they* would like to do to Penelope, but said nothing. In fact, it was Dunfield who stepped forward.

"There are six of us here," he said with a grin. "And we each have a certain reputation. Surely *one* of us could change her mind, put a stop to her meddling somehow."

"How?" Wharton snapped with a peevish scowl. "What is your plan, if you even have one?"

Dunfield shrugged. "Seduction is one way. It would open the door to blackmail or exposure."

"Seduce her?" Chartsford barked with an incredulous shake of his head. "Not bloody likely. She's not called the Ice Queen for nothing."

"Tried with her and failed, did we?" Jeremy asked as he tipped up his glass and took another slow sip of port.

Chartsford glared at him, but didn't refute the charge. As the other men began to debate the subject, Jeremy let his mind slip, once again, to Penelope Norman.

He had never felt the epithet of Ice Queen fit her. She might appear cold and distant at first blush, but he'd observed the young woman many times over the past two years. He saw her watching everyone around her. And sometimes, when she thought no one was looking, he saw a hint of burning lust in her pretty eyes. *Unsatisfied* desire, even before her husband tipped up his toes a year before.

No, Penelope Norman was no ice queen. Or if she was, she could easily be melted by the right man.

"Come on Kilgrath, draw a straw," Anthony barked, stirring him from his thoughts.

Jeremy looked at his friend in wide-eyed surprise. Some time during his private musings, his friend had collected a batch of matchsticks and was now holding out a fistful expectantly.

"You are not serious," Jeremy said as he stepped away.

Anthony advanced forward, his fist tightening. "Hell yes, I am! That little bitch Penelope Norman stole my mistress, and if she keeps up her crusade against men like us, it could be more than just Chartsford and me who suffer. I want her stopped. One way or another. And we are the only ones who have the balls to do it. Draw."

Normally Jeremy would have made some pithy statement, but since his friend looked so angry and serious, he refrained. Instead, he reached out and pulled a matchstick from the bundle. He winced when he saw how short it was.

Anthony smirked and moved on to Dunfield. Each man in their circle drew a straw, and each one was larger than Jeremy's. By the time Anthony opened his fist and revealed the last matchstick, Jeremy had already guessed the outcome of his friend's little game.

He stared at the short little stick in his hand, a thin piece of wood that had sealed his fate.

"You don't have to take Dunfield's ridiculous suggestion to seduce her," Anthony said as he threw himself into a chair and took a swig of whiskey. "You could threaten her. She's alone in the world now that her husband is dead. She only has one other association with any influence and that is her sister, Countess Rothschild. I have heard they've been estranged for at least as long as Lady Norman has been in London Society."

Jeremy paced to the fire with a shake of his head and tossed the splinter of wood into the flames. "I may be many things, gentlemen, but I've never been reduced to threatening a woman. No, I'm sure I can find many more pleasurable ways to convince the lovely Lady Norman that her quest against illicit sensuality is one she should abandon."

He stared at the flames as they devoured a log and thought about what he had been conscripted into doing. Seduce Penelope Norman for the purpose of manipulation.

He waited for a wash of dread or a slap of anger to fill him. But neither one came. Certainly, he normally bedded far more willing partners, but he had never turned away from a challenge.

And Penelope Norman was the ultimate challenge. Beneath her starchy exterior, he guessed there lurked a hypocritical, lustful woman. All he had to do was draw that part of her out. Once she succumbed to her own carnal desires, it would be easy to make her see how wrong she was to meddle in the affairs of others. Or, at the very worst, he could resort to blackmail, as Dunfield had mentioned earlier.

Either way, the entire seduction could be enormously pleasurable. Since Christopher had married, Jeremy had felt quite restless, even bored with his life. He'd parted ways with two mistresses in the past six months and had a decided lack of interest in the numerous opera singers, dance hall girls, and wicked widows who threw themselves at his feet.

Not that he didn't have his pleasure, but nothing felt quite the same. Yes, ruining Penelope seemed just the thing to put the spring back in his step.

"So what is your plan, Kilgrath?" Dunfield asked as he approached Jeremy with a fresh glass of port. "How *do* you intend to get into the Ice Queen's good graces?"

Jeremy smiled as he took a sip of wine. "My plan isn't complicated, gentlemen. I will simply convert to her cause."

Lady Penelope Norman stood in the corner of the ballroom, staring out at a sea of dancers who were swaying together to the music of the orchestra. Everyone around her looked so happy, so content.

And she was anything but. She felt . . . stretched. Sour. Sort of like an oddity on display. The feeling was entirely unpleasant.

"There, you see, Lord Billingham just snubbed you!" her mother, Dorthea Albright whispered, loud enough that everyone within fifteen paces heard her. "He is the tenth person to do so tonight."

Penelope sighed and didn't look at her mother. "Don't exaggerate, Mama," she murmured.

Her mother tugged on her arm and Penelope turned. Dorthea's round face was pink with indignation and her blue eyes, the ones that looked so much like Penelope's, were wide.

"It isn't an exaggeration! I have been counting." Her mother's fingers tightened around her arm to an almost painful degree. "Your behavior is exposing you to some pointed remarks and cutting you away from certain parts of Society."

Penelope pursed her lips. She hadn't even wanted to come to

this gathering, but Dorthea had insisted, saying the party was imperative to the future of Penelope's two unmarried sisters, Beatrice and Winifred.

Unfortunately, neither one of them were dancing. Which only seemed to upset her mother all the more.

"If you will not think of yourself and your own ability to obtain a new husband, think of your sisters. Your little crusade is hurting them by drawing the wrong kind of attention to you." Her mother suddenly released her and folded her arms across her chest. "Men like their wives to be pliable. Men like their wives to turn the other way. Men like their wives never to whisper the word," her mother's voice dropped, "mistress, let alone argue with him about having one. Penelope—"

Penelope rubbed her hand over her suddenly throbbing head. "Yes, Mother, I hear you. Half the room hears you," she hissed. "I'm getting a drink."

She pulled away from Dorthea before her mother could say another word and began to weave her way through the crowd.

How in the world had she become a crusader?

It was a question she asked herself at least once a day. She hadn't intended to become a voice against the sexual excesses of the Upper Ten Thousand. She had simply had a spirited discussion one day with members of her Ladies Aid Society. And then more women had wanted to talk to her about her thoughts on male behavior outside the bonds of matrimony. And then more.

Suddenly everything had snowballed, rolling out of control until she was being called a demon and a savior, sometimes in almost the same breath. There were men of the *ton* who hissed at her when she passed and women who squeezed her hand and told her how much they appreciated her "work."

Penelope shook her head. Well, it didn't matter how she'd gotten to this point. The fact was, she was now a voice against infidelity and rampant sexuality. And she believed in her cause.

She'd certainly seen and felt firsthand what kind of wicked power a man could wield with sex. Her life had been altered irrevocably by two men who did just that.

"Good evening, Lady Norman."

Penelope stopped walking, frozen in place by a voice she had come to know well, despite all her best efforts to avoid it and the man who owned it. She forced her expression into a chilly mask and turned to face Jeremy Vaughn, the Duke of Kilgrath.

Her breath caught, no matter how much she didn't want it to. That was something that always happened when she saw the man. He was beautiful. There was no other way to put it. With dark hair that curled lazily against his forehead, a harsh, strong jaw, sensual lips that seemed forever curled in a knowing sneer, everything about him was pure perfection.

But the one part that made him stand out, that frightened Penelope to her very core and also made her body shiver with a faint, undesired wanting, were his eyes. His dark brows and long lashes framed eyes that were the most striking green she'd ever seen. They were so dark they were almost emerald in color, and they sparkled with a sensuality that represented everything she was fighting against.

This man was sex and sin embodied. And he lived up to the things his handsome face and strong, well-formed body hinted at. Everyone knew his reputation, even the unmarried misses who were generally sheltered from such things. But who could look at him and not see that he was a man of lustful, searing appetites? A man who reveled in the attention of too many women to count.

Ladies of all rank and circumstance had thrown themselves at his feet over the years. There were stories that discreetly circulated about trysts in back hallways, sinful behavior at country gatherings, and even one public coupling on a London stage with a shameless actress when the play she had performed in was over and everyone had gone home.

This was her enemy.

And Penelope shivered as another little surge of desire made her a hypocrite of the highest order. Worse, Kilgrath smiled as if he knew exactly what she was thinking.

Penelope pursed her lips. "Good evening, Your Grace."

His smile widened, and the wickedness in his stare doubled as he let his gaze move over her in a lazy sweep. She fought an urge to fold her arms over her chest in protection and instead arched a brow.

"I admit I am surprised you are speaking to me, Lord Kilgrath," she snapped out. "Most of your friends are on the verge of throwing rotten fruit."

His smile fell a fraction and he tilted his head. "Yes, I have heard some whispers. It isn't often a lady of your rank takes up a cause at all, let alone one that affects the conquests of men of title."

"Perhaps it should happen more often." She shook her head. "I'm sorry to be rude, Your Grace, but if you have come to spit hateful words or threats at me, please refrain. I've heard enough to last me a lifetime. Consider your quarrel with me to be duly noted."

Turning on her heel, Penelope made to walk away, but before she could take one step, a strong hand wrapped around her forearm. She gasped at the feel of Kilgrath's touch and immediately spun back on him, breaking the distracting grip of his fingers.

"I apologize, my lady," he said softly, holding his hands up in mute surrender. "But you have misread my intentions entirely."

Penelope frowned. She had no trust in this man, although his expression seemed totally sincere. In fact, he appeared open and friendly. It was the first time she'd seen such a look from a man of his stature since she started her "crusade."

"Have I?" she asked, wary of giving him even a quarter.

He nodded. "May we speak privately?"

She sucked in a breath. Going anywhere private with this man was tantamount to stripping off her clothing and dancing naked in the middle of the ballroom floor. And he knew it.

"I am not some naïve little dancehall girl whom you can seduce, Kilgrath," she snapped, putting her hands on her hips. "You know the consequences of being seen leaving this room with you. If this is your plan to discredit me, it will not work."

He shook his head. "I'm not trying to discredit you, Penelope."

She jolted at the sound of her given name coming from his lips. It was as intimate as a touch. But before she could correct him, he continued.

"I'm trying to tell you that I support your cause."

Two

Jeremy smiled as Penelope's mouth dropped open and she stared at him in utter shock. Such a pretty mouth it was, too. One he could easily imagine closing around his length, or parting with a sigh of pleasure when he touched her in the most intimate ways.

Finally, she arched one fine eyebrow. "I don't believe you."

He stifled a chuckle. Damn, but he liked her spirit. No doubt she would bring a hefty dose of it to his bed when he finally had her there. He couldn't wait.

"I understand, my lady," he said, keeping his tone somber. "I have not given you any reason to have faith in my statement. My behavior has never been the kind that a lady such as yourself could approve of. But I am a changed man."

"Indeed." Her tone dripped with sarcasm as she folded her

arms, unwittingly drawing his attention to the perfect curve of her small breasts.

He struggled to maintain focus. "Perhaps you heard of my brother's marriage six months ago?"

She nodded slowly, almost as if she was uncertain if agreeing with him even in this was some kind of trap.

"Seeing his marital bliss has changed me," Jeremy continued.

The words tasted bitter, perhaps because there was some truth in them. Christopher's sudden and happy marriage *had* set him out of sorts.

He shook off the thought and kept talking. "And though I have tried to continue down the wicked path I was once set upon, I've found it less and less satisfying. Hearing your thoughts on the subject of sensual excess and marital fidelity altered my view on life. On many things. You are—" he leaned a little closer. "You are quite persuasive, Lady Norman, in ways you may not even fathom entirely."

She rolled her eyes. "And yet you say you have changed. You are flirting with me at this very moment."

This time he couldn't help but chuckle. "Indeed, I may be. Old habits, you know. But I've never felt there was any harm in a flirtatious exchange."

Her face suddenly grew hard. "Of course you wouldn't see the harm. But I have never known a man who didn't use scx as a weapon."

Jeremy drew back slightly at the heat in her tone. So that was it. She had been used or hurt by a man in the past. Her husband, perhaps? Or some other man? Or both? He would have to ferret out that secret as part of his plan.

He tilted his head in acquiescence. "You see, my lady, I need your help. This is exactly the kind of insight I require as I make my transformation into a respectable gentleman."

Penelope stared at him, her blue eyes almost impossibly wide. She was utterly silent for a long time, longer than a minute. Long enough that Jeremy began to wonder if she had been stricken mute with shock. But finally she shook her head.

"I do not know what game it is you are playing at, Your Grace. But I will be no part of it. Your 'transformation' is no more authentic than Lord Norwich's wig." She tilted her head. "I have no time for your foolishness. Good evening."

She turned away a second time, and Jeremy allowed her retreat with a smile. She was one step away when he said, "I shall change your mind about me, Penelope."

She sent a glare over her shoulder and continued into the crowd. Jeremy watched her hips twitch away with the heat of desire curling in his stomach.

Oh yes, he was going to change Penelope's mind about so many things. And enjoy every moment of it.

Penelope stepped into her chamber with a loud sigh. As she closed her door behind her, her lady's maid, Fiona Clifton, entered from the adjoining bedroom. Penelope forced a smile for the woman.

Fiona had once been a mistress. Penelope wagered she was probably a very sought after one at that. With her shiny brown hair, porcelain skin, and light blue eyes, she made a stunning picture to behold. Just watching her, Penelope could feel the sensual power her maid was so very aware of. Fiona knew exactly how to move, to look, to speak in order to gain masculine attention. Half the men on Penelope's staff were in love with her.

But Fiona paid them no mind. Abused by her so-called protector, she had willingly taken a place in Penelope's household after the two women met accidentally at the opera when Fiona's angry lover had deserted her after a particularly vicious argument.

Fiona's past, what she had been through, were part of why Penelope had started talking to her friends about the sensual excess of the men in their sphere. No woman should be forced to bear what Fiona had, no matter her place in life.

"Good evening, Penelope," Fiona said as she stepped forward to start unlacing Penelope's gown.

Penelope winced as the other woman pinched her. A good mistress she might have been, a good lady's maid she most definitely was not. But one did not save another person, then complain about her skills.

"How was the party?" Fiona asked, and Penelope thought she heard a wistful hint in her maid's voice.

She cast a quick glance over her shoulder, but the young woman was focused entirely on the task at hand. Perhaps she had only imagined the longing.

"Honestly?" Penelope sighed. "Quite horrid. I was given the cut direct by more people than not. Even the ones who whisper that they support me will not stand up with me in public."

Fiona wrinkled her brow. "I'm afraid I know the feeling."

Penelope nodded. She supposed that was true. Fiona had occasionally come to various parties on the arm of her protector before she ran away from him, and she had never been accepted, either. Everyone knew what she was. What she did.

And they punished her for it.

"What's worse is that now some of them are attempting to play me for a fool," Penelope said as Fiona pulled her gown away from her shoulders.

Instead of folding it properly, the former courtesan tossed it aside. In silent dismay, Penelope watched the yards of fine silk crumple into a pile in the corner.

"How so?" Fiona asked as she came around to the little bench in front of Penelope's dressing table and flopped down on it as if the action of undressing Penelope had worn her out entirely.

"I was approached by the Duke of Kilgrath," Penelope admitted with a roll of her eyes.

"Jeremy?" Fiona asked, straightening up. Her eyes lit up. "Oh, I always liked Jeremy."

Penelope went still. She had all but forgotten that Fiona had once been part of Jeremy's crowd. In fact, her former protector, Anthony Wharton, was one of the Duke's best friends. She pursed her lips. Was that why Kilgrath had approached her? Was he trying to wheedle his way into her good graces so that he might speak to Fiona? Penelope had never thought of him as the kind of man who would condone violence against a woman.

But perhaps he wasn't acting on behalf of his friend, after all. Kilgrath might simply want Fiona for himself now that Wharton no longer had her. Penelope had heard the small group of men who called themselves The Nevers had shared lovers in the past.

"How close were you to Lord Kilgrath?" Penelope asked, hoping she sounded nonchalant.

"Not as close as I would have liked," Fiona laughed. "My, he is a handsome devil, isn't he?"

Penelope remained silent. God yes, he was handsome. Too handsome. Just looking at him made her think things she was sworn to fight against. When she smelled that clean, masculine scent of his skin, it made her weak. When he smiled at her, it made her want.

But she also knew he was a complete liar. Especially about his supposed conversion to her way of thinking.

"Handsome or not, he's trying to make a fool of me," she said as she slipped her fingers into her hair and began taking her locks down. Normally her maid would perform that duty, but Fiona seemed far too interested in chatting.

"How?"

One by one, Penelope tossed the pins she was removing onto her coverlet. "Kilgrath wanted me to believe that he is no longer interested in the debauched life he has enjoyed for so long. That he has been changed by the things I've said about the consequences of excess."

Fiona covered a giggle with her palm. "Jeremy Vaughn? No, I've never known anyone who enjoyed his debauchery more. And with good reason. He can get anything he wants, any time he wants it with a mere crook of his finger. Why would he want to abandon that?"

"He wouldn't," Penelope conceded.

A little twinge of regret made itself known in the pit of her stomach. She frowned. Had she really wanted to believe him? In some tiny part of herself, had she wished he truly were changed and turning to her for guidance?

Stupid girl.

"Oh, I completely forgot," Fiona said, rising from her place at

Penelope's dressing table and digging in the pocket of her plain gown. She pulled out a letter and held it out to Penelope. The envelope had been crushed by the careless manner in which Fiona shoved it into her pocket.

Penelope sighed. "What is this?"

Fiona shrugged. "It was delivered just after you departed for the ball. I told Smickens I would give it to you when you arrived home. He still despises me, you know."

With a shake of her head, Penelope thought of her very proper butler. He, like the rest of the staff, had a hard time accepting a former lady of the evening as their equal. At least those who weren't swayed by Fiona's ample charms had difficulty.

"He will change his view in time, especially as you improve in your duties," Penelope said as she took the letter. "I wonder who this could be from. I do hope it's not another threat."

She broke the blank seal that held the pages together and opened the note. She scanned the words within and could not help the sharp gasp that escaped her lungs. The pages in her fingertips fell away, drifting to the floor as she stared at them with a hand clamped over her lips.

Fiona rushed over to gather up the missive. "What is it?" she breathed, turning over the letter.

"No!" Penelope yelped, jumping forward.

But Fiona was too quick. She sucked in a breath as she began to read out loud.

"'My dearest Lady Norman,'" she read, eyes widening. "'You do not know me, but I have watched you from afar for many a month. I cannot remain silent any longer. Please allow me to tell you of my admiration. Where shall I start? The lips that a man could easily imagine wrapped around his swollen cock? Or the throat I would spend an evening kissing, if only you would allow it? Your breasts, which would fill my hands. If I stroked my fingers over them, would you cry out? Sigh with pleasure?'"

Penelope stood frozen as Fiona read the words, the lascivious, erotic words that described in growing detail what the letter writer wished to do to her. It had been one thing to read them in a quick, shocked glance. It was quite another to have them recited to her in the sultry voice of a former courtesan.

"Stop," she whispered, surprised at how husky her own tone had become. She reached out a trembling hand and snatched the letter from Fiona's fingers.

Her lady's maid stared at her with parted lips. Her cheeks were flushed and her breasts lifted with each breath. "Who in the world wrote that?"

Penelope shook her head. "Someone who is playing a cruel, foolish jest, no doubt." She moved for the fire and held out the note toward the flames. But as she stared at the missive, she found she could not drop it into the devouring fire. Instead, she made a show like she had tossed it in, but in truth she hid it behind her back.

Fiona moved toward her. "It goes into great detail if it is only a jest," she whispered. "A man who wrote that would have to truly desire you, have truly watched you, to go into such lusty particulars."

The blood rushed to Penelope's cheeks. *Want* her? She didn't think a man had ever truly wanted her. Her husband had used her body, but for his own means, not because he wanted her particularly. And most of the men of the *ton* hated her at present, they didn't want to touch her unless it was in violence.

The words in that letter should have made her angry. Disgusted. But instead they . . . they moved her.

She blushed as Fiona tilted her head and looked at her closely. "Penelope?"

Penelope shook her head as if to dismiss the topic. "I shall not humor that kind of person with a response. Now, I am very tired. Is my bath ready in the next room?"

Fiona opened her mouth, but then shut it again, as if biting back a statement. "Er, yes. I did forget, but Smickens reminded me. It is ready for you."

Penelope nodded. "Very good. I shall bathe myself. You may retire to your bedchamber."

"Th-thank you," Fiona said softly, then backed out of the room with a strange expression on her face.

As soon as Fiona had gone, Penelope padded into the bedroom. There, behind a screen next to her bed, was the big tub her servants had filled with steaming water. Penelope approached the basin with a sigh of anticipation. It had been a trying night and all she needed was a good, long soak to put her to rights again.

She set the letter on the silver platter that contained her soaps and slipped out of her chemise and stockings. Then she put one foot into the hot water with a hiss of contentment. Ah, yes. This was what she needed.

The water rolled over her body as she settled back against the tub wall, covering her to the very tops of her breasts. She gasped as the water slapped against her tingling nipples and made her very aware of the ache that had begun in her body. But when?

Was it when she read the letter? No, it had been before that. Probably while she sparred with Kilgrath. As humiliating as it was, her exchange with him had started her body down a path of wanting that she could not allow. She had tried to ignore it at the time, but their exchange had been stimulating in more ways than one.

This was madness. She would not let the manipulations of a libertine like Kilgrath or the perverse scrawl of an anonymous "admirer" sway her from the morals she held so dear.

She grabbed for the soap on the little tray beside the tub, but her damp fingers touched the folded sheets of the letter instead. She yanked her hand back as if burned and stared at the white linen pages.

Who could have written those things to her? And how much more did that unknown person say? She had only skimmed the first page, which talked of her breasts, of her mysterious admirer's desire to see them in moonlight, touch them, strum the nipples until she cried out, lick the delicate curves. . .

Penelope shook her head with a start. Every word that unknown man had written was already burned into her mind. She picked up a fluffy towel from the tray and slowly dried her fingertips, never taking her eyes from the letter. It called to her. Taunting her.

What if the letter gave her some clue as to the author? What if it contained some valuable piece of information? She would be remiss if she didn't read it again. Read it fully.

Wouldn't she?

Her shaking fingers already reached for the missive and she sank down lower in the water as she unfolded the pages. With a furtive glance around the empty room, she began to read.

The familiar words on the first page washed over her just like the hot water in the bath. She lingered over each one, taking her time to absorb every description. And slowly she came to realize that she wasn't just reading the letter, but imagining in detail what the writer described.

She could almost see him now. A faceless man, his body strong and ready, crossing the room to her. Looking at her, watching her as this stranger claimed to have done for many months. Would he like seeing her in the bath as she was now? Her entire body only protected by a clear wave of clean bathwater?

She shivered at the idea of a man seeing her this way. One who wanted her. She imagined him touching her breasts as he had described in the letter. Holding their damp weight in his palms, covering them with his fingers, dragging his thumbs over her already distended nipples.

A little cry of pleasure escaped her lips and shook Penelope from her fantasy. What was wrong with her? What was she doing, allowing some stranger's vulgar words to arouse her?

And yet, her gaze fell back to the letter in her hand. Slowly, she lifted the first page away and read the second, the one she had only skimmed for a name earlier.

Have you ever felt your own arousal, Penelope? Not felt it in your gut or as a vague, passing thrill. I mean, have you touched yourself and felt how your body changes? Have you ever let your fingers play along your own skin and touch the slick evidence of your desire? Stroke your folds until you find the little clit hidden within. Played until your body spasmed with pleasure so intense that it borders on pain?

I have imagined you doing so. Longed to see you do so.

Penelope sucked in a harsh breath and shoved the letter away, throwing it back on the silver tray with enough force that the bar of soap there clattered.

Despite the warmth of the bath, she trembled at the words. They awoke memories she'd long hidden. Yes, she *had* touched herself, brought herself pleasure in the faraway past. Long before she saw how far desire would drive a person, she had been open to such activities in the furtive darkness of her bedchamber.

At one time, she had even looked forward to experiencing more sensual delights with some faceless future husband. But her eventual marriage had forced her to realize that passion was a weapon to be wielded. And pleasure wasn't inevitable, but something that could be snatched away at a whim.

And yet, reading her mysterious admirer's words didn't only force memory but sensation. Her sheath clenched at nothingness, her nipples tingled fiercely and her thighs clamped together, which served nothing but to increase her desire.

Almost of its own accord, her hand dipped beneath the water, sliding across her skin with purpose. She shut her eyes as she let her fingers graze her nipples, tensing when ricochets of pleasure rewarded her touch. God, it had been so long since she felt like this.

And she wanted more. Even though she knew it made her a hypocrite. Even though it went against the cold façade she'd worn so long in public.

Her hand slid over her stomach and finally her fingers slipped through the soft patch of hair between her thighs. She rested her hand against her mound for a long moment, eyes squeezed shut as the frank words the unknown author had written taunted her.

Have you ever let your fingers play along your own skin and touch the slick evidence of your desire?

Slowly, she dipped her hand down and touched the swollen flesh between her legs. A little moan escaped her lips as she stroked along the folds there. They *were* wet and from more than the mere bath. She pushed deeper and came in contact with the hidden nub of flesh the letter writer had alluded to.

Stroke your folds until you find the little clit hidden within.

Clit. She'd never heard it referred to in that manner before. She circled her fingers around the hard little bud and gasped as a warm wash of pleasure spread from the point of contact through her body. Focused and powerful, the feeling multiplied, widened, until it seemed her entire being was focused on that one tiny spot.

She circled harder, lifting her hips slightly to reach for the pleasure. It felt good, but she wanted more. More.

Shaking, she brought the opposite hand to join the other. Increasing the pressure, she turned her head, bit her lip to hold back the cries that might bring her staff to investigate.

There was something coming. She felt the wall of pleasure building to a crescendo, but she couldn't reach it. It was right there, over the edge.

She opened her eyes in frustration and found herself staring at the letter again. Somewhere in London, there was a man who claimed he wanted to watch her do exactly what she was doing right now. The idea made her hips arch helplessly and the pleasure jumped.

When she shut her eyes this time, she pictured that faceless man. Standing at the end of the tub, leaning over the water. His breath short, his bare, muscular arms straining in an attempt to maintain control. She could almost see him watching her. Waiting until she exploded to join her.

"Oh, oh," she couldn't help but groan.

Yet still, it wasn't enough. She pressed her fingers against her flesh, panting in frustration. The pleasure was so keen it was almost pain. She needed relief. She needed more.

She concentrated hard on the image of the man in her mind. What if his hands slipped beneath the water, strong fingers gliding up her bare legs, reaching higher and higher until they tangled with her own? Pushed her own aside.

Grinding down against her clit, she pictured him lifting her hips, spreading her legs wide, opening her body to him. She'd had very little experience with such true passion. Yet it didn't take much imagination to believe such a man would circle his thumb around her clit just as she was doing. And then drive his fingers deep within her womb.

She cried out as she did what she imagined that man doing. Still, she danced on the edge of utter madness. Tears pricked her eyes, tears of impending release mixed with wild frustration.

The man, he was the key. What kind of man would take her so wickedly? Play and toy with her? She needed a face for the faceless. A voice for the words he had written.

And suddenly a face appeared, a voice echoed in her ears.

Kilgrath.

The moment she overlaid Jeremy's handsome face on the blank countenance of her imaginary lover, her hips bucked wildly. Her sheath fluttered out of control against her driving fingers and she let out an echoing wail of relief that broke the silence in the room.

Her back arched and she was vaguely aware of the water slosh-ing wildly, churning over the edge of the tub as she rode out the intense pleasure.

Penelope collapsed back into the water with a final groan. She felt weightless, boneless. Utterly spent and satisfied.

For countless minutes, she laid in the rapidly cooling bathtub, simply feeling the aftereffects of desire and release. Then, slowly, she opened her eyes and faced her cold, empty room.

And the reality of what she had done.

The letter that should have been distasteful to her had instead aroused her to untamed, out of control levels. She had surren-dered to her base needs and wants, thwarting all her own im-passioned statements about the need for control from those who ruled the *ton*.

And worse, the very worst, she had done it all while imagin-ing Jeremy Vaughn, Duke of Kilgrath, as her illicit lover. A man she knew for a fact to be a flagrant seducer, a man who had lied to her face not three hours before. One who stood for everything she claimed to despise.

"What have I done?" she murmured as she sat bolt upright in the tub. More water sloshed over the edge and she looked down at the floor. The shiny wood was splattered with puddles, proof of how far her desire had taken her.

Rising, she stepped out onto the damp floor. She rubbed her-self dry swiftly and then went to work soaking up the pools of spilled water. She didn't want the servants to see the results of her passionate outburst. She didn't want any evidence to exist that she had utterly surrendered.

Utter surrender was a luxury she couldn't have. Even if she wanted it.

Which she didn't.

She only had to fight to remember that, despite the distracting presence of Jeremy Vaughn or the erotic words of her mystery author.

Three

Jeremy paced around his parlor, restless and agitated as he recalled the events at the ball tonight. Why, he could not say. All had gone as planned, perhaps better than planned. He'd managed to approach Penelope, garner her interest, and see, quite clearly, that she was hiding a most passionate spirit.

All in all, it was a successful night. So why did it feel wrong?

"Great God, Kilgrath," Anthony Wharton said from behind him as he set his fourth sherry of the evening down with a smack. "The entire room saw you with that little bitch. It is the talk of the *ton*, you know. The libertine and the crusader."

Jeremy turned to his old friend with a scowl. Wharton had followed him home, already half drunk. Now he was far past half and a large cause of Jeremy's foul mood. Wharton had been raging about Penelope and how she "stole" his mistress for at least an hour.

"If we are the talk of the *ton*, then I have done my job," Jeremy drawled as he returned his gaze to the dark night outside. "I want them to wonder what is afoot between Penelope and me. That way when I reveal her as a hypocrite, they will all be hanging on my every word."

"How are you going to reveal her as anything if you befriend her?" Anthony slurred.

Jeremy spun on his heel and strode across the room. Snatching the drink from his friend's hand, he downed it in one swig and snapped, "If she thinks I'm her friend, she'll trust me. All the better to catch her in my trap. And I have other plans already in motion."

His mind shifted to the letter he'd had delivered to Penelope's home right before he departed for the ball tonight. The missive detailed every observation he'd ever made about her lush body, about all the things he'd wondered if she'd ever allowed herself to experience.

What would her reaction to that be? He could only hope his erotic words would open Penelope further to an ultimate seduction. That his two assaults would work in tandem. By day, he would be the Duke of Kilgrath, her unexpected ally. By night, a mysterious, faceless lover who awoke her desires in the shadows.

"Plans? What, seduction like Crawford and Dunfield suggested?" Anthony barked, breaking the pleasant spell of Jeremy's fleeting fantasies. "Bah. I still say she won't change her mind, no matter how many orgasms you give her. If she can even find pleasure. Frigid—"

Jeremy cut him off with a scowl. "If seduction won't change her mind of its own accord, blackmail will."

Anthony let out a sigh. "And if those don't succeed, there *are* other ways to handle a woman like her."

Jeremy cocked his head, surprised by the suddenly lucid and utterly cruel glitter in his friend's drunken stare. That focused expression was troubling.

But no. He shook off the thought. Wharton was a hothead, nothing else. He was rambling without thought. The words were meaningless. But his friend was in a total drunk and needed to sleep it off regardless.

Jeremy turned Anthony toward the door. "Trust in me, friend. I have the situation well under control. Now, my driver will take you home and be sure you get inside without killing yourself. Good night."

Anthony pushed back against him momentarily, but finally acquiesced and allowed Jeremy to guide him to the parlor door and a waiting footman.

Once his friend was gone, Jeremy went back in to the parlor. Tonight he'd made the first step to conquering the beautiful and troublesome Penelope Norman. And he had no intention of failing in any way.

Penelope lifted her hands and raised her voice over the fray of chattering women. "Ladies, ladies, this chaos does us no good."

The babbling crowd quieted a fraction, and a few of the ladies turned their heads toward Penelope. She sighed as she looked over the small group of about ten women, half of whom had given her the cut at the ball a night before, but were now in her parlor to "support" her. But what was support when it was all done in secret?

"Each of you has the power to help our cause," Penelope insisted, harking back to the argument she had been making from the very beginning.

"Power?" Adela Forster, the Marchioness of Chartsford repeated with a sniff. "What power do *we* have?"

Penelope looked at the young woman with a sad frown. Although Adela sometimes seemed haughty and abrasive, she was a very pretty woman, dark haired and bright eyed, with the most beautiful skin Penelope had ever seen. But her uncommon beauty had not protected her from a highly unhappy marriage to one of Jeremy's best friends.

Jeremy. Color filled Penelope's cheeks at the thought of him. The thought of what she had done last night while fantasizing about him. No one could ever find out about that shame.

"Penelope?" Adela repeated. "Do you have no answer for me?"

Penelope shook off her thoughts with a frown. "The men of the *ton* will not change until their wives and mothers and sisters stand up and say that they do not condone their behavior."

An older woman, Lady Pendergrath, nodded. "Lady Norman is wise beyond her scant years. My experience has told me that men generally want peace in their homes. If we do not give it to them, they will ultimately change their wicked ways."

Adela shook her head and tears filled her eyes. Ones she blinked away with a scowl.

"I have made clear my thoughts on the matter of my husband's . . ." She blushed. "His activities outside of our marriage. Do you know what David said to me? He told me he liked me better when I was pliable and uncaring about what he did." The other woman clenched her fists. "I was never pliable, nor uncaring. Merely silent."

Penelope resisted the urge to touch Adela's shoulder, offer her comfort. She didn't think the other lady would appreciate the gesture, especially in front of others. She was far too proud.

The group began talking at once again, dissolving into arguments between those who thought they would only make things worse by standing up to their wayward husbands and those who felt it could change their world for the better. Penelope lifted her hand to her eyes and rubbed her temples. What good was fighting for something when half those in the war didn't dare go to battle?

Before she could make any attempt to silence the group a second time, they did so themselves. An unnatural hush fell over the group, punctuated only by harsh whispers whose muted words Penelope didn't understand.

Slowly, she lowered her hand and looked at the door. She staggered back at what she saw. Jeremy Vaughn stood there, leaning in her doorway, a smug smile on his handsome face. A smile that hit Penelope in the gut and forced her to recall her loss of control in the bath the night before. Heat burned her cheeks, and she wanted to run away.

But she couldn't. Instead, she strode forward, hands fisted at her sides.

"Lord Kilgrath," she said, her voice strained. As she drew nearer to him, she hissed, "What are you doing here?"

He looked down at her with a completely innocent expression. One that was woefully out of place on such a sinful face. "I heard

you were having a meeting regarding your thoughts on the behavior of the men of the *ton*. I thought I would come and see if I
could offer any insight."

Penelope's nostrils flared and she shoved her hands down
straight at her sides. As she kept a withering gaze on Jeremy, she
called over her shoulder, "I believe we have covered a great deal
of ground today. Why don't we adjourn to the Rose Terrace for
tea?"

The women in the room got to their feet slowly, still whispering and glaring at Jeremy as they passed by. As the last few fil-
tered from the room, Kilgrath gave Penelope a smile and offered
her his arm.

Penelope reeled back at the idea of touching him. She wanted
nothing to do with his heat. It would only court more images for
her dark, forbidden fantasies.

"What are you doing?"

His smile fell a fraction. "Going to the Rose Terrace. I could
use a spot of tea."

Her jaw fell open in shock. "*You* are not joining us, Your
Grace."

"You mean you wish to talk to me privately?" he asked, tilting his head closer. Close enough that she caught an intoxicating
whiff of his spicy male scent. It was a pleasing and dizzying combination of sandalwood and something that was purely Jeremy.

"Yes," she said.

He smiled. "I thought a woman of your caliber couldn't take
the risk of speaking to me alone. What did you tell me last night?
That it would discredit you? And yet, less than twenty-four

hours later, you demand I stay with you alone in this parlor. Has something changed?"

She pursed her lips. Damn him. Even though he couldn't know just how much had changed since her verbal exchange with him the night before and this afternoon, his words still reminded her of that fact.

In just a few short hours, she had become an utter hypocrite.

"You certainly have not changed, my lord," she said, hoping her voice was cold even though her heart was throbbing madly. "So please stop trying to convince me that you have."

She made to push past him, but Jeremy caught her arm and held her in place. Just as she had feared, heat equal to that of a furnace rushed from his touch and settled in the worst possible places. She looked up at him, her throat dry and full, her traitorous mind taking her to places she ought not allow.

"You have not permitted me to convince you of *anything* yet, Lady Norman," he said softly as he released her and took a step back as if to prove he wasn't touching her out of any attraction.

Her stomach sank unexpectedly at the thought.

"Why should I believe in your miraculous alteration?" she asked, rubbing the place where he had touched her. It felt . . . burned. Branded.

He cocked his head. "Because it proves you are correct in your assessment that a man *can* change. Think of it, my lady. What a boon I could be to your cause. I know of my own reputation. If I came out on your side, in support of you, it could change the tide of your movement. Are you so proud and do you hate me so much that you will not even consider my offer to assist you?"

Penelope's lips parted in surprise. "I-I don't hate you. Hating you would imply I knew you or cared for you. I-I don't."

He looked at her for a long, charged moment. Then he shrugged. "I would like to prove myself to you. I can help you if you let me. If you do not know me, nor care for me, you cannot truly know my heart nor my intentions. And yet you still judge me?"

Penelope stared at him. Damn him, he was correct on so many levels. If Jeremy were truly changed and worked beside her, it would add needed credence to her words.

But how could she believe he had changed? Or even wanted to change?

"And how do you intend to prove yourself?" she asked, slowly.

A little hint of a smile tilted his lips, arrogant, like he already knew he'd won. "I can show you exactly what it is you are fighting against. Secretly. Anonymously. Then you will understand your enemies all the better."

She tilted her head, both confused and intrigued. *Show* her? What in the world could he possibly mean by that?

"I don't know what you are talking about," she said, pacing away from him and trying to look bored by their conversation. She didn't want him to realize just how aware of him she was. Just how curious he made her. About what he could reveal. About who he was.

When she peeked over her shoulder, he was smiling again, but this time it was feral. Despite herself, her stomach clenched. Her nipples hardened in an instant. He was looking at her with such . . . desire.

And even though that fact only proved he was lying about the changes to his wicked personality, she wasn't angry. Not at him, at least. No, her anger was all self-directed because she was drawn to him.

"May I take you somewhere tonight?" he asked quietly.

She started at the question. "What?"

"I think I can better explain my meaning by *showing* you, rather than explaining." He moved closer. Just a fraction. "Allow me to take you somewhere, and I think everything will come clear to you."

Penelope shook her head. This was a game, but she couldn't understand the rules, or even the goal. What was he trying to gain?

"If this is some way to get near me——" she began.

He stared at her in shock, like he'd never even considered such a thing, and yet again she blushed.

"Please," he said softly.

Penelope stared at her hands, fisting them together reflexively. Her mind spun both with all the reasons she should refuse and the reasons she should accept his offer. Of all the dangers and all the benefits.

And most of all, it spun with the fact that she *wanted* to take his offer. To see whatever he would show her. To be alone with him, if only for a little while. Perhaps if she did, he would reveal himself to be the cad she knew him to be, despite his grand claims of change. Then this silly spell of desire would be broken and she could return her attention to matters at hand.

At the very least, doing as he asked would appease him, and perhaps she could convince him to stop trying to play her for a fool, especially in the inconvenient presence of others. She couldn't afford any scandal or misunderstanding his sudden interest in her could cause.

"Very well," she finally murmured, letting her gaze come back up to his face.

He smiled, this time something more genuine. "Very good. I shall send a carriage for you at eight tonight."

She nodded wordlessly. "And now you should go. Your presence is of some upset to my guests, I think. Until I'm certain of your true intentions, perhaps we should keep our association a secret."

He tilted his head. "Very well. Then I shall see you later tonight. Until then, Penelope."

With a little salute, he backed from the room. It was only when he was gone that Penelope realized her breath was short and her hands were shaking.

Four

Jeremy leaned back against the plush leather seat of his carriage as it pulled to a smooth stop in the darkened shadows behind Penelope's London estate. He peeled back the curtain and watched as she slipped from the servant entrance and hurried across the lawn to the vehicle. His footman bowed quickly, then opened the unmarked carriage door to allow her entry.

Jeremy leaned forward, offering her a hand in. Penelope looked up at him from below, her eyes wide as she stared at the offering. But finally, after a very long moment of hesitation, she took it. When he touched her soft fingers, sparks of awareness ricocheted through him, taking him off guard.

They seemed to take her off guard, as well, for she released his hand as if it burned her the instant she settled into the seat across from him. The door shut behind her, and the carriage jolted into motion.

He took in the sight of her. Though her gown was not as re-vealing as those she would see tonight, it was still quite lovely. A deep blue with a plunging neckline that showed him the tempt-ing upper curve of her lovely breasts. He wondered if she was aware of just how provocative that fine, firm curve was. Did she show herself on purpose, proving her heated nature?

Or was she so innocent that she couldn't fathom how utterly charming she was?

Another mystery to ferret out.

"Good evening," Jeremy drawled. "I actually thought you might not come after all, so I'm pleased to see you."

She was quiet for a moment, but then she shrugged. "I consid-ered it. But I assumed you would come to my window and throw pebbles until you made the entire neighborhood aware of your presence, so I thought coming with you was the lesser evil."

"You would rather do something naughty than have people believe you were doing something naughty?" he asked, watching her face in the shadowy light.

Her gaze jerked to his. "I would rather not have to make the choice. But if I must, then my reputation is all I have. Protecting it means something to me, yes."

Jeremy nodded. It was a good piece of information, for it meant that he could likely blackmail Penelope into silence in order to protect the reputation she held so dear. And that was definitely preferable to him rather than revealing her as a hypocrite and ruining her irrevocably.

Why, he didn't want to analyze too closely.

"I suppose that seems silly to a man like you," she murmured, staring out the window again.

"Protecting your reputation?" he asked. When she nodded, he laughed. "No, it makes perfect sense. After all, I have a reputation of my own to uphold."

"Except you claim you want to change that reputation. Perhaps with my help."

Jeremy looked at her sharply again. She wasn't looking at him, but he could feel her scrutiny nonetheless. He had to give her credit. No fool was Penelope Norman. Despite his charm, she refused to take his change of heart at his word.

Which meant he would be forced to prove himself to her, even while he seduced her. A challenge, indeed. One he thrilled at.

"Why don't you tell me where we are going?" she asked, not waiting for him to answer her comment. "And how do you intend to keep me anonymous?"

Jeremy sat up straight. Yes, it was time to get to the point of tonight. Without preamble, he moved across the carriage to sit beside her. Penelope caught her breath at the sudden action and stared up at him with wide eyes. Jeremy couldn't help but catch his own breath. God, she smelled good. Like cinnamon, a spicy heady scent that tightened his gut and hardened his cock.

Hopefully she wouldn't notice that.

"What are you doing?" she breathed, her voice broken by what he instantly sensed was desire.

She wanted him. Despite everything.

He smiled as he drew an intricate mask from the inside pocket of his jacket. He'd chosen blue, a turquoise color that matched her eyes perfectly. It was sewn with little jewels and tiny feathers that framed her bright eyes.

He wrapped the soft satin fabric around her face, positioning it against her nose before he glided his fingers around the back of her head. Wicked, he leaned in as he tied it into place, moving far too close to her to be proper. He could actually feel the ragged swell of her breath and the tickle of her hair against his cheek.

Her fingers clenched against her legs and she muffled a little sound of . . . well, it was either distress or desire. Probably a combination of both.

Jeremy pulled away and smiled down at her. God, he just wanted to push her back against the cushions and slip his hands beneath her skirts. He would wager his best mount that she was already slick and ready for him, her thighs clenching and tingling.

And he could have. In her current state, it was likely he would be able to overcome her protests, awaken the core inside of her that wanted to be touched, licked, fucked. He had never doubted his own prowess before, there was no reason to start now.

But as much as he wanted to do that, as easily as he believed he could, his plan was far more intricate than a mere screw in a carriage that she could later dismiss. No, he needed to *change* Penelope. If he wanted to win, he had to make her question every belief she had. Force her to see her true, sensual nature, not just in one situation, but in every moment of her life.

That was the only way to end her little crusade.

So instead of dragging her against his chest, he leaned away. "Tonight, we are going to a Cyprian masked ball," he explained.

Penelope's lips parted in surprise. With the rest of her face covered in blue satin and lace, her mouth stood out all the more. Damn, but they were tempting lips. Full and plump, a little wet from where she had licked them.

"No!" she cried, breaking the spell. "You must be jesting. I cannot go to such a place."

Jeremy pursed his own lips as he moved back to his side of the carriage. Being so close to her was having an odd effect on his normally solid control.

"I told you I wished to show you what you were fighting against. Help you understand your enemy. This gathering, it is exactly what you claim to despise."

"And that is why I cannot go!" she repeated, her tone that which he guessed she would use with a slow-witted servant or small child.

He arched a brow. "You want to see your enemy, don't you?"

Penelope was silent for a long moment, tilting her head as she stared at him across the shadowy vehicle. Jeremy shifted a bit under her scrutiny. It was almost like she could truly see him. See more than he was on the outside, more than his public persona. See *him*.

"*You* are my enemy, Jeremy," she whispered.

He might have been disappointed, he might have felt that he had made no progress with her, except that she called him by his given name. And hearing it from her lips was utterly arousing. It also showed him that despite all her protests, she was beginning to trust him . . . if only just a little.

"I *was* your enemy," he said softly. "But no more."

The carriage stopped, but none of his servants came to open the door, just as he had ordered. He wanted Penelope to be the one who made the decision to go inside. She had to guide her own journey. If she could point to anyone else as the catalyst later, it would detract from her utter surrender to her own heart.

"Come inside with me," he said, "and see what it is you are fighting against. No one will know who you are. They will assume you are just another woman I've claimed as my lover. You can watch the men of the *ton* in action and see what kinds of women they choose to philander with."

Penelope swallowed hard enough that he could see her throat working. Such a delicate throat indeed, her pale skin nearly translucent it was so fair. She stared at the carriage door, then back toward him.

"Fine," she finally said with a frown. "I will go inside. But I don't want you to do anything that would make someone think we were lovers. No . . . touching me in a way that is familiar."

Jeremy drew back. He could hardly contain his chuckle. He didn't think he could remember the last time a woman had denied him. It spurned him on, drove him to make her change her mind all the more.

And it also piqued his curiosity. What had happened to Penelope Norman that put so much starch in her spirit? Who had made her fear sensuality and sin rather than embrace all its pleasures?

"I promise, I will do nothing more than take your arm," he said softly.

At least for now.

She nodded, the motion jerky. "Then let us go inside. I want to see this infamous Cyprian ball."

"Would you like a drink?"

Penelope jolted at the soft seduction of Jeremy's voice. It raked across her raw senses like satin over her skin.

"W-Will I be safe here alone?" she asked, hating how her voice trembled.

Jeremy looked around. He had brought her into the Cyprian ball half an hour before. But when too many masked revelers identified him and wanted to know who his new companion was, he had escorted her to this small, private terrace that overlooked the ballroom below. Penelope was just as happy. Amongst the partygoers she felt surrounded, stifled. Exposed.

"You will be quite unharmed, I assure you. And I shall be back in a few scant moments." He smiled down at her, and Penelope shivered.

She felt protected by her mask, but she also felt protected by Jeremy's presence. Like he would keep anyone from harming her. Even though she knew the greatest harm could come from him. Despite all his declarations to the opposite, she still sensed a feral, animal quality that lurked beneath his proper attire.

"Very well." She nodded. "My throat *is* parched."

He nodded, then left her alone on the terrace. Penelope turned back to the scene below. The home they were in was large and very beautiful, although it didn't belong to any gentleman she was aware of. She'd certainly never been here, in this room with tall pillars decorated by writhing, naked sprites and lewd mystical figures with swollen phalluses. Great God, the things some of the women in her acquaintance would say if they saw such erotic images.

But it wasn't the sinful craftsmanship of the pillars that was the real shock to her. It was the behavior of the participants. Unlike at a ball that had been sanctioned and was attended by ladies of her own social sphere, there was an air of unabashed sexuality that permeated the room. Men and women danced and laughed together, staring openly and analyzing the physical attributes of their partners.

Everyone wore masks, though it seemed many knew the identities of their partners without seeing their faces. Or at least, they acted familiar enough. Their hands roamed over each other shamelessly, boldly, as erotic music lilted around them.

The women . . . *Cyprians*, wore shocking gowns. More than a few had bodices that dipped down *below* their breasts, revealing the pale, bare globes of flesh. Others wore gowns with strategic slits up the sides so that they could flash their admirers shocking glimpses of thighs and even more.

None of the women seemed ashamed of what their clothing revealed. Or embarrassed by the blunt appraisal of the men in their company. In fact, they appeared to like the attention.

In comparison, Penelope's own gown, which was one of her more daring ones, seemed drab.

She leaned forward and stared over the crowd. As the night wore on and the drinks flowed freely, the behavior of the guests below seemed to be deteriorating. She sucked in a gasp when a gentleman leaned down to lick the naked nipple of his dance partner before he laughed and spun her away to another leering gentleman who cupped the same firm breast and ground his hips against her suggestively.

Penelope tore her gaze away, instead staring toward a corner of the room that was hidden behind a white linen screen. It wasn't visible from the dance floor, but from her elevated position she could see over the top and to the empty space behind it. As tempting as the sensual images before her were, her senses were beginning to be overwhelmed by the blatant eroticism all around her.

Overwhelmed and . . . and titilated. Penelope squeezed her eyes shut. She would never admit it, not to anyone, but watching the couples writhe together, kiss in full view of everyone around them, touch each other . . . it was all infinitely arousing.

It was so wrong to feel this way. These women were being used, weren't they? They might laugh and moan and preen, but they had no other choices . . . did they?

She opened her eyes with a sigh and found that a couple had slipped behind the screen in the corner of the room while she mused on her own reactions to what she saw all around her. The woman was a pretty dark-haired lady, decked out in a beautiful red satin gown with lacy swirls around her shoulders. Her companion was a well-built gentleman wearing a bull mask that matched the shocking red of his companion's dress.

Penelope watched as they whispered to each other for a few minutes. The lady leaned up toward the gentlemen, resting her hands against his chest with a familiar touch that spoke of a deep and physical relationship. And when he guided his hands along her spine and began to gently massage her backside through the silky dress, it became clear to Penelope that the two were lovers.

As they began to kiss with a passionate abandon that sent a wicked thrill through Penelope's body. She knew she should turn away. It wasn't right for her to watch such a thing, to be aroused by the very activities she was fighting against. And yet, she couldn't stop herself. It was as if she were frozen, held still by some invisible power that forced her to observe from afar.

She glanced around. No one was nearby to see her shameful voyeurism. And the couple below had no idea that they were being observed. Perhaps they wouldn't care even if they were aware of her presence, since they had chosen to begin their love play behind a thin screen at a busy ball.

No, no one ever had to know what she was doing. So Penelope surrendered herself to the images below.

The lady had broken the full, wet mouth kisses she and her companion were sharing and started to trail her lips along the front of his coat, then lower, lower until she had dropped to her knees before the gentleman. Penelope gasped as the two loosened his trousers together and the lady drew out his hard shaft into her hand. Even from a distance, Penelope could see the hard thrust of muscle curling up.

Then the woman leaned forward and wrapped her dark red lips around her companion, taking him as far into her mouth as he would go. The gentleman clutched at the wall behind him to brace himself, even as his fingers tangled in his companion's hair to guide the speed and depth of her mouth.

Penelope shifted as she watched the scandalous activities below her. Warmth spread through her as she observed the lusty way the mysterious lady took her lover's erection into her mouth. A tingling sense of desire and power made Penlope shiver against her will when she watched the man tilt his head back, his neck straining with pleasure.

Penelope's husband had never wanted this act. Never asked for it. But she could see just how much power it gave a woman. And how much pleasure it gave a man.

The gentleman below suddenly caught his partner's arms and

pulled her up and away from his erection. He slipped his fingers beneath her mask and tossed it away, then did the same to his own mask so he could drop his mouth to hers. They kissed, wild and passionate, as he shifted her around so that her back was to the wall.

He pressed her against the wall, pulling at the low neckline of her sheer gown until both her breasts bobbed free. He lowered his mouth and suckled each nipple while the lady's fingers dug at his wool-encased shoulders.

Even as he pleasured her breasts, he pushed at her skirts, gliding them up and up until he had access to her legs and the naked mound between them. Penelope gasped at the woman's lack of chemise and other undergarments, but before she could grasp that shock, the couple had maneuvered into position and the gentleman's hips thrust.

Penelope couldn't hear them from high above, but by the way the woman's lips parted and her eyes closed, it was clear she had let out a long, low sigh of pleasure as she was taken. The couple held there, still, their foreheads pressed together for a long moment. Then the gentleman drew back and thrust forward, his hips working in hard, harsh circles against his companion, who arched into each one, her face contorting with silent pleasure.

Penelope's fists gripped against the terrace wall, clenching as she watched the scene. Her own breath was short, her body reacting to their coupling with wet heat and clenching tingles of frustrated pleasure. She leaned forward, gritting her teeth with every thrust and trying hard not to picture herself as the woman being taken.

She didn't want that. She didn't.

Suddenly there was the clink of glass along the terrace wall and a masculine hand set a champagne glass beside her hand.

Penelope jumped, spinning around to find Jeremy standing there, watching her intently. His dark eyes glittered in the candlelight, focused on her face. She felt heat on her cheeks and raised cold fingers to cover them.

"H-Hello," she stammered, refusing to meet his eyes.

One dark brow arched in response. "Are you quite well? You are flushed."

She nodded. Perhaps he hadn't seen what she was staring at when he approached her. Perhaps he didn't know that she'd been watching—

"Pretty young woman, isn't she?" he asked, inclining his head toward the couple.

Well, so much for that hope. Without even looking, she knew which young woman he was referring to. The lady in red who was being taken so lustily.

Penelope spun away with an even darker blush and caught up the glass of champagne. Her hand shook as she took a long sip of the bubbly liquid. "I-I suppose."

Her gaze flitted back to the corner. The couple was still mating furiously, but the end seemed near. The gentleman's neck strained on every thrust and the lady had put the back of her hand against her lips, likely to muffle her mewls of pleasure. Finally the man caught her mouth for a hard kiss and stiffened, his legs shaking as he reached completion. They parted for a brief moment, then their lips met again, this time for a gentle kiss before he set her down on the floor and helped her smooth her dress over her bare legs.

Penelope turned away. Somehow watching their postcoital gentleness seemed more of an intrusion than observing them have sex had been.

"Who is she?" she managed to ask.

"Her name is Cecilia Charles. She is the daughter of a very famous courtesan and has followed in her mama's footsteps." He tilted his head as the couple exited from behind the screen. "And she's made a good match in Rannoch."

Penelope stared at the retreating back of the gentleman and the twitching hips of the lady as they circulated back into the crowd. "That is Peter Rannoch?"

She hadn't even recognized the popular gentleman. Her own excitement had blinded her.

Jeremy nodded. "Second son of the Duke of Turnberg."

"That woman shouldn't be forced to do such things at a ball," Penelope murmured. But even as she said it, she thought of the expression on Cecilia Charles's face. Never had she looked *forced* into anything.

Jeremy turned toward her, and she felt his gaze on her face. She couldn't help but blush once more. Did he know what kind of thoughts had drifted to her mind while she watched the couple? Could he read how aroused she had been and still was?

"Do you think she was forced?" he asked softly.

She swallowed, looking at him, but never meeting his eyes. "Wouldn't she have to be to do something so bold, practically out in the open?"

He smiled, just a slight expression, but it made her feel very young and inexperienced. "Haven't you ever done something naughty? Something you knew you shouldn't? Something you might get caught at, but you did it anyway? Perhaps the idea of being caught only made the act all the more exciting?"

She caught her breath. "Are you implying that I ever—"

"It's not all about sex, Penelope," he said softly, and took a small step toward her. Close enough that she could smell the intoxicating combination of sherry and mint on his warm breath. "I mean any little thing you knew you shouldn't do. Take a cookie from a housekeeper when she wasn't looking. Ride a horse astride just out of the view of your Mama. Have you never done anything that involved a little risk?"

Penelope thought of her own childhood. Her overbearing mother. Her often absent and completely irresponsible father. Her elder sister, Miranda had often been forced to take the reins and make sure everything was all right. Penelope had never had the heart to do anything naughty and make her sister worry over her, as well.

"No," she finally admitted softly. "I did was I was supposed to do. When I was supposed to do it."

Jeremy stared at her for a long, quiet moment. "Then it might be difficult for you to understand if I explained to you why a lady would agree to doing something so taboo in public. But it is a predilection many have."

Penelope clenched her fists. Again, she felt completely naïve. "Are *you* included in that group?"

"Who have a predilection for pursuing their conquests in

public?" he asked, eyes widening. When she nodded, they went even wider. "I will admit to being swept away by the moment a few times over the years. However, I have always preferred to take my lovers in private, where I would have more time to savor the surrender."

Penelope wet her suddenly dry lips and forced herself to look up into Jeremy's eyes. They were such a pretty green. So sensual and dark. And his mouth also drew her attention. How many women had he kissed with that mouth? His lips were very full; she had to assume they would be nice to kiss. They were standing so close now that it would be so easy just to lift up on her tiptoes and indulge. That would be very naughty. A stolen kiss from one of the *ton*'s most talked about rakes.

Would he be swept away or want to savor the moment if she did so?

"But that was before I was reformed," Jeremy said, and took a long step back.

Penelope shook her head to clear her mind. Great God, what had she been thinking? Standing here in the midst of a Cyprian's ball, contemplating kissing this man?

"I-I think I have seen enough," she said, voice shaking. "I want to go home."

Jeremy nodded. "Yes, you have probably seen enough for one night." He hesitated before he held out his arm. "Come, I will escort you home."

Penelope took his arm, ignoring the spark of awareness that shot through her at his touch. As they weaved their way back down and through the crowd, she thought of what Jeremy had said.

Was he truly "reformed"? Or had he escorted her here for the exact reason that he wished for her to see such titillating sights?

And if the second were true . . . did he know just how fully she had fallen into his trap?

Five

Jeremy watched Penelope closely as she motioned him into her parlor and said a few soft words to her servant. He had been surprised she asked him to come into the house for tea, but he'd been in no position to refuse. Not if he wanted to follow through on his plan.

Although tonight, perhaps, his plan had succeeded all too well. When he came onto the balcony at the Cyprian ball and saw Penelope staring at Cecilia and Rannoch's frantic coupling, her breath short, her eyes glazed with desire, her legs shaking, it had taken all his willpower not to sweep her against his chest and kiss her until she couldn't breathe. And that had been even more difficult to resist when she stared at his mouth, asked him questions about his own conquests that he hadn't been ready to answer.

As much as he wanted this woman, those things weren't part of his plans. No, he had to be careful. Prudent.

And it couldn't be Jeremy Vaughn, Duke of Kilgrath, who seduced her. If he did, she could curl up into her shell and fight him. He *would* have her, but it would be in the guise of her mysterious secret admirer. So when he was with her, he had to remember that fact.

No, when he was Jeremy Vaughn, he had to play her friend. Someone she could trust.

"May I ask you a question?" he said as he took a seat by the fire.

Penelope paced restlessly to the window and stared outside for a long moment before she whispered, "What question?"

"You have always seemed to be a very proper lady," he began, choosing every word carefully. "However, taking up a public fight against sexual excess brings the kind of attention to you that most women of your station shun."

Slowly, she turned to face him. Her cheeks were pale and her eyes wide. "Yes. It's true that having this crusade thrust upon me has altered my life in so many ways. Friends I've held dear for years have cut me. And people I never had any association with suddenly know my name. I've been praised and threatened, sometimes simultaneously."

Jeremy tilted his head. "Thrust upon you? Are you saying you don't truly believe in your cause?"

If that were the case, "convincing" her to end her intervention would be all the easier.

Penelope looked at him for a long moment, and Jeremy could sense the fight within her. She did not yet trust him, which he had to give her credit for, and yet there was a longing in her eyes. A desire to tell him things that perhaps she couldn't tell anyone else. All he had to do was cultivate her desire for a confidante free of judgment.

He stepped a little closer. "I understand your hesitance. But I promise you that I only ask from mere curiosity in how you came to this place."

Her expression relaxed a little, but triumph was not Jeremy's reaction. He had manipulated her by saying what she needed to hear, but that fact felt . . . empty. Cold. For the first time, he wasn't proud of his ability to turn any situation to his own benefit. Especially when he knew what the ultimate outcome would be for Penelope.

"I only said a few things," she said softly. "I only spoke out of irate frustration. And then it all spiraled out of control."

He tilted his head. "I don't understand."

She paced the room restlessly. "It was a few months ago. I was almost out of mourning, at a tea with a few friends. One of them was very upset because she had found out her 'perfect' happy marriage was a lie. Her husband had secretly kept his mistress, who was now expecting his illegitimate child. Seeing my friend so heartbroken, so wrenched by her husband's thoughtless actions, made me *angry*."

Jeremy remained silent, observing the way her face lit up when she spoke. Her cheeks darkened with heightened color, her body became animated, her eyes glowed. If this was anger, it was worth inspiring. Suddenly she was more than just pretty. She was magnificent.

"I don't know why I said it, but I launched into a tirade about men of the *ton* and their foolish, selfish actions. Once I started, the words flowed. I talked about their sexual freedom and how we women could curb their out of control habits, if only we banded together." She shook her head. "It was only talk. But the women who were in attendance seemed utterly mesmerized. It was as if none of them had ever thought to tell their husbands how they felt about their philandering, let alone demand something more."

"Probably none of them had." Jeremy chuckled. Certainly, he had never met a woman so bold as to think she could control him. "So you became their champion."

She nodded. "Somehow word of my ideas that day spread. Suddenly I was being approached, ladies were seeking me out to have me repeat my thoughts. And then a few women began to actually put my words into action. That's when the men began to hiss at me, glare at me . . . even threaten me."

Jeremy's smile fell. Although he understood the anger and frustration of men like his friends who had had their lives turned upside down by Penelope's crusade, the idea that any of them would threaten her gave him no pleasure. As frustrating as Penelope was, she did not deserve to be harmed. Or even frightened.

It had always been his belief that if a lady was angry at a gentleman, it was the gentleman's duty to use his charm to appease her. If his friends were incapable of that, that was their failing. Not Penelope's.

"Do you think any of the threats are serious?" he asked, suddenly quiet. If Wharton could become so impassioned by her, it was reasonable that other men felt even more strongly about stopping her. By any means necessary.

She shrugged, but the way she dipped her chin and refused to meet his eyes told him that she had been frightened by the threats. "I think most are not any more than blustering talk. But I cannot pretend I haven't angered some very powerful men."

"You do not have to continue to pursue this," Jeremy said, carefully testing the waters. "If you feel it endangers you, you could easily end it. I think if you simply left off, soon everyone would forget."

Penelope sucked in a breath and shook her head. "No. Now that I have begun, I cannot stop."

"Why?" he asked and moved closer, yet again. She stiffened at the movement and her turquoise stare came up to his face, filled with anticipation and trepidation in equal measure. "Why are you so driven?"

She fisted her hands at her sides. "I have seen the consequences of men's actions," she whispered, her voice harsh. "More than once."

The moment the words escaped her lips, Penelope broke her stare with a little gasp. Jeremy started. That was the second time she had eluded to some kind of personal pain in her past that had to do with her crusade. Perhaps ferreting that pain out was the key to silencing her.

"Penelope—" he began.

But before he could finish the door behind them opened, and a woman stepped inside. "Good evening, Penelope—"

The woman cut off with a gasp and staggered back, even as Penelope's gaze jerked up and her wide eyes moved to him, filled with fear.

Jeremy drew back. What could cause such a reaction? He stared at the woman who had entered the room. She seemed familiar, with her pale blue eyes and brown hair. Where had he seen her?

Wait. He knew exactly where he had seen this woman before. Although she no longer wore the shocking, expensive gowns or sultry makeup that had once drawn men to her like flies to honey, there was no hiding the sensual sway to her hips or the familiar pout of her full lips. It was Fiona Clifton. The mistress who had left Jeremy's best friend, Anthony Wharton, because of Penelope's prying.

The woman whose desertion had driven his friends to force him into stopping Penelope.

Why had Fiona come into the room?

Penelope clenched her fists in utter terror. Dear God, any other lady's maid would have inquired whether her mistress had a guest before she barged into the parlor to interrupt.

But that was the trouble. Fiona had no training in any of the little nuances that separated a servant from her mistress. And now she had walked into a very dangerous situation. Jeremy was staring at her friend, and it was perfectly clear that he recognized the former courtesan. He knew she was his best friend's former mistress.

"Fiona?" he stammered. "Great God, is this where you scurried off to?"

If Fiona was a terrible maid, Penelope had to give her credit for having other talents. Although fear sparkled in her blue eyes, the young woman never missed a beat. She simply stepped up to Jeremy with a smile that could only be called flirtatious and laughed.

"Kilgrath! Goodness, how long has it been? And you are looking simply devilish, as usual."

Penelope pursed her lips. The woman couldn't learn the proper etiquette of serving tea, but she still had all the lessons of being a courtesan firmly in hand. She was looking at Jeremy like she could devour him right in the middle of the sitting room. And worse, Jeremy was staring back like he wouldn't mind that in the least.

And thoughts of "devouring" only made Penelope think about the sinful scene she'd witnessed earlier and struck her mute as a hot blush colored her cheeks.

"And how do you know Lady Norman?" Jeremy asked with a quick side glance for Penelope.

Fiona smiled, but there was a tightness around her lips that spoke of her own nervousness. Penelope stuffed her shaking hands behind her back.

"Lady Norman was kind enough to offer me a position in her home," Fiona said, and she gave Penelope a glance filled with genuine gratitude.

It was that gratitude that made it easy to overlook Fiona's other failings.

"Is that right?" Jeremy said, his surprise evident in both his expression and tone.

Fiona nodded. "Yes. Actually, I came to deliver this for you, Penelope."

Penelope winced as Fiona used her first name. She hadn't corrected the young woman before, mostly because it seemed difficult for the sweet but flighty girl to remember any more than one or two things at once. But hearing Penelope's name from a servant's lips made Jeremy's eyebrows arch. Damn, he would certainly have questions. And if she wanted him to keep Fiona's presence here a secret, she'd be forced to answer them.

Penelope stepped forward, hand outstretched.

"What is it?" she asked, finally finding her missing voice.

Fiona handed over a folded sheet of paper. When Penelope turned it over, she gasped. There was the sensual, swirling handwriting of her mysterious admirer. Damn, it was another letter from *him*.

"Thank you," she stammered as she jammed the letter behind her back. "You are dismissed."

Fiona cast Jeremy a quick glance. "Good evening, Your Grace. It was very pleasant to see you again."

Jeremy inclined his head politely, but there was no denying the curiosity and interest in his eyes as he murmured, "And you, Fiona. Good evening."

The moment her maid had left the room, Jeremy turned on Penelope, a dark eyebrow raised in question. "Fiona is under your employ?"

Penelope straightened her shoulders. "Yes. She is my lady's maid."

Jeremy nodded slowly, then looked at her with a hint of wicked humor. "Is she any good at that?"

Penelope's eyes widened in surprise. She hadn't been expecting that question and found herself blurting out, "Not very." She covered her mouth, smothering a nervous giggle. "But she *is* trying to learn."

He laughed, and the sound was entirely pleasant. Deep and rich. She stared at him, despite herself. His entire face changed when he laughed. He seemed less the sensual devil and more just a man whose smile was . . . warm. Inviting. He had a little dimple in the corner of his lip on the right side of his face.

She blinked. Great God, what was she thinking?

"I, er, I would like to ask you not to mention Fiona's presence here," she said, forcing herself to maintain a very businesslike tone.

Jeremy stopped smiling. "May I ask why?"

She faltered, her doubts about the man before her rushing back. Fiona had told her terrible stories about the abusive anger of Anthony Wharton. Fiona's past was part of why Penelope had continued on her quest, even when it felt like too much for her to bear. Was it truly possible that Jeremy wouldn't be totally aware of Wharton's abuse?

Or did he simply not see it as a problem, since Fiona was merely a woman—and a courtesan at that?

She pursed her lips at the thought that Jeremy would stand by while a woman was beaten. That she wasn't certain what he would or wouldn't do was a painful reminder that she couldn't trust him.

"I simply wouldn't want the people who come to my home to treat her with anything less than respect based upon her past indiscretions," she explained. "It is the one favor I will ask of you."

Jeremy shrugged. "I'm quite certain that the subject of the servants you keep will not come up in polite conversation, Penelope. But if it does, I shall not be the one to reveal that Fiona is under your employ, or the nature of her previous life."

"Not to anyone?" she pressed.

He stared at her, his eyes lighting up with understanding. "Ah, do you mean Andrew Wharton, her former protector?"

She nodded slowly.

With a shrug, he said, "I see no reason why he should be told about Fiona's whereabouts unless she chooses to tell him about them, herself."

Tentative relief flooded her. Now she only had to hope that Jeremy would be good to his word.

"She brought you a letter," he said with a little smile. "One you hid behind your back."

Penelope darted her gaze to him, and her grip tightened on the letter behind her. "It is utterly impolite for you to point out something like that, you know."

Jeremy laughed. "Is it? You must forgive me, I am still learning to be a reasonable man." He hesitated, leaning to the side as if to peek at the missive she had hidden. "Is it a love letter?"

Penelope's lips parted. Was it that obvious? Except, she wouldn't really call it a love letter. What the man who wrote to her had said last time had very little to do with love. Desire, yes. Passion, certainly. Love . . . no.

"No, and even if it was, it would be none of your affair!" she snapped as she backed away from him.

He laughed again, and Penelope stopped backing up with a start. He was only teasing her. Like they were close. Like they were friends.

But were they? Could they ever be?

"Very well, forgive me," Jeremy said with a gallant bow. "I shall not torment you any further. If you wish to keep your counsel on the letter, I won't force your confidence. I merely hoped that I had ferreted out some weakness in you, my dear. If some-one of your stature has one, it might give me hope that I may one day overcome my own."

Penelope stared at him. Was he still toying with her, or was he, in some part, serious? The man was so utterly confusing, she wasn't certain what to think of him at any given time.

"I have many weaknesses, Jeremy," she whispered.

His smile fell. "You would not be human if you did not."

He reached for her and caught her hand before she could draw it away. He lifted it to his lips and brushed a featherlight kiss across her knuckles. She jolted at the firm contact of his warm lips against her skin. She had a sudden urge to feel them in other places. All over her.

With a jolt, she snatched her hand away and drew it up to her suddenly heaving breast. "Good-bye, Jeremy- er, Your Grace," she stammered, her cheeks flushing.

One dark brow arched. "Until later, Lady Norman. Enjoy your letter."

Then he released her and backed from the room. Once he was gone, Penelope sank into the nearest chair. Her legs were trem-bling and her stomach was doing flip-flops. It didn't matter that it was utterly stupid or that she still wasn't certain she could trust Jeremy Vaughn; something about him still shook her. Moved her from her foundation. Made her question herself.

Much like the letter writer did. Penelope pulled the missive from behind her back and stared at the swirling handwriting. What would he write to her tonight? What fantasies would he weave?

And would she be strong enough to resist their pull?

She already knew the answer to that question, even before she broke the wax seal and unfolded the pages. She didn't possess that kind of strength. Before the end of the night, she knew full well she would be writhing in her bed alone, thinking of the author's words, remembering the wicked things she'd seen at the Cyprian's ball. . .

And picturing Jeremy's face all the while.

With a sigh, she began to read:

Dear Penelope:

If you were mine, I would spend an eternity simply touching your skin. And then I would spend another tasting you all over . . .

Six

Penelope sat on her bed, staring at a small pile of letters that she had placed there. Their presence mocked her. Tormented her.

They were all letters from *him*, her mysterious admirer who wanted to do such wicked things to her. Each night for a week, they had arrived at exactly the same hour. In fact, Penelope had become so accustomed to receiving them that when the time grew near, she found herself watching the door and waiting for the next missive. She grew restless and dull until she held the folded sheets of expensive paper in her hands.

I want to take you, Penelope. Hard and fast. Slow and easy. . .

Each one detailed more and more about the author's fantasies about her. In truth, they had become her fantasies, as well. She'd read his pointed, poetic, and often pornographic words so many times that she could summon every sentence from memory without even trying.

And I want you to want me as desperately as I crave you. . .

Some of the letters had concentrated on what her admirer wished to do to her in detail. She had been forced to think about nights where this faceless man simply kissed every inch of her body. Of his hands and fingers stroking over every curve and invading every hidden, forbidden crevice. And finally, of the crescendo of him taking her in every position imaginable . . . and some she hadn't even thought possible.

Would you surrender if I pressed you to a bed and opened you wide for my touch? Do you ever imagine I am doing so?

But some of the letters had been less blatant about activities. They were more about her charms. One letter had been entirely about the erotic beauty of her hair. Of his fantasies that she would take it down in front of him, let it tickle his body, wrap it around his cock. . .

Penelope surged to her feet and paced away from the letters. She had no illusions that those heated words weren't altering her. Ruining her. Making her into something she didn't understand.

She should burn them, but she couldn't manage it. They brought her too much sinful pleasure. Haunted her nights. She had given up the pretense of resisting their erotic draw. The past week had been sleepless and restless as she brought herself to completion again and again, and yet felt less than satisfied each time.

She clenched a fist against the mantel. A deep hunger, one she had never allowed herself to feel before, had been awakened in her. A dark desire that made her thighs clench against empty wetness when she thought of the letters or the sinful things she had seen on Jeremy's field trips.

"My lady?"

Penelope turned with a hot blush to face the door and a wait-ing footman. She refused to meet his eyes, fearful anyone who looked at her now would see her wicked thoughts.

"What is it Appleton?"

"The Duke of Kilgrath has arrived, my lady. He awaits you in the west parlor."

Penelope started. Her brain was becoming so addled, she had completely lost track of time and utterly forgotten the appoint-ment Jeremy had made to visit with her.

"Please inform him I will be down directly."

As the servant bowed away, Penelope moved to the full-length mirror in the corner of her dressing chamber. Although she was probably silly to think her servant would read her outrageous thoughts and fantasies with a look, Jeremy was a different story. He would surely see something sinful in her demeanor if she didn't clear her mind.

She smoothed her hair and ran her hands over the high waist of her pretty blue gown. She looked like a lady. She could behave and think like one, as well.

Slowly, she made her way down the stairs to the comfort-able parlor where Jeremy waited. Drawing a calming breath, she pushed the door open.

He was not sitting, but leaning against the wall beside the fireplace when she entered, one of the books from her library in hand. She caught her breath at the sight of him. His slightly too long hair swept over his forehead, his green eyes were utterly focused on the words he was reading.

Her knees began to shake at the sight of him. If her admirer's words and the sinful images she'd been exposed to had haunted her, so had Jeremy's face. How many times had she pictured him while she pleasured herself in the furtive darkness of her empty bed?

In how many dreams had it been Kilgrath who slid beneath her covers and woke her with the shattering pleasure another man wrote about in such detail?

"Byron," he said, jolting her from her thoughts as he closed the book. "Rather sensual for a woman who leads the fight against excess."

Penelope blinked. "I've always thought of Byron as romantic rather than sensual."

He smiled as he set the book on a nearby table and approached her. "In my experience, sometimes romance and sensuality are close to the same thing."

Penelope swallowed hard as he stopped no more than a foot in front of her. He stared at her face, then tilted his head to the side.

"Are you quite well?"

She blinked. "Of course."

"You look . . ." He hesitated, as if searching for the correct word.

In the brief silence, Penelope tensed. She could think of a few to describe herself. Hypocritical. Wanton.

"Tired," he finally finished.

She shook her head. "No, I'm fine. I simply lost track of time. I'm sorry if you were forced to wait overly long for me."

"Not at all. But are you ready to depart now?"

She drew back. "Depart?"

It was the middle of the day. Where in the world could he possibly want to take her in the middle of the day? No Cyprian ball or courtesan's bed or erotic opera could be going on now, could it? If any of those things were, she wasn't sure she could bear them in her present state.

"Yes." He nodded. "Will you do me the honor of riding with me? Come to my home."

Penelope staggered away from him a step. "To your home? No, that would be utterly improper. Your reputation, our being alone together. If that were discovered . . ."

He frowned. "I would insure we weren't seen, Penelope. I'll protect you."

Penelope sucked in a harsh breath. Protect her. That was the one thing she couldn't afford to believe, that this man could be her protector. And she found, now that it had been said, that it was the one thing she wanted, perhaps more than anything else in the world.

She hadn't had a true friend, a real confidante, since . . . since she and her sister broke faith years before. And that had been because of a man almost exactly like the one standing before her. Yet now, looking at Jeremy, she felt like she *could* whisper her most intimate secrets to him and find no judgment. She could tell him her pains and be comforted.

And no matter how much she tried to convince herself that those appearances were nothing more than an illusion, she couldn't bring herself to break from him, as she knew she should.

"You promise that you will not let me be seen?" she whispered.

He hesitated, then nodded. "I do."

Her head dipped. She was defeated by her own secret desires and a loneliness that felt so keen when she was near this man. "Very well. I will gather up my wrap and we can go now, if you would like."

Jeremy glanced down surreptitiously at the hand Penelope had slipped into the crook of his arm after he snuck her into the back servant door of his opulent London estate. She seemed so-so *fragile* today. Shaken and quiet as they rode in his carriage to his estate. She had barely met his gaze the entire time they were together.

He supposed he should take pride in that fact. It was perfectly clear that he was breaking her every time he exposed her to the erotic and she responded with muted arousal. And his anonymous letters moved her, as well. He was certain of it. Now it was almost time to progress to the final stage of his plan.

And yet, he felt no pride. Looking at her, so pale and quiet, feeling her cling to his arm as if she thought he would support her, he felt . . . *guilty*.

And that was not an experience he'd ever had before. Certainly not associated with a woman. His life was his to lead. He'd never led it thinking much of other people. If they didn't like him, they could move out of his way. If they were hurt by his actions, that was their failing, not his own.

But with Penelope everything was . . . different.

"Why did you bring me here?" Penelope asked.

Jeremy started. He'd been so tangled in his own confusing, unwelcome thoughts, he had forgotten his purpose. Well, he couldn't allow for that. He couldn't allow for Penelope's strange appeal to manipulate him into abandoning his sworn duty. He had some honor, although his promises were so dishonorable.

"I wanted to show you something," he said, letting go of her arm. Distancing himself was best. After all, he was supposed to be her convert, not her friend.

She stared at him for a brief moment, then broke the gaze with a blush as she forced her hands behind her back. "What is it?"

"I will, of course, be ridding myself of these things shortly, but before I did, I thought you would want to see them. They represent all you fight against," he said as he stopped in front of a door.

Penelope tilted her head in question, but before she could speak, Jeremy gave a push and the door swung open, revealing his private gallery.

Penelope stepped past him, her mouth slightly open as she moved into the large, sunny room. Jeremy shut the door behind them and leaned back against it, watching her as she stared in awe at what she saw.

Jeremy had started collecting these pieces five years ago, when a friend returned from India with a few shocking statuettes that depicted couples intertwined in blatant acts of sexual hedonism. He'd bought one from his friend and immediately set out to find more erotic art.

Over the years, he'd added paintings, some of which he had commissioned, and others that had simply caught his eye. He'd also taken an interest in other forms of art. Pottery engraved with scenes of lovemaking, silverwork whose handles depicted nude women or were phallic in nature.

In a short time, he had gathered one of the most extensive

collections of such art in London. From time to time, he even allowed tours of the work.

But this "tour," with Penelope as his only guest, was his favorite so far. What she saw around her would have been scandalous to most women who had been raised to be "good" and "proper." Certainly this room wasn't one he shared with just any guest.

This kind of art took a certain kind of personality to truly appreciate. He had thought Penelope would hardly be able to look at the statues and paintings, but to his very happy surprise, she did not cower.

In fact, she stared openly. Her fists were clenched at her sides and her body was stiff as she lurched closer, but she couldn't hide the rapt expression on her face as she moved toward the large marble statue that was the centerpiece of the room.

He had commissioned that work a year ago and paid a very pretty penny for it. It featured a woman, long hair blowing back from her enraptured face. Her nude body was wrapped around the one of her marble lover. Her legs were clasped around his waist, his stone fingers pressed into her thigh, his mouth pressed to her breast. It was beautiful and arousing all at once.

And whether she liked it or not, it was clear Penelope reacted the same way he did. She was enraptured. With a shiver, she turned toward him, her face a flaming red, her blue eyes cast anywhere but his.

"What is the purpose of showing me these-these things?" she asked. "Is this a game to you?"

Jeremy swallowed back a chuckle. Sometimes it did seem like they were playing a game. A complicated chess match where she maneuvered and he countered, but neither one gained ground.

But he could feel her defenses wavering, and it was only a matter of time before he put her in checkmate.

"Of course not," he lied, doing his best to sound affronted. "When I approached you, I told you I could safely expose you to the underbelly of the Society that you wish to fight against. I've lived it for most of my life, and I am intimately acquainted with it. You agreed that you would like to see that underbelly first-hand, so that you could be better equipped to battle it. Have you changed your mind?"

She shook her head, but there was hesitation in her movements. Subtle, but undeniable. Penelope was beginning to question her fight, question *herself*.

"I cannot change my mind now," she murmured, turning back to stare at the intertwined lovers and their passionate embrace.

"Do you wish to?" he asked, his own voice as low as her own.

She looked at him over her shoulder and his stomach clenched. Dear God, she had no idea how alluring she was in that position. Little strands of blond hair curled around her pink cheeks, framing her face. Would her face be that pink if he was gliding in and out of her slick body as he bent her over the marble statue?

Damn, how he'd like to find out.

"No," she said, this time more firmly.

She smoothed her gown and it seemed that the questioning he had sensed in her bled away. Covered, at least temporarily, by the stern, cold exterior Penelope presented to most of the world around her.

"Tell me, does every gentleman in your position have such a gallery?" she asked, sidestepping the statue and moving to look at the paintings.

Jeremy laughed. "I know of a few collectors, but nothing as extensive as this. I have pieces that I've commissioned, as well as works going back thousands of years."

Her eyes widened when she looked at him in shocked disbelief. "Thousands?"

Motioning to a glass case along the back wall, he nodded. "Yes, most of these pieces are quite old."

She stepped up to the case like she was approaching a ready executioner, but finally she leaned over the glass and gasped. Most of the ancient items were pieces that would have had a household use. Spoons with naughty images on their handles, a tarnished mirror with mating gods and goddesses on the cracked frame, even a piece of women's jewelry that featured a decorated gold devil pleasuring a writhing maiden with his tongue.

"Sensuality, sex, debauchery," Jeremy said, moving a tiny bit closer to Penelope. "Those things aren't new. They were even celebrated by some societies."

"And how many of those societies ultimately fell?" Penelope continued to stare at the items, her fists clenched along the cool glass top of the case. "These things, these images and the dissipation they represent may not be new, but they were dangerous then. Even as they are dangerous now."

"Dangerous?" Jeremy repeated, surprised by her use of the word.

It could easily seem as though she meant dangerous to Society, dangerous to those who surrendered to their baser drives, but there was something in her tone and a sadness to her expression that made him think her statement was more a personal one than a broad reference.

He leaned down. "Penelope, what happened to you?"

Her fingers curled against the glass before she spun around, her face pale. She wouldn't meet his eyes, but Jeremy saw powerful and dark emotions in the blue depths regardless. There was raw pain reflected there.

And for the first time, he actually cared about that pain.

"Someone I cared for—" she gasped out a breath, as if the mere act of speaking the words hurt her, "—was seduced in order to protect me."

Jeremy drew back a fraction. That was the one confession he hadn't expected. Who could she mean?

He caught his breath. Her sister. Lady Miranda Rothschild had been the subject of many whispers after her now husband, Ethan Hamon, the Earl of Rothschild, threw himself at her feet at a ball . . . wait, it had been Penelope's engagement ball, hadn't he heard that?

Could Rothschild have seduced Miranda? Jeremy wouldn't put it past him. The two men had run in similar circles for many years, though Ethan had left all that behind once he married. Many of Jeremy's friends had said the Earl's wife had ruined him, though the man seemed happy enough whenever Jeremy saw him.

He searched Penelope's face. There was more to her pain than something from her sister's past. By all accounts, Miranda was now happy, and she certainly wanted for nothing. Rothschild showered her with gifts on a regular basis, to the point that even the women placed wagers on what magnificent bauble the beautiful Lady Rothschild would be given next.

No, Penelope's pain went much deeper. It was personal. Caused by something that had no happy ending.

"But what happened to *you*?" Jeremy pressed, his fingers itching to cover her hand. But he wouldn't allow himself that. He wouldn't touch her, mostly because he feared once he did, it wouldn't end with mere comfort.

And if he gave her more than comfort, it would ruin his plans.

Penelope finally lifted her gaze to his. Her eyes shone with unshed tears and her bottom lip quivered just slightly.

"H-he-" she began, then cut herself off.

She backed away from him three long steps, shaking her head. "No. I never should have said anything. I apologize for my lack of decorum. I want to go home now. I will be attending the Trimble ball tonight, and there is much for me to do."

Jeremy could have pursued her, but he stayed put, partly because he felt that pushing her would only hurt his cause. And partly because being so close to her was disconcerting.

"Very well. I will escort you home."

He motioned for the door, and Penelope stood at least two feet away from him as they made their way to the hall.

"Will you be there?" she asked, her voice full of forced lightness.

"At the Trimble ball?" he asked.

She nodded.

He glanced at her from the corner of his eye. He had been invited to the ball, of course, and had intended to be present. But now he wasn't sure that was the right course of action.

Penelope was ripe for the taking, but not by him. No, she couldn't think it was Jeremy Vaughn, Duke of Kilgrath, who seduced her into surrendering her senses.

She needed the anonymous stranger who had already weakened her with his shocking words. And Jeremy was more than willing to play that role.

"I'm afraid I'm unable to attend," he lied. "But perhaps we could speak tomorrow?"

"Yes," Penelope said as he helped her into his carriage. "I would be happy to see you tomorrow."

And as Jeremy climbed up and took his seat across from her, he couldn't help but smile. Whether she knew it or not, Penelope would see him. And he would see her.

All of her.

And perhaps by the time the night ended, he would have completed his duty to his friends and purged himself of the strange draw that this pretty little miss had on him.

Seven

Penelope looked at herself in the mirror, watching as Fiona brushed her hair in long, even strokes. It felt like she was looking at a stranger, for she had no idea who she had become in just a fortnight.

Since her husband's death, since she started talking about the Upper Ten Thousand and their vices, she had begun to see herself in a particular light. She was Lady Penelope Norman, a woman who spoke her mind, who didn't care what others thought of her. She had accepted that her unpopular opinions would likely preclude her from another marriage. And her moral code would keep her from having her baser desires fulfilled by a man's touch again.

She'd believed she had accepted all those consequences.

But the more time she spent with Jeremy Vaughn, the more she realized her acceptance was nothing more than a pretty lie.

She might have been able to *ignore* her darkest, most secret and sinful desires, but in truth, she hadn't cut them away. They still lurked there, making her ache, making her weak.

Between Jeremy's erotic influence and the secret author who left no detail to the imagination of what he would do to her wet body, she was dangerously close to the edge.

"Are you quite all right, Penelope?" Fiona asked, her voice cutting through Penelope's thoughts. "You are so very pale."

Penelope focused on the other woman in the mirror image. "Your life before," she said softly, blushing when Fiona winced ever so slightly. "Your life with Wharton, do you ever miss it?"

Fiona placed the brush on the dressing table with a clatter. "Wharton . . . did things to me that I will never forget," she said softly. "And never forgive."

Penelope nodded. The look on Fiona's pale face reminded her of everything she believed in. And she stiffened her spine. She *could* fight her desires, she could battle her weakness. Tomorrow, when she saw Jeremy, she would tell him she no longer desired to meet with him. That she had seen enough. If he was truly changed, her denial would be enough for him.

And if he wasn't, she would no longer be his fool.

The door to her chamber opened, and a footman stepped inside. "My lady, a missive for you has just arrived."

Penelope spun around to look at the servant. Even from across the room, she could tell who the letter was from. Her secret admirer. Her tempting vice.

This was the first test to her newfound resolve.

"Bring it here," she said, rising to her feet with a stern frown.

The young man delivered the letter. As he left the room, she stared at it. At the familiar handwriting. At the blank, round seal of wax on the back. Even before she read it, her body weakened, her breasts felt heavy. Her legs shook.

Her fingers clenched around the paper, wrinkling it as she stepped toward the fire silently.

"What are you doing?" Fiona asked, drawing in a harsh breath.

"I am burning it," Penelope said through clenched teeth as she held the pages out to the flames. The heat warmed her shaking hand, but she couldn't release the letter, as she knew she should. She stared at it, the orange glow of the fire turning the ecru a strange yellow.

"Penelope?" Fiona whispered.

Biting back a sob, Penelope yanked the letter back. She couldn't do it. She was too curious about what the mysterious man would say next. If she burned the letter, she knew full well that it would haunt her.

"Damn," she whispered beneath her breath as she broke the seal with enough violence that the sheet beneath tore. Holding the ends together, she read the message.

Penelope, you must know how seeing you without being able to touch you is a torment. I will be at the Trimble ball tonight. I will wait for you in the first parlor in the west wing of the estate. Come to me at midnight. Please.

"What does he say this time?" Fiona asked, stepping forward.

Penelope clutched the letter to her chest. Since Fiona saw the contents of the first letter, Penelope hadn't allowed her maid to read the others. But she had no illusions that the former courtesan wasn't utterly aware of the kind of sinful things the mystery author was writing in every letter that had followed.

"He wants to meet me. Tonight. At the Trimble ball," Penelope admitted, her breath short as she crumpled the pages.

Fiona smiled, her bright eyes sparkling. "How exciting!"

Penelope stared. Dear God, she agreed. It *was* excitement that swelled her chest and made her wet and needy.

She shook her head. "No!" she snapped, angry at herself, as much as Fiona. "It is not exciting. It is utterly inappropriate and foolish and outrageous!"

Fiona drew back at her shrewish tone. "I-I apologize, my lady," she whispered. "I did not mean to offend."

Penelope dipped her chin in shame. It wasn't her right to take her problems out on Fiona. That made her no better than Wharton.

"No, I apologize. The last few weeks have been *trying*. And this newest development only causes more confusion."

Her servant smiled as if she understood Penelope's feelings. "What will you do?"

Penelope considered the question. "Part of me wishes to hide here, avoid the party altogether like a coward."

Fiona stepped forward with a shake of her head. "You, a coward? No, you are the strongest woman I have ever known."

Penelope blushed with pleasure at the compliment. She wasn't sure she deserved such glowing praise when her mind was so weak.

"Thank you. But whether I am strong or a coward cannot dictate this decision. I am expected at the gathering by Lady Trimble herself. She is influential. I cannot cry off."

With a sigh, Penelope began to pace. "I suppose I could simply ignore the letter, as if I'd never received it. Then this man will wait for me in vain, and that will be the end of it."

The idea of which gave her an unwanted sense of dismay that she crushed down deep inside her.

"But what if he doesn't simply wait?" Fiona asked.

Penelope tilted her head. "What do you mean?"

"I've spent many years around men who are bold and sensual like the one who is writing to you," the former courtesan explained. "He might not just wait for you and then fade into the crowd when you ignore his summons. He might approach you in front of all in attendence."

Penelope swallowed hard. Dear God, she hadn't thought of that possibility. If a man approached her in public, demanding to know why she hadn't kept a secret rendezvous with him in the private area of her hosts' home, the scandal could be quite vicious. There were those who would gladly capitalize on any mark against her character.

"That is true." She paced the room twice, picturing every hideous scenario that could result in such a thing. Finally, she looked at Fiona. "I suppose I have no choice but to meet with him. I can tell him, without question, that I do not wish to receive his correspondence any longer. Perhaps that will end this madness."

The other woman stepped forward, placing a hand on Penelope's forearm with an expression of concern. "Are you certain he won't . . . hurt you?"

Penelope placed her own hand over the other woman's with a smile. Of course Fiona would fear for her physical safety after everything she had been through in her own tragic life.

But Penelope didn't worry for her bodily safety. The way the stranger wrote to her wasn't threatening or crude. It was simply bold and erotic.

Her fears were more grounded in her own lack of control, rather than his. But perhaps, once she saw the man she had built up so fully in her mind, she would no longer desire him. Perhaps he would have bad teeth and padded calves and she would find him repugnant.

"He won't hurt me," she promised. "I won't let him hurt me."

And all she could hope was that she wouldn't end up hurting herself when she came face-to-face with the man whose words had haunted her.

Jeremy stood in the long shadows that filled the darkened, empty expanse of Lord Trimble's parlor. It was a family parlor, not a public one, far away from the buzzing crowds that flowed in the sparkling ballroom just a few twists in the halls away.

Although he hadn't seen her, he knew Penelope was there. His driver had informed him of her arrival as he waited in an un-marked carriage outside. Jeremy had slipped in through a side door and was now waiting for her.

Waiting for the inevitable.

He thrilled at the thought. In just . . . he glanced at his pocket watch . . . just ten minutes, he would be with her. She wouldn't be able to see him in the dark room, but he would finally touch her. Seduce her.

He hadn't felt so needy since . . . actually, he couldn't truly remember the last time. Raised the eldest son of a powerful Duke, Jeremy had grown accustomed to having what he wanted, when he wanted it. Whether it was blunt or horses or women, he could count on one hand the times he'd been refused.

It was rather boring, truth be told. There was no challenge in simply snapping his fingers and having a woman fall at his feet.

Penelope was a challenge. Pursuing her had been hard work, and tonight he would receive the benefit of that labor. It was an infinitely satisfying thought, and his cock hardened.

The click of the door latch being turned brought him from his reverie and focused his attention. He stared as the barrier slowly swung open, and a gloved hand curled around the edge.

Penelope.

She stepped inside. The moonlight washed down from the window in a long column that illuminated the doorway perfectly. In the misty glow, Jeremy could see every detail of Penelope's form and face, but she could not see him in the shadows.

And look, he did. She was wearing a pale green gown with a fashionably low neckline and short, puffed sleeves. A darker wrap was draped around her forearms, the tassels brushing the curve of her hip as she moved farther into the room.

"Hello?" she said, her voice hoarse and weak. She pursed her lips and repeated it, this time with more conviction.

Jeremy continued to stare, watching her full lips form the word in fascination. Her face was almost as pale as the weak moonlight, her eyes wide and filled with emotion she wasn't practiced enough to hide. She was afraid. She was anxious.

She was needy. Desire was sparkling in her gaze, along with those other emotions.

Her face fell when there was no answer from the room within. She looked down with a blush before she began to go.

Jeremy shook off his unexpected reaction to her appearance and whispered, "Penelope."

He was careful to keep his voice low, disguised by its level and a slight roughness that he forced.

She jumped at the sound of her name and spun back, stumbling out of the shard of moonlight to join him in the almost complete darkness.

"What——?" she began.

He didn't allow her to finish. Stepping forward, he caught her hand. She jolted at the touch, but didn't stop him when he tugged her forward and pulled her into his arms. He wrapped himself around her, pulling her flush to his chest, her hips to his hips, her legs to his own. God, she felt good. An unexpected heaven that entered his seductive hell.

"Please," she whimpered, but the intent of her plea was anything but clear. He didn't know if she was saying please touch her or please don't.

But it seemed she didn't know, either. She at once bunched her fists against his chest to push him away and subtly arched her hips against his to bring them even closer. With a little chuckle of pleasure, Jeremy took advantage of her confusion by dipping his head down and pressing his lips to hers.

For a brief moment, she was completely still, her hands fisted against his chest, her mouth pursed beneath his own. But then she let out a little moan and clutched at his coat. Her lips parted, inviting him in and when he took the invitation, her wet tongue greeted him with hot and hungry fever.

Jeremy crushed her closer, forgoing technique for raw passion. He sucked her tongue, he stroked his hands down her spine, he cupped her backside to lift her up against his aching cock. He rocked into her as he backed her, step by step to the wall across the darkened room.

When her back flattened to the hard surface, Penelope moaned again and lifted her hips to his in a mute entreaty.

All the waiting had been worth this. Her surrender was sweet. True surrender, not a put on play like courtesans or even widows did. Jeremy had truly conquered Penelope, overcome her resolve, buckled the strength of her resistance. Every time she made a little sound of pleasure, it made his cock ache all the more.

Until he was almost mad with the wanting.

Moving his mouth from hers, he dragged his lips down her chin, over the curve of her throat. He slipped a hand beneath the neckline of her pretty gown and felt the beaded tip of her breast already straining toward his fingers. He rolled the bud between his thumb and forefinger as he dropped his mouth lower, over the silken fabric of her gown, lower to her stomach. He dropped to his knees as he glided his mouth even farther, blowing hot breath against the juncture of her thighs and reveling in the way her hips surged to meet his mouth while she let out a cry of pleasure.

He didn't speak, didn't ask as he shoved the layers of silky gown up, up until he revealed the delicate cotton chemise beneath. He pushed that away, too, and found the split in her satin drawers. He worked a finger inside, stroking the tip of his index finger along the wet, sweet slit hidden within.

"Oh God," she groaned, her fingernails raking against the expensive wallpaper behind her.

He added a second finger, spreading and teasing her slippery folds, opening her until he could scent her desire, until it coated his fingers with the proof that she had been aching for him as much as he had ached for her. Even if she didn't know who he was.

Penelope fought for purchase against the slippery wall. Everything was happening too quickly. She'd had every intention to end this madness. To demand her mysterious admirer cease his unwanted correspondence. Instead, she found herself half naked, his fingers now plunging into her wet channel and dragging out sensations unlike any she'd ever felt before, even with the furtive touch of her own hands.

He stroked her with a combination of wicked intent and infinite gentleness. He stretched her body, opening her for. . .

She knew what for. He had every intention of taking this heated, unexpected, animalistic coming together to its end. He was going to have her. Against a wall in the parlor of one of the most influential and stern leaders of London Society.

And Penelope couldn't find her voice to stop him. Especially when his fingers curled inside her and she felt the whisper of his breath against her bare skin.

She jolted her gaze down and watched as the shadow of his head moved in. She squinted but could make out no features in the dark and still room. Just a shadow lover, as he had been in all her fantasies.

But this was real. The brush of his lips against her thigh was real. The way he tugged against her draws, ripping the fine satin until it hung useless around her legs and then brought his mouth up to give her the most intimate kiss was real.

She braced her legs, rolling her head against the wall behind her as exquisite sensation roared through her. His tongue stroked her outer lips, teased the little nub hidden within the folds of her sex, sucked it until the dull, warm throb of desire roared into a mounting crescendo. She thrust against him, against both her will and her reason, and reached wantonly for the release she wanted so badly. A release of her body. Of her spirit.

A release of everything she fought for.

That thought brought her up short. Her body teetered on the edge of madness and she could not allow herself to fall. With a sob of anything but pleasure, Penelope detangled her fingers from his hair and skirted away from his wicked tongue.

"No," she moaned, turning to face the wall. She sagged against it as she smoothed her skirt down between the cool surface and her body. "No, no I can't."

Jeremy stared up at Penelope, wishing he could see the details of her face in the darkness. He could only hear her ragged breaths, the ones that matched his own panting. Her body had been so close to release, he had already felt the first flutterings against his tongue. He'd tasted the desperate neediness of her flesh, felt the liquid relief as it poured over him.

And he had ached for more of it. In that moment, he hadn't been thinking about anything but making her sob with release. Feeling her rock with pleasure. And doing it again and again until she lay weak and satisfied on the floor beneath his hard body.

The idea that she would refuse him without even allowing her own pleasure hadn't entered his mind. Not when she had reacted so powerfully to his kiss, his touch, his heat.

Apparently, he had underestimated her dedication to her foolish quest and strange moral code.

He pushed from his knees and stood watching her shadow as she continued to lean on the wall, her back to him.

"Penelope," he whispered, and this time it took no effort to make his voice rough and strange. "Why do you push me away when all your body's reactions tell me how much you want my touch?"

She spun around and in the dim shadows he saw her shake her head. "My wants, they are not all I must consider. You must know that, since you know my identity. I don't know why you chose me to write your . . ."

She hesitated and he heard her breath release in a shuddering sigh.

" . . . to write your letters to."

He stepped closer and her body stiffened. "Because I have wanted you since the first moment I saw you."

"No," she whispered, but he had the distinct feeling she was saying it to herself, not denying him. "I can't. I cannot allow you, I cannot allow this."

She sidestepped him, staggering across the room until she stood in that shaft of moonlight by the door again. She rested her forehead on the barrier, her shoulders rolled forward.

"Please, I don't know who you are. I don't want to know. But you cannot write to me again. You cannot seek me out. Just . . . just leave me be."

Then she threw open the door and rushed into the hallway, leaving Jeremy alone. He stared at the place where she had stood and let out a low curse, though he wasn't angry.

No, there was some other feeling. One he rarely experienced. Disappointment, mixed with a tinge of regret. His body was so hard that he ached all over, and it was clear he wouldn't have satisfaction tonight unless he sought it from another woman.

He licked his lips and tasted the sweet ambrosia of Penelope's body on his tongue. Another woman would only satisfy him temporarily. It was Penelope he wanted.

She had run away tonight, rushed back into the crowd unsatisfied, but that did not mean she had been unchanged. Even if she had not allowed either one of them to find release, she had surrendered, given herself over to a man who existed only in shadow. To a stranger who had seduced her with words.

Her shaking body, her moans of pleasure, they had been proof that the lovely Penelope hid desires that were polar opposites of the proper code she lived by.

Jeremy smiled as he took a quick glance into the hall and made his way back to his waiting carriage. He might go home hard and aching tonight, but he had no doubt that with a little more time, a little more pressure, he would have Penelope. First her body, then her soul. And her cause would soon be crushed in the wave of pleasure he would surely introduce her to.

Eight

The frayed satin edges of Penelope's torn drawers stroked her still trembling thighs beneath her gown. The gentle brush of ragged fabric tormented her already edgy body. It was a constant reminder of what she had done. Of what more she *still* wanted to do with a stranger whose intent she didn't understand.

But that hadn't mattered the moment he brushed his lips to hers. She had thrown away all hesitation and surrendered like a reckless wanton. She blushed as she recalled every pleasurable sensation that had washed over her in the dark. As she recalled that she hadn't made any effort to stop the faceless stranger when he touched her.

Her hands shook as she took a glass of wine from a passing servant's tray. As she swallowed a hefty gulp of the liquid, she willed herself to be calm, but it was all in vain.

She wanted to go home. She wanted to hide from her memories.

And worst of all, she wanted to talk to Jeremy, of all people. Even though she doubted his intentions, even though his presence made her nervous and needy, she wanted to see him. To tell him what had happened and ask his advice.

He wouldn't judge her. He wouldn't think she was disgusting. He would understand.

Wouldn't he?

"Penelope!"

Penelope's shoulders stiffened at the piercing sound of her mother's voice coming across the ballroom behind her. Great God, of all the nights she didn't want to see her mother. Spending time with Dorthea Albright was already trying enough, even when Penelope didn't have ragged nerves and an aching, empty body that kept reminding her of her sins.

With a grimace, Penelope turned. Her mother was shouldering her way through the crowd with Penelope's younger sister Beatrice at her side, a glower on the other girl's face.

"Hello, Mama," Penelope said. "Beatrice. Where is Winifred?"

Beatrice folded her arms with a frown. "*She* was asked to dance. Which isn't fair. I'm older than her by a whole year. If a young man wants to dance with an Albright, he ought to choose me."

Penelope bit her tongue. It would do no good to point out to Beatrice that her superior attitude and sour expression likely kept young men from pressing a suit for her hand. Beatrice had always been her mother's child, raised with a sense of entitlement that did not fit her station in life. She was cold and spoiled, and her attitude alienated women and men alike.

Penelope had often thought her sister must be awfully lonely in the ivory tower she had built around herself. But there was no stopping her, or their mother's encouragement of such vanity and superiority.

"Don't worry about Winifred," Dorthea shushed. "That boy she's with is *only* a baron's son. Not worth your time, certainly."

Penelope bit back a gasp. Her mother had spoken so loudly that certainly a few families around them had heard her disparaging comment.

"Mama," she whispered, clasping her mother's arm. "You speak out of turn."

"I do not," her mother insisted, shaking herself free. "Your sister should not marry anyone less than an earl like her sister has married."

Beatrice nodded. "Yes, and you shouldn't talk, Penelope. After all, you've been working on landing a duke."

Penelope's jaw dropped open, and she stared at her mother and sister. "First, we are not a family who is titled, and even though Miranda married an earl, it does not follow that Beatrice and Winifred will marry men of that rank." She turned on her sister. "And as for me marrying a duke, I have no idea where you heard that rumor, but I am not marrying anyone!"

Her mother smiled. "Come now, Society is buzzing with talk of how you and the Duke of Kilgrath have been spotted talking very closely. The man has six estates and at least fifty thousand pounds a year, Penelope! You will exceed even Miranda. I am so proud!"

Penelope swallowed hard. Her head was beginning to spin. Great God, were people truly saying such things? With her mother, it was hard to tell the difference between truth and hopeful delusion.

"The Duke of Kilgrath has shown an interest in my thoughts on the behavior of the men of his circles," Penelope insisted. "We are not courting."

Although that was something she occasionally had to remind herself of, like she had earlier in the day, when they had toured the sinful gallery where he kept his erotic art.

Her mother's smile fell. "Your ideas. Dear Lord, child, you shall ruin everything if you continue your incessant babbling. You are garnering a reputation, my dear. One just as damaging as if you were cavorting around in dark corners like a woman of easy virtue."

Penelope bit her lip. She had been doing just that not an hour before. A bit more than cavorting, actually. She had very nearly surrendered to the sinful touch of a man whose face she hadn't even seen.

And she had liked it. Which made her the biggest fraud in the land.

". . . and when you talk to Miranda and Ethan, I hope you will do just that," her mother continued.

Although Penelope didn't know what her mother had been rattling on about, the mention of Penelope's sister and her husband made Penelope jolt back to attention.

"Speak to Miranda and Ethan?" she repeated as her heart jolted to her chest. "I have no intention of speaking to either one of them."

Her mother frowned. "I do not understand what made you

break ties with your sister. The two of you were thick as thieves until her marriage. It's silly to be jealous of her accomplishments when you know her husband could be very influential in your life."

Penelope bit back a bark of unladylike laughter. Oh yes, Ethan Hamon, Earl of Rothschild, could be very influential. She'd seen firsthand just how *influential* he could be. And if her mother knew just exactly how he had "wooed" Miranda, she wondered if Dorthea would approve of him so much.

Sadly, her mother might see only the money and influence the match had garnered their family. Perhaps she wouldn't care about the means to the end.

But Penelope did.

"They are here tonight and you *shall* speak to Miranda!" Dorthea insisted as she snapped her fan shut and rapped it against her palm. "This feud between you must end."

Penelope gasped as her gaze moved around the room. Sure enough, no more than twenty paces away stood her eldest sister Miranda, her hand curved into the crook of her husband's arm. She was leaning against him ever so slightly, looking up at him as she whispered something to him. It wasn't hard to guess the topic of the conversation from the way Rothschild returned her smile with a wicked one of his own.

Penelope broke her stare away.

"I am going home," she said through clenched teeth.

"No, you are not," her mother snapped, reaching for her.

Penelope dodged her grip. "I am."

She found her sister a second time and saw that the couple was moving toward them. From across the room, Miranda met her stare. Penelope's heart ached. Miranda had once been her best friend, her closest confidante. Or at least, she'd *thought* they'd been that close, but it had turned out to be a lie.

Still, when she looked into Miranda's eyes she saw the close relationship they'd once had. She saw the warmth and care of her oldest sister.

But when she looked at Miranda and Ethan together, Penelope saw all the lies, all the deceptions. And she also saw a reminder of everything she couldn't even want, let alone have. It was another shameful reminder of how close she'd come to throwing away the virtues she extolled.

"Good evening," she stammered, before she rushed away, her mother's calls of her name still ringing in her ears.

Jeremy paced his bed chamber, his robe flapping around his bare thighs with every step. Although it was almost noon and nearly twelve hours had passed since his powerful encounter with Penelope, the intensity of their exchange still rocked him. And the memories . . . well, he had perfect recall. He could still smell her light perfume, could still feel the warmth of her skin beneath his.

He could still taste her on his lips. An earthy, sweet combination that made his cock rock hard no matter how many times he found release at his own hand. It had been more than once since she left him, and yet, even now, his arousal taunted him from beneath his robe.

Allowing Penelope to go when he knew he could have coaxed

her back with another kiss, another touch, had been very difficult. Almost impossible.

And that was troubling. He hadn't felt this strongly about a woman in a long time. Desire was a hunger that he fed and then forgot. But with Penelope, it was different. Thoughts of her tormented him.

As did the knowledge that he could have very easily fulfilled his duty last night. He could have arranged for the two of them to be interrupted in that room. Any of his friends would have been happy to bring respected witnesses to the parlor at some prearranged hour and interrupt the passionate scene within.

If anyone had seen the wild, erotic display, Penelope would have been ruined. The ladies who were so enthralled with Penelope's thoughts on the evils of Society's unfettered sexuality could not have overlooked their leader's wanton display.

His own friends would have been fully satisfied in Penelope's ruination.

But Jeremy hadn't made any arrangements of the kind. He hadn't *wanted* to be interrupted. He hadn't *wanted* to end his pursuit of Penelope.

He'd only wanted to touch her. And he still did.

"Your Grace, Lady Norman awaits you on the Sunset Veranda."

Jeremy jolted at the sound of his butler's voice from the door. He spun around to face the man. "Lady Norman?" he repeated, ignoring how his cock hardened even more at the thought that she was here.

"Yes, sir," the servant said with a nod, keeping his eyes on Jeremy's face.

"She is early, I did not expect her until two," he murmured, more to himself than to the servant.

"Should I tell her you are not in house, sir?"

"No!" Jeremy said, a bit more forcefully than he had intended. He caught his breath. There was no need to allow his eagerness to show in everything he said and did. "No. Please tell her that I will be down when I have dressed. And prepare luncheon. I believe the lady and I will dine on the veranda together, since it is such a pretty day."

He didn't mention that he also looked forward to seeing the early afternoon sunshine dance off of Penelope's golden hair.

"Yes, sir. I will send in Paddington, as well," the butler said as he bowed from the room.

Jeremy grinned as he moved to his dressing room to await his valet. If Penelope had come to his home almost two full hours before their appointed schedule, it could only mean she had something important to share with him.

And he had a sneaking suspicion that the *something* had to do with last night.

He wasn't dressed. That was what Jeremy's servant had said before he bowed away, leaving Penelope to wait in the warm sunshine of the summer's day. She wrung her hands in her lap as sinful thoughts bombarded her.

Thoughts of Jeremy's naked body. Thoughts of the things Jeremy could do to her with that naked body.

She pushed to her feet and paced to the veranda wall. She fisted her hands against the railing and looked down to the gardens below. What was wrong with her? Last night she had let a total stranger kiss her in the most intimate way imaginable, twelve hours later she was fantasizing about allowing Jeremy Vaughn to do the same thing.

Her principles were eroding at a shocking rate.

She dipped her head, shutting her eyes as shame washed over her. How had things come to this? She hadn't grown up wanting to be some kind of crusader. She had dreamed of passion and pleasure just like any young girl.

But things had changed. They had changed when Penelope realized just how far Miranda would go to protect their family. They had changed when Penelope married and her husband's concept of passion was far different from her own.

They had changed when she made a few frustrated comments about the sinful excess of the men of the *ton*. Somehow those things had turned her into the woman she was now.

But it all felt like an illusion. Now, standing in the revealing sunshine of Jeremy's terrace, she wasn't certain of herself any longer. And in the darkness of the room last night, with a stranger pinning her to the wall, his hot, rough tongue coaxing wicked moans from her lips, she hadn't felt like a crusader. She hadn't felt wrong.

She had felt alive.

She covered her face with a shuddering sigh. She wasn't even sure who she was anymore. Or what she wanted. She'd come to Jeremy Vaughn's house two hours before their appointed meeting time, violating social niceties and opening herself up to even more remarks like the ones her mother had insinuated the night before, but she didn't care. It was like she was no longer in control of her own heart, her own body, her decisions.

"Penelope, I'm sorry I kept you waiting."

She spun around to face Jeremy as he strolled onto the veranda with a broad smile. But the instant he saw her face, that smile faded into a look of pure concern that made her heart ache even more.

"Are you well?" he asked as he closed the distance between them in a few long steps. He caught her hands and drew her closer to look down into her eyes. "You are pale. Are you ill? Can I summon a doctor for you?"

Penelope blushed as she slowly extracted her fingers from his. It was almost impossible to think when he was touching her.

"No, I-I am perfectly well," she stammered as she backed away a step. "I am simply tired. I had a trying evening."

He frowned. "The ball was not pleasant, I assume. Did more people make impertinent remarks? Were you threatened again?"

She shook her head. "No, not last night." She struggled to regain her composure. "My mother was in attendance, though. Did you know that some people are apparently whispering that you and I may be courting?"

Jeremy drew back, and Penelope didn't miss the slight flicker of panic that darkened his already dark eyes. Even if he claimed to be changing his attitude, it was clear he had no interest in settling down with only one woman. Or at least not with her.

Which was fine, of course. She still wasn't certain of this man's motives. Even if she *were* looking for a new husband, which she wasn't, Jeremy Vaughn was the last man she would ever consider.

"Your mother said as much?" he asked.

She nodded in response as she avoided his eyes. Just speaking to him, calmly, quietly, seemed to soothe her ragged nerves. It was strange that this man, of all men, could cause such a reaction.

"I do not mean to offend," Jeremy said with a little chuckle. "But I would think your mother might say such a thing for her own motives."

Penelope snapped her gaze up to his. Her blush deepened. "I suppose her mercenary desire for each of her daughters to marry powerful, rich men is no secret. Certainly, we must be mocked for her behavior in many circles."

Jeremy didn't respond, but motioned to the chair she had vacated earlier. "Come, sit down. Have a drink and we'll share luncheon."

She hesitated. Breaking bread with this man seemed so *civilized*, so *normal* after all the sinful things they had seen together. And despite how many erotic images he had shown her, sharing the meal also felt more intimate in some way.

"Please," he urged, placing a hand on her back to gently guide her to the seat. "Clearly there is more going on here than a mere encounter with your mother. Perhaps I can be of some assistance?"

Penelope sat down and stared at the starched linen tablecloth that decorated the round table before her. The lines of the fabric blurred as she considered her options.

She needed to talk to *someone* about the troubling encounter last night. Penelope didn't want to remind Fiona of anything unpleasant in her past, and she certainly couldn't speak to any of her other friends about the mysterious man who had seduced her with words and aroused her with his dark, faceless touch.

"I need to know something," she whispered. She looked up into Jeremy's eyes, seeking the truth there. Looking for his intentions, his honor. "Are you toying with me?"

Nine

Jeremy jolted at the pointed question. From the focused, sensual expression in Penelope's blue eyes, he initially feared she had determined the truth about her mystery lover's true identity. But as he examined her expression, he realized that that was not the case. He had already surmised that Penelope wasn't capable of hiding her emotions, no matter how hard she tried. She wore her pain, her fear, her happiness, and her desire on her face.

If she had guessed the truth, he would have known it from the first moment he stepped onto the terrace.

"Toy with you?" he repeated, letting the words create sensual images of last night in his mind. "What do you mean?"

She frowned, the expression causing little creases around her lips that he wanted to soothe away with a touch. Last night he hadn't been able to see her face clearly once she stepped out of the moonlight. How had she looked when he touched her? When pleasure rushed over her in a wave?

"Your miraculous transformation from a man of vice to a man of honor. Is that real, or are you playing a game?" she asked.

Jeremy drew back a fraction. Though he'd always known Penelope didn't fully believe in his change, a fact he respected, he had not expected her to put her doubts on the line so plainly.

"You may trust in me."

He looked at her evenly. Unlike Penelope, he had *always* been able to mask his true emotions. Never before had he felt guilty for that fact. Now he pushed that unwelcome reaction aside.

His deceptions were for the best. For his friends, of course, but also for the woman before him. If he managed this situation properly, he could stop her war against sin with blackmail, not exposure. Once she ceased her battle, Society would accept her fully again. Her life would be much easier, and certainly safer.

And yet guilt continued to plague him when her face relaxed a fraction. She believed him.

"I hope that is true," she whispered. "For both our sakes."

"Tell me what is going on, Penelope," he said as he reached out to take her hand gently. "Please."

She nodded, a jerking motion. "Do you recall that letter you teased me about after we returned from the Cyprian's ball?"

He inclined his head. "Yes."

"You implied it was a love letter," she said with a hard swallow. "But it wasn't. I have been receiving letters that are . . . *seductive* from an author who keeps his identity a secret."

Jeremy arched a brow. This honesty, he had not expected. "Seductive. You mean they detail—"

"Yes," she interrupted, her cheeks darkening beyond pink.

His cock swelled as he again wondered if her blush had been so dark last night. "I see."

She turned away. "Last night, before the ball, I received another. This time the author wished to meet with me."

"And did you?" he asked, leaning forward with anticipation. How far would Penelope go? Would she confide in him what she had done? What she felt when he touched her?

She nodded, her motions slow and jerky.

"And who was he?" Jeremy asked, leaning away like he was only half interested in the answer.

"I-I don't know," Penelope stammered. "He hid in the shadows. He kept his face a mystery."

"Interesting," he mused, observing her expression for every reaction. She was watching him from the corner of her eye, doing the same. "He must have some reason for his anonymity. Tell me, what did you discuss?"

She clenched her fists against the tablecloth. "Nothing. I had every intention of telling him to stop writing to me, but instead . . . instead he-he . . ."

Jeremy leaned forward with a practiced look of concern. "Did he hurt you? Force you to do something you didn't want?"

She shook her head instantly, and he felt a strange sense of relief that she wouldn't accuse him of forcing her.

"No, I-I liked it when he touched me." She covered her face. "Everything spiraled out of control, I don't know what happened. It terrified me how quickly I let go of my manners, my morals. It was only in a brief moment of clarity, when I realized I would let him do anything, *everything* to me, that I pulled away. I told him I wanted him to leave me alone, and I ran."

Jeremy swallowed. It was taking a lion's share of his control to keep from flipping the table out of the way and hauling Penelope into his arms. Hearing from her lips all of her emotions and reactions was almost as erotic as touching her.

"And do you," he asked, his voice a little hoarse, "wish for him to abandon his pursuit?"

She jerked her head up and looked at him strangely. Then she shook her head. "No," she admitted on a sob. "I don't want him to leave me alone."

Jeremy stared at her. Her face was so sad, so lost. *He* had done that to her by drawing out the wanton she hid inside, the woman of fiery desire that Penelope insisted on tamping down out of some misguided fear.

"I didn't know who else to confide in," she admitted as she composed herself. "I don't think anyone else could ever understand. But I thought . . . oh, you must think me the worst fraud after everything I said to you about the evils of desire and sin."

Jeremy shook his head. "No, Penelope, I don't think you are a fraud. And I'm pleased you are putting your trust in me."

The fact that he was sworn to betray that trust was something he tried to ignore, even though it ate at his belly.

"What should I do?" she asked. "You are trying to change, yes? How do I ignore these feelings? These things I have never felt before, never understood."

Again, he drew back a fraction. Penelope had been married. Yet she acted as though desire was a foreign concept to her. She had implied before that her marriage was unhappy, now Jeremy wondered just how broken it had been.

"Not long ago, we spoke of your past," he said, his voice gentle, soft to soothe her like he would an untamed mare. "And I was under the impression that someone . . . perhaps your husband . . . had caused you pain."

Penelope jerked, her hand slipping from the table into her lap as her wild eyes met his. She was so pale he reached for her on instinct, steadying her by touching her forearm.

"What happened?" he asked.

She stared at the hand that rested on her arm and again her stare was heated. Jeremy felt his body react to the look, hardening, growing heavy. Thank God for the protection of the tabletop over his lap, lest the intentions Penelope was forever trying to read would be more than clear, and all would be lost.

"Did you know my father?" she asked, her voice soft and shaking.

He nodded. "A little."

"Then perhaps you knew a little about his . . ." She hesitated and her mouth hardened a fraction. "His lack of control?"

Jeremy frowned. He *had* seen Thomas Albright in the gambling hells a few times, many years before, when he had been little more than a green boy, himself.

"If you didn't know, you weren't the only one," she whispered. "Very few were privy to the extent of his problems. Even our own family was quite in the dark until his death. It was only when my sister Miranda took over the household finances that we realized how deeply in debt he was. 'Gentlemen' came out of the woodwork, demanding payment."

She shivered. "Some wanted their repayment in very disgusting terms. But Miranda refused them all. I thought her so strong. But we knew one of us, at least, would have to marry far above our station, however we had no funds to finance such a thing. But suddenly, two summers ago, Ethan Hamon, who was our neighbor, offered us money for a Season for me, as well as Seasons for my sisters, later. He claimed he had owed my father a debt, and this was his way of repaying it."

Jeremy frowned. He might not recall much about Thomas Albright, but Ethan Hamon was another story. The Earl of Rothschild had once been notorious for his vices, his wicked way with women, his sexual prowess. He had not been known, however, for his charitable works. The idea that he would offer Seasons for the daughters of a neighbor didn't ring true.

"Why did he do that? Was he close to your family?"

She barked out a laugh that was anything but pleasant. It was harsh and hard, just like her expression. "I did not think so. But it turned out . . ." She hesitated, and her gaze snagged his. "My sister had made a bargain with him. He promised to pay for our Seasons, and she-she . . ."

Jeremy's eyes went wide. So Miranda Albright *had* sold her body to protect her sisters. There had been discreet whispers about the Rothschilds' relationship prior to their marriage, but Jeremy had dismissed them as idle chatter. Miranda seemed so very proper, and she had certainly tamed Rothschild in the short time they'd been wed.

"I understand," he said, holding up his hand. He wanted to hear how this story affected Penelope, and saying out loud what her sister had done was obviously difficult for her.

"Miranda and I had always been close," she continued. "But she never confessed this wicked little arrangement to me. Instead, I uncovered it myself, when I stumbled upon them in an . . . an *embrace* during a ball to launch my Season."

Jeremy jerked his head up to stare at her. An embrace? No, he thought it was much more than that. Penelope had been an innocent, and she clearly loved her sister deeply. To see Miranda in the height of passion with a man like Rothschild, of all people . . . he could see how that might alter her.

"Later, Miranda confessed to me that she not only made the bargain of her own volition, but she *liked* it. She had turned down the proposals of very suitable men simply because she wanted that kind of passion." Penelope frowned. "I was so . . . angry."

"Angry?" Jeremy repeated, genuinely confused.

She nodded. "Our family was in dire straights, our very lives were at stake, and my sister was willing to barter her innocence for some-some fantasy she built in her head. I vowed that night that I would make the sacrifice she had not. I would marry the first man of title and wealth who offered for me, no matter who he was. If only to prevent Miranda from making more mistakes. If only to protect my younger sisters from the consequences of her selfish actions."

Jeremy looked at her. She was sitting so stiffly that he feared if he touched her, she would shatter.

"And that is when you met Viscount Norman," Jeremy encouraged softly when Penelope had been lost in thought a few moments too long.

She jerked out a nod. "He was in attendance at the party that night. When I stumbled back into the ballroom after my confrontation with Miranda, I threw myself into what I saw as my duty. I felt nothing toward any of the men who surrounded me. And I *never* felt anything for George. But he had a title and he had funds and he promised me that he would assist my family. So when he made an offer for my hand, I accepted."

"But ultimately, Rothschild and your sister married," Jeremy said with a shake of his head. "And the Earl has holdings and influence that outstripped Norman's wealth by far. From all appearances, he would catch the moon if your sister asked for it, so why did you not break the engagement when it was clear Rothschild intended to do the honorable thing?"

Penelope caught her breath, and it was clear from her expression that the marriage between Miranda and Ethan was a source of much confusion and even jealousy. Yes, that was jealousy Jeremy saw flickering in her clear blue eyes. Interesting.

"My sister and I had shared such harsh words. After what he had done, I didn't think I could truly trust Ethan. I certainly didn't want to pin my future on his honor, nor did I wish to live under his roof." She gritted her teeth. "And I admit, I was stubborn. I thought my life with George would be no worse, so I went forward with the wedding. But it was—" She caught her breath. "It was a terrible mistake."

Jeremy saw the tears beginning to gather in the corners of her eyes, and his chest tightened at the sight. Hesitant, he lay a hand over hers. "Why?"

She shook her head. "I was a trophy for him. A way to prove his prowess, despite his advanced age. But he cared no more for me than I did for him. The prowess he was trying to prove, it was failing. When he couldn't become aroused, he blamed me. He said," she faltered. "He said unimaginable things to me. Words that will ring in my ears until the day I draw my last breath."

Jeremy's lips pursed. He could well imagine the kinds of things Norman would have said. He'd never liked the bastard. Now he liked him even less.

"When he *could* perform," she continued, and now one of those tears fell, silent. "He thought nothing of my pleasure. My only comfort was that those nights were few and far between, and his attentions were short in duration."

Now Jeremy's anger doubled. The idea that any man would have such a goddess in his bed and not worship her body rightly was a disgusting tragedy. That he would hurt her was an unforgiveable offense.

"I saw my sister, who had sacrificed everything for her own pleasure, settled into a happy marriage," Penelope whispered, her voice harsh. "And here I was, sacrificing myself for everyone else, and I lived in a hell. It seemed so desperately unfair. The rift between us grew wider, I became more and more alone. And when George died, I was left with a large inheritance, a respected title, and an empty life. And now I don't even have that life anymore. These past few weeks have changed me, Jeremy." She shook her head. "I don't know who I am or what I want or what I should do. This mysterious man is offering me pleasure and I find I want to take it, despite how wrong it is. Despite how I have spoken out on this very topic time and again."

Jeremy nodded, pretending to consider how to respond. In truth, he was thrilled that Penelope wanted him, especially after the torment of her marriage. It made him all the more driven to bring her pleasure unlike anything she'd ever imagined. To seduce her and make her see that the sensuality she fought against wasn't only exploitive and cruel.

But it also made the fact that everything she thought was happening was in truth a manipulation all the more bitter. She had already been caused so much pain, and he was bound to bring her even more.

He shook his head. What was he thinking? A month ago, he wouldn't have given a damn about her pain. Or her past. He had to forget the fact that he was beginning to *like* this woman and focus on the duty at hand.

"Do you want my advice?" he asked, rising and pacing to the veranda wall. He leaned back against the barrier and looked at her.

She nodded. "Yes. You have far more experience in these things. And you claim you are trying to improve yourself. Tell me, Jeremy, what should I do? How do I stop this madness?"

He tilted his head. "I don't think you should make any attempt to stop it. I think you should take the pleasure you are being offered, Penelope."

Ten

Penelope stared at Jeremy, her eyes as wide as saucers, no matter how she tried to pretend she was unmoved by his suggestion.

"Take the pleasure?" she repeated, hoping her utter confusion and the temptation of that permission wasn't clear in her voice and expression. "You cannot mean that."

He nodded. "I absolutely mean it. This man is offering you a gift, and I think you would be a fool not to take it."

She frowned. Somehow she had thought Jeremy would tell her to fight her inner urges. Or even be . . . *jealous* that she had allowed another man such liberties. Although they were not courting, she had sometimes sensed a connection between them. A sizzling fissure of heat that drew her closer.

But perhaps she had misread the situation entirely. Perhaps Jeremy felt no attraction to her whatsoever. At this point, his bored expression and utter lack of emotion were proof of that fact.

"I don't understand," Penelope said. "If I surrender to this man, it will go against everything I've said and done. It will fly in the face of my arguments against the sexual excess of our class."

He nodded. "I can see why you would see it that way, but I am thinking of it from an entirely different point of view. Let me explain."

Penelope hesitated. Again, she wondered if she were being played a fool by this man. He had vowed that she could trust in him, but now he told her to throw all her ideals to the wind.

"Please," she finally whispered, her curiosity overwhelming her reason.

"You are fighting a war, Penelope," he said, moving toward her slowly. "It isn't a pretty war, either. When you speak about the lack of morality in the men of the *ton*, when you encourage unhappy wives to confront their husbands and demand better treatment, there are some in my circles that see that as an underhanded tactic. And they feel no compunction in fighting back with little regard for you. And the fact is, you are unarmed."

"Unarmed?" she repeated, shaking her head in confusion. "What do you mean?"

"When I first spoke to you about my . . ." Penelope thought he hesitated a moment, but then he continued on, his face never registering any uncertainty. "About my change of heart regarding my activities in the past, I offered to show you a little of the world you were fighting against. I thought that would help you know your enemy better. But until this afternoon, I didn't fully realize how ill equipped you are to fight them. A few nights hiding in the shadows while you see for yourself the sensual excess of the underground is not enough."

Penelope got to her feet. "I still don't understand."

"You don't, I know." He sighed. "You see, I assumed because you were married that you had felt, firsthand, the pleasures of sex. That you had a basic understanding of why sins of the flesh would draw a person, and that when you saw the darker side of that pleasure that it would simply round out your education. But you have just told me that your husband's bed was never a place of desire for you. Never a warm and pleasurable hideaway."

Dark blood colored her cheeks and she moved to turn away, but Jeremy reached out to catch her arm, keeping her in place. He cupped her chin with his opposite hand and tilted her face up until she couldn't avoid his pointed, dark stare.

"It wasn't your fault," he whispered. "What Norman did wasn't because you weren't desirable."

She caught her breath. Without being told, Jeremy had struck upon the very fear that had plagued her for so long. One she had never spoken of to anyone, just as she had kept the bitter secret of her empty marriage to herself. But he saw through her.

He knew her. Without having to ask. And that was a terrifying prospect.

Did it also mean he knew what was best for her when it came to the stranger who had offered her seduction and sin in the cover of darkness?

"You said you liked it when that man, whoever he was, touched you last night," he continued.

She nodded.

"You felt pleasure?"

"Yes," she said, the word torn from her tight throat. "I stopped him before I could feel even more, but there was pleasure."

He swallowed hard enough that she saw his Adam's apple work with the action. "Good." She tilted her head and he hurried to explain himself. "I only mean that feeling the pleasure will help you. I say that you should surrender to what this man offers because after a few nights under his tutelage you will fully understand the desires that drive others to sexual excess."

Penelope slowly pulled her arm from his grip and backed away. When he explained his logic like this, it almost made sense. He was right that she had never fully understood why women surrendered to men or why men strayed with no thought to the consequence. Understanding that could give her great power, as long as she didn't lose herself.

"But there are so many risks," she murmured, more to herself than to him.

Jeremy shook his head. "Not really. What this man offers is temporary. It is secret."

"No," she said. "It is secret to me, but he knows my identity. He knows my name and my face. He could easily betray me."

Jeremy pursed his lips and seemed to be pondering that thought. She found herself leaning forward, waiting for him to explain away that final fear. Hoping, in some secret part of her, that he would find a way to allow her all that pleasure.

Because she wanted it. She hated herself for it, but she wanted it.

"I suppose he might have some kind of nefarious motive," he conceded, and Penelope's heart sank. "But he had every opportunity to expose you last night and chose not to."

Penelope stopped. "Yes, that is true. If he had arranged for someone to stumble upon us . . ." She tapered off with a shiver at that thought. "I would have been ruined. And yet, he did not."

"Then that is probably not his purpose in seduction." He turned away suddenly to look out over the estate grounds behind him. "It is more likely that he simply wants you."

Penelope sighed as she moved to stand beside him and look out over the cool green grass behind the garden below. "He may have wanted me last night, but I pushed him away. I told him to leave me alone. It is entirely possible he might not want me anymore, even if I knew of some way to contact him."

Jeremy turned to face her. She drew back at the intensity in his eyes, the sudden focus that pulled her into the darkness she saw there.

"He would be a fool if he didn't still want you," he said, his voice low and seductive.

Penelope's lips parted. Here they were, talking about her going to bed with some other man, indulging in a secret affair for the sole purpose of understanding pleasure, and yet she still felt that connection with Jeremy. Her treacherous body warmed under his gaze, beneath her skirts she grew wet and ready.

She found herself leaning forward, her trembling hands lifting up. He watched her every movement, though he didn't step toward her. But just as she was about to wrap her fingers around the fine fabric of his lapels, the terrace door opened behind them, and a servant appeared, carrying a tray laden with food.

"Your luncheon, Your Grace," the young woman said as she set the tray on the table behind them.

Penelope jolted away from him, staggering back. She stared at Jeremy, stunned by her lack of control. She had wanted to *kiss* him. And she very well might have if not for the interruption of the servant.

"I-I cannot stay," Penelope stammered as she backed toward the door. "I'm sorry. I must go."

Before he could respond, she ran, not daring to look behind her. Not daring to see if he beckoned her back to him. Not daring to test if she would be able to resist him if he did.

Jeremy strummed his fingers along the smooth wooden surface of the sideboard, staring with unseeing eyes at the glass of whiskey he had just poured himself.

"Whiskey so early in the day?" his brother asked from behind him. "Is there something you would like to discuss?"

Jeremy turned to look at his younger brother. Christopher Vaughn was sprawled across his settee, looking every bit as debauched as he had just a year ago when the two of them had prowled London together, seeking out vice and pleasure of all kinds.

Except now his brother's appearance was only an illusion. Six months before he had married. Not a forced marriage, not one for show. He had married because he claimed to have *fallen in love*, of all things.

And the brothers had not shared the same relationship since then. In fact, Jeremy more often avoided his brother's company than sought it out. He simply didn't know how to handle Christopher's newfound fidelity and peace.

And yet, after Penelope fled from his side, he had been driven to come here. To see his brother. To talk to him as they once had.

But now the words wouldn't come and awkward silence filled the space between them.

"Jeremy?" his brother repeated, straightening up. "*Is* something wrong?"

He shrugged as he threw himself into a chair across from Christopher. "No, of course not. What could possibly be wrong? I live the perfect life."

His brother's eyebrow arched, but if he had arguments against that statement, he blessedly kept them to himself.

"I only ask because normally you avoid my company unless Mama is in town. And she is on the Continent for another month, at least."

Jeremy tightened his grip on the still-untouched drink. "Do you not desire my company?" he asked, his voice strained.

Christopher shook his head. "Of course I do, I miss our times together. I simply wasn't expecting you today. And now that you are here, you seem distracted. Distant. I feel like there is something you want to share with me, yet you hesitate. If there is some way I can help you, you know I would do it. No matter how things have changed, we are still brothers, Jeremy."

Jeremy stared at his brother. Christopher was younger than he by a year, and Jeremy had spent their entire growing up lording his elder-brother status over his head. Even as grown men, Jeremy by contrast had always felt a little more worldly, a little more experienced.

But now Christopher looked at him as if he were a child. And he felt like his brother *did* understand more than he. It was a strange feeling.

Could he tell Christopher of his plans for Penelope? Of his interactions with her and the odd way they made him feel? Would his brother even understand his motives anymore, or would he just be horrified by the lengths Jeremy had gone in the name of protecting their once mutual friends.

"I doubt you would understand," Jeremy said with a wave of his hand that didn't reflect his inner turmoil in the slightest fashion.

"Because I am in love?" Christopher asked blandly. He had a little knowing smile that Jeremy didn't particularly care for.

"Love," he snorted.

"You ought to try it," his brother said quietly. "There is much to be said for the feeling."

Jeremy shook his head. "You mean have only one woman, no one else? *Bah!* Sounds like a prison to me."

Christopher's smile fell, and the knowing glint in his eyes was replaced by something even more irritating. Pity.

"If that is truly how you see a union of souls, then that is your misfortune. I hope someday you will find a woman who changes that. Otherwise, you shall live an empty existence, indeed."

"You lived that 'empty existence' yourself, not that long ago," Jeremy snapped, more emotional than he wished to be.

Christopher nodded. "Yes. And I do not miss it."

Jeremy stared at his brother. How could that be true? Christopher had been the one who celebrated his freedom most. Could he truly be content settled into the boring day-to-day life of a marriage?

As if on cue, the parlor door opened, and Hannah Vaughn stepped inside and interrupted their conversation. Jeremy stared at her as she moved into the room.

Christopher's wife was a beauty, there was no denying that fact. With a heavy mass of auburn curls bobbing around her cheeks and bright, lively green eyes, she was exactly the kind of woman his brother had always been attracted to.

Except Christopher hadn't merely seduced her as he had so many before her. He'd married her.

Jeremy staggered to his feet out of politeness as his sister-in-law gave a wide smile and pressed a kiss to her husband's cheek.

"There you are, dearest," she said. Then she turned on Jeremy. There wasn't an ounce of hesitation in her eyes, despite Jeremy's having spoken to her only twice in six months. She stepped forward, holding out both her hands.

"And Jeremy, how lovely it is to see you." She squeezed the hands he held out briefly. "I'm so pleased you could come. Christopher and I think of you often."

Jeremy shifted uncomfortably. "Th-thank you."

He stared at Hannah as she took a seat beside his brother. Jeremy had not always thought of her in the kindest of lights, yet she was never anything but welcoming to him. He had disparaged her for being nothing more than a lady, yet her ladylike behavior shamed him.

She was a woman of Penelope's class. And though Penelope was more jaded by the circumstances she had related to him just a few hours before, he had a sneaking suspicion the two women would get along quite well. He could almost picture the four of them, sharing tea together in this very room.

With a jolt of shock, he shook away that troublesome thought. Dear God, he was going mad to think that kind of thing would be satisfying in the least. That was because of his brother's words, not some true desire.

"Have you heard from your mother lately?" Hannah asked, completely oblivious to his internal thoughts, though Jeremy thought he saw Christopher's concerned expression.

Jeremy nodded. "I had a letter from her two days ago."

"She is enjoying her tour enormously, it seems," Hannah said, then laughed. "Who knew she would become such an adventurer?"

Jeremy wrinkled his brow. Their mother had been traveling since just after his brother's wedding, and she'd written him many letters. But like the one sitting on his desk at home right now, most had been left unopened and others he had only skimmed. It wasn't that he didn't adore his mother, he simply didn't have much interest in her doings. As long as she was safe, he was content to live his own life and leave her to hers.

This was the first moment he realized just how selfish that was. Dear God, did he even know where his mother was? Was it Italy? Or perhaps it was Spain.

Why hadn't he cared enough to remember?

He watched as Christopher reached over and placed a gentle hand on Hannah's knee. She absently stroked the hair on the back of his neck. There was something so intimate about those touches. Something so easy and comfortable.

For months, Jeremy had mourned the loss of his brother's company and secretly resented Hannah for taking Christopher away from him. But looking at his brother now, he could see Christopher was *happy*.

And it put a troubling question into his own mind. Was he?

Was he *happy* carousing about London? Was he *happy* with the meaningless couplings and the hazy, alcohol-filled nights? Was he happy doing the bidding of friends whom he sometimes didn't even like all that much?

"Jeremy?" his brother said.

He started and looked at the two. Both Hannah and Christopher were leaning forward, looking at him with twin expressions of concern.

"I'm sorry," he mumbled as he surged to his feet. "I forgot an appointment I must keep. Thank you for seeing me, Christopher." He gave Hannah an awkward bow. "Hannah. Good afternoon."

He hardly heard their good-byes as he strode from the room, feeling the flames of hell licking at his heels with every step. His brother only confused him, that was all. Jeremy wasn't interested in giving up the life he led. It was fulfilling enough for him. It was what he wanted.

He was right. And he was going to prove it.

Eleven

How did one find a man with no name? A man with no face? It wasn't as if Penelope could put out an advertisement in the *Times* describing the stranger's sinful touch and ask for him to send her another shocking note. That would create a scandalous stir that would be talked about for decades.

Penelope paced her bedroom, clenching her fists open and shut at her sides. When had she become this . . . this *wanton*?

No, she wasn't a wanton. Jeremy had made perfect sense when he said that she needed to experience pleasure in order to understand what drove others to sacrifice everything for it. If she was going to surrender to the touch of her admirer, she would do it for research purposes, and research alone.

"Liar," she murmured with a shake of her head.

It certainly hadn't been *research* that had driven her to want to touch Jeremy yesterday afternoon. It hadn't been a sense of mere curiosity that had made her whisper her darkest secrets to him, even though she remained uncertain of his trustworthiness.

Those things had been caused by her weaknesses. Nothing more.

And yet, she didn't regret either one. She had kept the particulars of Miranda's marriage and the nightmare of her own to herself for a long time. Those secrets had festered inside of her, poisoning everything she said and did. Now that she had stated them out loud, she felt . . . free.

Perhaps it hadn't been intentional, but that was a gift Jeremy had given her.

And now she would take one more gift from him. His permission to surrender to the stranger who wrote to her.

If only she could find that man.

With a sigh, she covered her face just as the door behind her opened.

"I don't require anything, thank you," Penelope said through her fingers.

"I'm sorry, but you have received a letter."

Penelope spun to find Fiona standing in the doorway, a folded missive held out in her hand. Penelope crossed the room in a few hurried steps and snatched it away. She stared at the handwriting and her heart leapt. It was from *him*.

"Are you quite all right?" Fiona asked, tilting her head. "You are so pale and you hardly ate anything last night or this morning."

Penelope looked at the other woman in distraction. "What? No, I'm fine. Thank you. If you'll excuse me, I want to read my letter."

Fiona hesitated, her gaze flitting to the papers in Penelope's hands. Penelope blushed. Fiona was the only one who had any idea of the kind of things those letters said. And her maid's concern was plain.

"I-I know I'm not a very good lady's maid," Fiona said softly. "I don't know what I'm doing, even though I'm trying to learn. But I *am* a good friend. And I *do* understand certain things, certain impulses and feelings."

Penelope gripped the letter tighter as she stared at Fiona in surprise. She hadn't thought her maid would want to revisit old impulses and feelings. Certainly, she had to regret her choices now.

"It may be out of turn to say it, but if you need to talk to someone, I hope you'll think of me," Fiona continued.

Blushing, Penelope turned away. "I . . . thank you, Fiona. I appreciate that offer."

She heard her maid murmur a response and then exit the room. Penelope sighed. She *couldn't* talk to Fiona, even if she wanted to. After everything the other woman had been through, after Penelope had convinced her to leave the life she'd once led? There was no way she could then explain how she, herself, was being lured by the pleasures of the flesh. She was certain such a confession would horrify Fiona, and rightly so.

In fact, there was no one but Jeremy whom she could talk to about the matter. And after her initial confession, she hesitated to think about giving him even more details. Especially if the letter in her hand led to the seduction he suggested she allow.

With shaking hands, she broke the seal and sank into a settee by the fire to read what her mysterious admirer had to say.

One taste, one touch is not enough. I know you said you couldn't, but Penelope, reconsider. Let me give you pleasure. Such pleasure you have never known. If you want me, put a candle in your window tonight and leave it unlocked for me. If I do not see the candle, I will do as you asked and abandon all hope. But my greatest wish is that you will let me in.

Penelope crushed the unsigned sheet to her breast with a strangled groan. A war was raging inside of her. A war between her desires and her hesitations. A battle between the personal rules she had adhered to for so many years and the secret, burning needs that she had stifled over and over.

What should she do? How could she take the pleasure this man offered, understand it, and yet keep herself separate? Was it possible to allow this man his liberties and yet remain unchanged?

She didn't know. But she would have to decide her course of action quickly. Because in a few hours she would either need to open her window or close herself off from her deepest desires forever.

Jeremy swung up onto the small terrace high above Penelope's gardens. It was after midnight, and the house was dark and silent except for one glowing light that flickered in the bedroom window in front of him.

Penelope's window.

It had taken some doing getting up to her room, but it was going to be well worth the trip. Jeremy smiled before he slipped a dark mask over the top half of his face to protect his true identity. As he settled it over his nose, he couldn't help but think of seeing Penelope in her fancy mask at the Cyprian ball.

He shivered in desire before he drew a deep breath in an attempt to calm his ragged nerves. Tonight had to be about his plans, nothing more. He would put both his confusing visit to his brother and his conflicted emotions about Penelope's reactions and painful confessions aside.

Tonight was about breaking down her final barriers. Then he could end this charade and return to his normal, carefree life.

Quietly, he tapped her window and the pane swung out. He stepped over the ledge and into the darkened silence of her room.

He looked around. Aside from the candle, the only other light in the room was the low fire across the room. In front of it stood Penelope. Jeremy sucked in a breath.

She was wearing a thin cotton night rail. Broad straps covered most of her delicate shoulders and the white fabric hung around her curves like an unshaped sack. But with the firelight coming through the cotton, he could still see every single curve of Penelope's body outlined in tantalizing shadow.

And his cock went hard as steel in an instant.

"Hello, Penelope," he murmured, and this time it took no effort to make his voice low and rough with desire.

She turned to face him, obviously startled by his voice. In the dim firelight, he saw her expression relax with relief. She had thought he might not come to her, as he had promised. Thanks to her past, disappointment and humiliation had become her expectation. The realization made his chest ache with unwanted empathy.

"I notice you didn't raise the light in your room," he said softly as he stepped forward, still cloaked in shadow. "You make no effort to see my face."

She shoved her hands behind her back. "Y-Yes," she stammered. "I mean, no. I think it is best if I don't know your identity. In some ways, I wish you did not know mine."

He stopped moving as that unwanted guilt he'd felt the day before returned. She feared he would betray her. And now he had to promise that he wouldn't when there was no bigger lie. He *would* do so. He had to.

"So you want a secret lover," he purred, ignoring her fears instead of telling a direct untruth. "You want someone you can pretend away in the cold light of day."

She bit her lip and nodded slowly. "Yes, I suppose that is true. In the day, I don't want reminders. I don't want distractions from the actions I must take. The things I must do."

"I am most happy to oblige you," he said as he closed the final gap of space between them and reached for her hand. Lifting it, he pressed his mouth to her knuckles. His tongue darted out, and he stroked it between her fingers.

Penelope shivered, a movement that worked from her head to her toes. "But I do have some stipulations," she said, breathless.

He hesitated. There was something unexpected. "Stipulations?"

She pulled her hand away, pressing it against her chest. "I cannot simply throw away all caution and responsibilities. I must retain *some* level of control."

Jeremy held back a chuckle. So that was her game. How entertaining it was going to be to wrest every semblance of control from her.

"And how do you propose you do that?"

She backed up and her tone was businesslike, despite the remaining tremor in her limbs.

"I do not want to know your name nor your face," she said, ticking off her statements on her fingers. "I see you are wearing a mask. I ask that you continue to do so, and I will keep my room dark when you come to me. Will you promise not to reveal yourself?"

He bobbed out a nod. That was an easy promise to make. He didn't want her to know who he truly was. At least, not unless it was absolutely necessary.

"If you promise not to ask me who I am, I promise not to reveal myself to you."

She didn't hesitate. "Agreed. You must also vow you will not approach me in public again. When we were at the Trimble ball, it was too great a risk. We must keep our-our—"

"Trysts," he offered, noting how she shivered again at the word.

"Yes." The word came out as a strangled croak. "We must keep them private."

He folded his arms. "I can agree to that."

"And my final stipulation," she said, shifting uncomfortably, "is that I do not want you to-to breach my body with yours."

Jeremy rocked back on his heels and he was surprised enough that he didn't alter his voice when he burst out, "What?"

Penelope tilted her head and looked at him in questioning. For a moment, he thought he had been found out, but then she shook away her doubts and said, "I do want what you have to offer. I want it more than I probably should. But I can't go that far. I shouldn't."

He pursed his lips. "Let me make sure I understand you. You want me to touch you, but never breach your body. You don't want my tongue, my fingers, my cock . . ."

She turned away, but he wasn't sure if it was in embarrassment at his boldness or because she wanted to hide her arousal.

"No, I want your mouth." Her voice broke. "I want your fingers. I want everything except I don't want you to put your . . ."

She stopped, and Jeremy bit back a growl of frustration. "You don't want me to put my cock inside your body, where you ache most. Is that it?"

She nodded without turning back.

He shook his head in wonder. Did she really think that would keep him from changing her? If she protected her body as if she were a virgin, then the rest somehow wouldn't count?

He stopped short. That was it. She thought that if she allowed him everything but the final act of sex, she could somehow keep herself distant from the connection two lovers invariably formed. That the experiences he introduced to her wouldn't be as intense. As meaningful.

Looking at her, he considered his options. If he refused her harsh, frustrating terms, she might shy away from his offer entirely, and that would do his cause no good. If he took her bargain, though, he would have every opportunity to prove her wrong. Prove that there was no way to protect herself from desire.

Prove that denying herself the ultimate physical act would only make her crave more, not less.

"Very well," he conceded as he reached out and caught her elbows. She didn't resist when he drew her back against his body, molding her into him until he felt his cock rub between the smooth globes of her backside.

Penelope gasped at the feel of him so tightly against her, but she didn't run.

"And I have one term of my own," he murmured, letting his tongue trace the shell of her ear.

She moaned instead of answered.

"If I agree not to fill your pussy with my cock," he said, loving how she jolted with the pointed words. "Then you must grant me full access otherwise. I want you in every other way. Is that fair?"

As he asked the question, he smoothed his hands around and cupped her breasts, letting the soft mounds fill his palms as he massaged her gently.

"Oh God," she moaned, her knees buckling just a little.

"Is that a yes?" he asked, blowing his hot breath against her sensitive neck.

"Yes, yes," she cried as he plucked her nipples to hard peaks beneath the cotton.

Jeremy stifled an urge to say thank God, and instead spun Penelope around to face him. Her blond hair, which had been bound loosely away from her face, now threaded down around her cheeks in little loose waves. The dim light showed just how wide her blue eyes were. And her ragged, uneven breathing let him know how much she wanted him even more than any words could convey.

With another low growl of pleasure, Jeremy caught the straps of her gown and yanked them down from her shoulders. The oversized night rail fell away with little urging, bunching around her ankles and leaving her instantly exposed.

If her reaction was any indication, that was not a state she was comfortable being in. Unlike the experienced women who had graced his bed more recently, Penelope didn't thrust her breasts out or coo and simper to show herself to the best advantage. Instead, she lifted her hands to her breasts, turning her face so that her expression was hidden by shadow.

For a powerful moment, Jeremy hated George Norman with his entire being. As a husband, the man should have taught Penelope how beautiful she was. He should have made her proud of the power she had been given with her desirable body. Instead, the bastard had made her tremble, not in pleasure but in fear and humiliation.

But her mystery man wasn't supposed to be privy to those facts. Only Jeremy, her friend and confidante, knew the truth of her past. He would have to be careful to make sure he didn't reveal that they were one and the same.

"Don't look away," he whispered, turning her face back. "Look at me."

She didn't obey him, instead keeping her gaze focused firmly on the floorboards beneath her bare feet. Jeremy clenched his teeth.

"Remember, you promised to give me anything I desired. Look at me."

Penelope couldn't hide the way she flinched, but finally she lifted her chin. It was too dark to tell if she looked at his face or not, but he didn't press her. Not yet.

"You are beautiful," he said softly. "You don't know how much you drive me mad. How deseperately I want to taste you, touch you, how much I want to claim you. You do that by merely standing there."

Her breath caught on a ragged gasp that bordered on a sob.

Jeremy ignored the tightness around his heart and cupped her chin to tilt her face up at just the right angle. "I'm going to kiss you now," he promised as his lips drifted down to hers. "And then I'm going to finish what we started at the ball."

Her groan was lost as he caught her mouth. He meant to overwhelm her, overpower her with his passion and draw out her own in equal measure. But somehow, it didn't work out that way. Instead, he barely brushed her lips, dragging his mouth back and forth against hers in a gentle, soft rhythm.

When her mouth opened on a sigh, that was the first time he breached her lips. He dipped his tongue inside, tasting mint and a hint of some kind of liquor she'd probably drunk for liquid courage before his arrival. He smiled against her mouth as he traced her tongue with his own, sucked her in ever so gently.

Penelope dug her fingers into her faceless lover's forearms as her knees began to shake. How could a kiss so fully arouse her? Make her so weak? Kisses with her husband had never made her melt.

But she was beginning to realize, both through her conversation with Jeremy and with every touch from this other man, that her experience with George had not been one that represented everything sin and pleasure could be. For the first time, she understood there was so much more.

The stranger wrapped his arms around her waist and drew her closer, pressing her to his body until she could hardly tell where he ended and she began. He rocked against her, cupping her naked hips and grinding into her until she felt the very insistent presence of his harsh erection pressing between her thighs.

Penelope was shocked that her first reaction to the intimate touch was a shameful desire to open those same legs and offer herself to him. Despite her statement not ten minutes ago that she could not allow him to breach her body with his own.

Now that stipulation seemed foolish. Because she wanted to surrender fully. To give her entire body over to this man to do with as he pleased.

But before she could do something so foolish as beg him, he swept her up and deposited her onto her bed. His hard body covered hers, pressing her deep into the soft coverlet as his mouth found hers a second time. Penelope clung to him as wave after wave of pleasure washed over her. Gentle at first, but growing in intensity and fervor. Soon, she would be swept away.

She squeezed her eyes shut and surrendered herself to his ministrations. Lost on a sea of pleasure, her mind went blessedly still, quiet, for the first time in what might have been years.

Until one persistent image cropped up. A vision of Jeremy Kilgrath leaning over her, claiming her mouth with his.

With a gasp, Penelope wrenched her lips from her lover's. No! She couldn't, she wouldn't think of Jeremy. Not now.

"I have been dreaming of your taste for two nights," her mystery lover whispered before he dropped another kiss to her lips.

Penelope forced her focus back to the man who lay over her,

his breath teasing her skin with infinite gentleness. As her mind faded, she smiled, but then his words sank in. He wasn't talking about the taste of her kiss. He was talking about . . .

"So sweet," he murmured as his mouth slid down her flushed flesh. "And tonight I can't wait to taste you again. All over, Penelope. Everywhere."

Her hands bunched against the coverlet and her back arched against her will as his hot lips branded her throat. He sucked gently on the delicate, sensitive column, and she was shocked when heated wetness flooded her thighs. God, what he could do to her in just one touch.

And he was promising so much more to come.

His lips moved lower, lower until he hesitated at her breasts. She looked down at the misty shadow of his body. He was staring at her breasts, and she blushed. He might not be able to see her clearly in the dim light from the dying fire, but surely he noticed her shortcomings. George had often complained that her slender frame made her breasts too small. He'd told her how ugly and unwomanly that was. How her body was the reason he could not perform his husbandly duties.

The stranger cupped the small mounds, covering them completely with his big hands. She turned her face, unable to bear his scrutiny or judgment.

"Why do you look away?" he asked as he spread his fingers. Her nipples popped out between the didgits.

She blushed. "They are . . . they're not pretty."

His head jerked up. "Who told you that?"

She shook her head. She had already made humiliating confessions about her marriage to George to Jeremy. She wasn't about to repeat them to this man.

"It doesn't matter."

"Someone very stupid," he muttered and he lowered his head. "I think they are perfect."

His lips wrapped around one nipple and Penelope's hips bucked up against his stomach at the shocking, tugging, heated sensation that rushed from the point of contact all the way through her body, settling as a pounding pulse between her legs.

"So responsive," her faceless lover said, and she heard the smile in his voice. "So sweet."

He moved to the opposite nipple and suckled it, at first gently, then increasing the pressure until the tip was distended and throbbing with pleasure so keen she felt like she could fall over the edge just from this touch.

Hearing every pant, feeling every arch of Penelope's hips, made Jeremy mad with desire. There was something so seductive about giving her pleasure. She had never felt it before, at least not from the touch of a man. And he was giving it to her. Slowly, deftly dragging the feelings from her body until she was weak beneath him.

He'd never felt so driven to give that kind of pleasure before. Certainly, he had never been called a selfish lover. He knew how to make a woman come, and he prided himself on leaving a string of satisfied ladies in his wake.

But there was a difference between making certain a lover experienced pleasure and giving her something without thinking about himself. He was aware of his hard cock, of course. He felt that driving, pulsing need to take Penelope, even though she said she couldn't allow that. He *wanted* to drive home inside of her and come as she pulsed around him like a hot, wet glove.

For the first time, though, those desires weren't as strong as the need to bring her pleasure.

He looked up as he blew a slow gust of hot breath over her wet nipple. There was just an orange glow in the room from the fire now, but Penelope's eyes glittered in the dying light. He caught a glint of white as her teeth sank into her lower lip while she bit back little moans and sounds of encouragement.

She was so close to the edge.

Jeremy slid lower, dragging his lips over her bare stomach. Her skin was so soft, so smooth. Like satin beneath his tongue. Every touch made her quiver, each stroke made her hands fist into the coverlet with increasing force.

He glided down farther, nuzzling the bare curve of her hip. He could smell the sweetness of her desire already, and his cock hardened even further with the scent. She stiffened when his mouth grazed her thigh, her entire body going tense just as it had the first time he did this two nights before.

But this time, he was going to make sure she didn't run. He cupped her hips, keeping her steady as he brushed the faint stubble on his chin across her sensitive skin. She let out a little cry and her legs fell open out of instinct.

He took what she hadn't meant to offer, moving his hands to the inside of her thighs and opening her even further. She was wet already, swollen by his touch, her flesh quivering in anticipation of what would happen next.

His own fingers trembled as he cupped her sex and felt the heat burn into his skin. Penelope bucked against him, helpless to keep a loud, strangled moan from bubbling from her lips. Slowly, he opened her, peeling aside damp folds to reveal her in the low light. Her hips arched up and he took the silent invitation, pressing his mouth to her straining flesh and tasting the proof of how much she wanted him, wanted this, no matter how much she argued against it or worried over it.

He stroked her, tasting her honeyed sweetness, exploring every weeping inch of her slit. Her breath grew short and then ceased entirely as she trembled beneath his touch. He was relentless, purposefully driving her toward release at a speed and intensity he normally would have reserved for a second or third time he made love to her.

But with Penelope, everything was different. In part, this was an education. And he wanted her to feel with an immediacy, just how pointless it was to fight the tide.

And the other part was that he wanted to make her come. He wanted to hear her scream out her pleasure, to feel her hips crash against him, to taste the nectar of her release as it washed over his tongue. He wanted that with a powerful drive that bordered on obsession.

With gentle strokes, he moved toward the hard nub of her clit, exposed by the strokes of his fingers. When he licked over it, Penelope cried out and her head lolled to the side. He tasted it again, teasing her, playing with her like a cat with a mouse. She arched, whimpering her pleasure with weak mewls of pleasure.

He sucked her clit into his mouth at the same moment he slipped one finger into her clenching sheath. Penelope sat up partially, looking through the darkness as her cries grew louder. He delved into her with his finger, curling against the hidden bundle of nerves deep within her even as he sucked the hard nub of her pleasure with force. She wasn't even trying to stop her cries now. They echoed in the room around them as her hips arched up to meet his strokes.

The crescendo was approaching, her trembling body made that clear. But before she came, Jeremy wetted another finger in her juices and glided it between the globes of her backside. As Penelope exploded, he slipped the wet digit into her, filling her completely.

At the forbidden touch, Penelope's orgasm intensified. Her hips ground against his mouth and hands and her wetness doubled as she shivered and shook out her pleasure. Even after she collapsed against her pillows, spent, the tremors went on, little earthquakes of pleasure that exploded on his tongue.

Finally, he withdrew, reveling in the soft sound of distress that left her lips when he no longer filled her in every way. He slid up her body and kissed her. She opened to him immediately and he was well aware that she tasted her own essence on his lips.

But she didn't withdraw, and that left him certain that he had been right about Penelope Norman all along. She *was* a creature of sensuality and sin, despite her protestations to the contrary. And he was sure that after a few hot nights with him, she would be changed, altered enough that she would surrender her fight against excess. He might not even have to blackmail her.

"Did you like that?" he murmured, nuzzling her ear.

Her arms came around him and she stroked her fingernails along his spine through his linen shirt. He shivered at the feeling.

"More than I should," she whispered. "This is wrong. So wrong, considering who I am and what people believe I stand for."

He drew back, unable to determine her expression in the dark. But there was a resignation in her voice that he wasn't sure he liked.

"There is nothing wrong with pleasure, Penelope," he said softly. For so many reasons, he wanted her to understand that. *Believe* that.

"Wrong or not," she replied as her fingers tightened and she pulled him closer. "I want more."

Jeremy sucked in a breath at that confession. Damn, the woman was a natural temptress. How could she not know how irresistible her touch on his back was? How the heat of her flesh made him want to slam his cock into her and have her in every animalistic way possible? How he wanted to make the room blaze with light and see her body in all its glory?

How could she not understand that she was torment embodied?

"I would give you everything," he said, rolling onto his back and pulling her to straddle him.

Although he was fully clothed, his cock immediately settled against her wet pussy. He could feel her ready heat through the woolen fabric and he rocked up against her. She made a strangled moan at the friction.

"Not everything," she whispered as she leaned down and captured his lips. "Just more."

Twelve

Dawn's first light was starting to pierce into the room when Jeremy rose from his spot beside Penelope and began gathering his discarded clothing from around the bed. As he dressed, he couldn't help but relive every sensual moment.

He had brought her to orgasm three more times with his mouth and fingers before she collapsed into a shaking, exhausted pile and fell into a deep slumber.

But he hadn't come. Watching her awaken to intense, powerful pleasure had been enough for him at the time. Once she was asleep he hadn't wanted to find completion in his own hand. So he had simply lain there, watching her sleep for the last hour.

He still burned with desire, but he was also . . . at peace somehow. He had debauched the woman his friends called the Ice Queen. He had made her arch and beg and rock with pleasure. It would be easy enough to blackmail her now. End this madness.

Except, as he fastened his trousers, he realized he didn't want to end it. Not yet. He felt like he was at the beginning of a journey, not the end. Like there was so much more pleasure to be had and to teach.

There was no harm in a few more nights of pleasure with her. Perhaps he would even convince her to beg for his cock.

After that . . . *then* he would be satisfied. He was certain of it.

He bent to press a kiss against her bare shoulder and Penelope rolled onto her back with a sigh that brought him to rock hard readiness in an instant. The sheets were tangled around her legs, her bare breasts offered up in the dawn light so beautifully that it took every ounce of strength in him not to simply capture one hard nipple and make her cry out in pleasure one last time.

But no. Not now. If she woke, she might recognize him in the rapidly increasing light, and he didn't want to be discovered. So instead, he bent down to press a second kiss against her lips, then he moved to the window and made his escape.

As he picked his way down the window ledge to a tree branch and finally to a remarkably sturdy trellis, he couldn't help but think about last night. The details of Penelope's surrender, of course, but more than that. He thought about the catch of her breath, the pleading of her voice, the way she'd said she was wrong for submitting to his touch, despite wanting more of it.

He was unsatisfied with the evening's events, he finally decided as he walked down the alley behind her home to the well-hidden carriage that had been waiting for him all night long.

Unsatisfied physically, yes. As he settled into the plush leather seat, he was forced to shift around his still hard erection, a harsh reminder that he hadn't coaxed full surrender from his adversary.

But it was more than physical need that made him feel restless. Penelope, despite her acquiescence to his touch, her needy moans, her cries of pleasure, still held back a great deal. She'd found utter completion at his skilled touch, but in her mind, she had been able to keep herself separate from him.

He most definitely needed another night with her. Two nights, perhaps, to whittle away at her final shreds of resistance. To make her see, for once and for all, that she was not the proper, cold woman she wanted the world to believe her to be. To make her feel wanton and alive and needy.

Once he had done that, she would be forced to see herself in a new light. Then his final duty would be easily accomplished. It would be simply to convince Penelope to stop encouraging her friends' uprising against the men.

Yet even with that comforting thought in his exhausted mind, Jeremy still didn't feel completely at ease as his carriage turned into the wide drive of his London estate.

Penelope picked absently at the lacy edging of her mother's tablecloth. Dorthea's voice echoed loudly around her, yet Penelope wouldn't have been able to repeat even the broadest topics of her mother's never-ending tirade if her life depended upon it.

She was too distracted by her increasingly troubling thoughts. Thoughts of last night. Thoughts of her mysterious lover, whom she had surrendered to without hesitation. Well, one hesitation. She had stuck to her stipulation that the man not breach her body with his cock. Somehow she had hoped that would make the experience less intimate, less altering.

But she was wrong.

And yet, it wasn't the memory of the faceless man's heated touch that kept her frustrated and confused. It was because the Duke of Kilgrath's handsome face had intruded into her over-stimulated mind again and again. No matter how she tried to fight it, his image came back while her lover did so many wicked things to her body. Seeing Jeremy's face in her mind had only made the experiences all the more intense. In fact, his image had pushed her over the edge of release not once, but multiple times.

So she was not only a hypocrite with her body, but with her mind. She was a woman who railed against sexual excess and yet let a stranger touch her intimately while she fantasized about another man. Unfaithful, even to a stranger.

She rubbed her eyes in an attempt to ease the sudden pounding in her head.

"You are not even attending, Penelope!" her mother said as she slapped her palms down on the table in front of Penelope.

She jumped at the sudden action and jerked her gaze up to her mother's. "I'm sorry, I did not sleep well last night. But honestly, Mama, this is not a new conversation!"

Even without being fully aware of the topic, Penelope could say that with certainty. Her mother only ever spoke of three subjects: Miranda's fortunate match to Ethan Hamon and his huge annual stipend; the belief that her as yet unmarried daughters must make equal, or even better, matches, as soon as possible; and she desired that Penelope remarry. *Now.*

None of the topics inspired Penelope to respond. She didn't share her mother's view on any of them.

"How can you be so cold to your sisters?" her mother wailed as she sank into a chair next to her.

Penelope sighed. Well, at least she knew which subject her mother was going on about this afternoon. "I don't know why you insist that my status has any bearing on Beatrice or Winifred. I was married to a respectable man with a tidy fortune. I am accepted in the correct circles of the *ton*. What more could you possibly want of me?"

"I told you, I want you to stop your foolish conversations about the behavior of the very men your sisters are likely to wed."

Her mother shook her head, and for a brief moment Penelope saw true concern in Dorthea's often blank expression. She was such a flighty, mercenary woman, and yet Penelope had long ago realized that all her mother's rantings sprung from some kind of misguided beliefs. She wasn't trying to be wicked or horrible. She simply could not help her behavior.

With a sigh, Penelope reached out to cover her mother's hand. "I never intended for my thoughts to launch some kind of movement, Mama. Truly, I was only talking. The fact that others have taken up this . . . this *banner* was as much a shock to me as it was to anyone." She shook her head. "But Mama, surely you do not really wish for either of my sisters to marry a man who would flaunt his mistresses in front of them? Or treat them with utter distain except when he wished to create heirs and spares? Would that make them happy?"

Her mother's lips thinned. "You must remember what it was like to be poor, Penelope. If your sisters had money, had stability, they could learn to live with other disappointments in their marriages. It is what women do."

Penelope patted her mother's hand absently. Dorthea had not been born into the upper sphere of the *ton*, but entered it after her marriage. Penelope vaguely remembered some unpleasant scenes in which her mother had been given the cut direct. It must have hurt Dorthea terribly.

How many other disappointments had she endured in the years before her husband's death? As much as the family had adored him, Thomas Albright had not been perfect.

"I would wish more for them than that," Penelope whispered. "Living a loveless marriage just for the sake of financial comfort . . . it is a poor trade."

Dorthea pulled her hand away with a scowl. "You are impossible!"

Penelope sighed. "This is a subject upon which we will never agree, I am afraid, Mama."

"Then what about Miranda? You know that people talk about your estrangement," her mother said, rising up and pacing the room again with frantic energy. "And yet you refuse to speak to her."

Penelope shut her eyes. "That is complicated."

"Ha! Complicated my foot. You *will* reconcile with her. She will be arriving any moment and I expect you to——"

Penelope shot to her feet as her heart lodged firmly in her throat. "What? Miranda is coming here today?"

Her mother nodded.

"Yes. It is far past time you end your silly feud. You must get over your jealousy over her marriage," Dorthea said with a definitive glare.

"I am not jealous!" Penelope gasped. "I was *never* jealous."

Except, there was a little voice in Penelope's head that said that wasn't true. For the first time, she realized perhaps she *had* been jealous of Miranda. After all, her sister had surrendered to her baser needs, gone against every rule, been utterly selfish . . . and had ended up with a seemingly happy marriage to a man she adored.

While Penelope had sacrificed herself on the altar of familial responsibility, done what was expected, and been unhappy. Unfulfilled, Penelope had wilted for years, even while she watched Miranda bloom.

And perhaps jealousy *had* been as much a part of their estrangement as Penelope's reaction to the passionate scene she had intruded upon between Miranda and Ethan.

As if on cue, a footman stepped into the doorway. "Lady Rothschild."

Penelope gripped her hands behind her back as Miranda stepped into the dining room. She wore a stunning peacock blue satin gown with a low neckline that would have been shocking if not for the mass of translucent white lace that provided some modesty. Miranda's eyes shone, partly from the flattering color of the gown, but partly from a happiness that burned bright from the inside.

Penelope shifted uncomfortably. It was most definitely jealousy that burned in her chest presently. And the bitter, horrible feeling had nothing to do with Miranda's pretty gowns or Ethan's large fortune or anyone's higher title.

It had to do with love. Passion. Contentment. Her sister possessed what Penelope could not even fantasize about.

The two women met eyes across the room. Miranda's gaze softened, gentled as she stared at Penelope, and Penelope had a strong urge to rush across the room and wrap her arms around her sister. To whisper her secrets to Miranda as they had just a few years before.

To trust her, even though Miranda hadn't trusted Penelope with her own dark secrets.

Instead, Penelope turned aside. "I-I cannot stay."

"Penelope!" her mother snapped, glaring at her when she pressed a brief kiss to her mother's smooth cheek.

"I have some things to attend to," she lied. She shot Miranda another glance as she edged around her to the door. "Good-bye."

Bolting into the foyer, she motioned to the butler that she needed her carriage. As the man stepped outside to summon the vehicle, Penelope heard the dining room door snap shut behind her. Slowly, she turned to find Miranda leaning against the barrier, staring at her.

"You look tired," her sister whispered.

Penelope squeezed her eyes shut, fighting to keep the distance she had maintained for so long. It was almost impossible when Miranda was close enough to touch.

"Thank you," she managed to say with a chill to her voice. "I appreciate the compliment."

Miranda ignored the snipe and stepped forward. "You don't look physically tired. If anything, you are more beautiful than ever. But you are . . . *soul* tired." Her sister shook her head. "And there is such pain in your eyes."

Penelope caught her breath as she spun back around to stare with unseeing eyes out the open front door. God, Miranda knew her. Even now, when Penelope hadn't allowed a civilized word to pass between them for over two years. Her sister could still pierce through her outward appearance, just as had always been the case. Except for the one secret Miranda had been able to hide.

Penelope had judged her sister for lying about Ethan. For making a trade of her body for his money, for his assistance. She had been angry, she had been cold.

But after what she had experienced last night, she could no longer judge Miranda for anything anymore. She couldn't judge anyone. And if Miranda looked closely enough, she would see that fact, too.

Her sister's hand closed on her upper arm, a gentle touch that brought tears to Penelope's eyes.

"You know if you need me . . ."

Penelope shook her off as her carriage pulled around to the door. "I must go."

She bolted without a backward glance, running out into the warmth of the afternoon and ducking into her waiting carriage without even waiting for assistance from a servant. As the door shut behind her, she dared to peek out the window to see Miranda walk up to the doorway and stare after the carriage as it slowly pulled away.

Penelope covered her eyes. How had her life become so complicated? So confused? And how was it that she had no one in the world to confide in.

No one but Jeremy Vaughn, of all people. He knew about the

man who had written her. He knew the man wanted her. He hadn't judged her for that correspondence.

Perhaps he could help her make sense of the topsy-turvy existence she had somehow found herself a part of. A world where the desires she feared were suddenly acceptable, the choices of the sister she shunned were now understandable, and in which she wanted one man while coveting another.

Thirteen

Jeremy took a deep breath as he paused before the door to his parlor. He hadn't expected Penelope's arrival, but he had no intention of sending her away. He just had to be very certain that she wouldn't grow suspicious. He couldn't show his remaining desire for her on his face. He couldn't let her guess that he was the same man she had allowed such liberties the night before.

Slowly, he pushed the door open and stepped inside. Penelope sat on the very edge of the settee in the middle of the room, her hands clenched in her lap. When she heard the door, she glanced up and Jeremy rocked back. She looked so upset. A mixture of fear and disappointment and sadness that hit him hard in the gut.

Was her emotional turmoil all because of him? Could he really have developed such influence over her? It was a sobering thought.

"What is it?" he asked as he moved toward her.

She staggered to her feet as he approached and backed away, lifting her hands as if to ward him off. He stopped instantly. Invading her space, forcing her boundaries was the role of the mysterious man. During the day, Jeremy was her friend. As much as he wanted to touch her, force his comfort until she accepted it, that wasn't the right tack to take if he wanted to continue on the delicate tightrope of their relationship.

Penelope looked at him for a long moment, her pale face drawn down. She opened and shut her mouth a few times, struggling for words.

Jeremy found himself leaning forward, waiting for her explanation, wondering how much she would tell him about her heated encounter with the man who had been writing to her.

"It is nothing," she murmured finally, turning her back to him. She paced to the window and looked outside.

Interesting.

He shook his head. "You are pale as a bedsheet and clearly upset. Something must have happened. Did you have another encounter with the man who wrote to you?"

She spun around with a harsh gasp. Her hands gripped the windowsill, and she stared at him, lips trembling. Again he waited for the inevitable confession. Penelope had never been very good at hiding her emotions, at keeping secrets. It wasn't in her nature.

But today, she fought that nature.

"I-It isn't that," she said, dropping her gaze to the floorboards.

"*Hmmm.*" Jeremy tilted his head.

So, she had no intention of confessing, even though he already knew so much about this supposed stranger. Why would she want to keep last night a secret when she had already revealed so much?

Unless she regretted what had transpired in her bed.

His stomach turned at the thought.

"I saw my sister today," she whispered.

Jeremy drew back. "Did you?"

"My mother secretly arranged for us to meet at her home. She wants us to end our 'feud.' I have not been that close to Miranda since . . . since my marriage, I suppose. Years." Penelope shut her eyes, and Jeremy sensed she was fighting tears.

Again, he wished to move forward and offer comfort, but this time he held back for his own sake, rather than hers. Her confession about her emotional reaction to seeing Miranda made him more uncomfortable than any sexual secret would have. Penelope's pain felt more *intimate* than hearing about her tryst.

"I wanted so much to talk to her." Penelope opened her eyes. "I wanted to tell her—" She cut herself off.

Jeremy moved forward a step, almost against his will. "Why didn't you?"

"I couldn't. I once judged her so harshly. If she talked to me for a few minutes, she would see . . ."

Jeremy reached for her, finally allowing himself to touch her for the first time since he left her bed early that morning. He took her hand. She stiffened but didn't draw away. Instead, she stared up at him, a little rabbit trapped by a wolf.

Only the wolf was just as affected by her as she was by him. Jeremy had the strongest urge to kiss her. Kiss her until she forgot her pain. Kiss her until she would allow him anything. Until she realized that *he* was the man to whom she had surrendered her body last night. He wanted to demand she surrender even more.

"What would she see?" he asked, his voice low.

His question jolted Penelope from the spell and she tugged her hand away. "She would see what a hypocrite I've become."

Jeremy stared at her. This self-doubt and self-loathing she was experiencing was exactly what he had planned for when he agreed to stop her. When he began, he had *wanted* Penelope to realize she was a charlatan, a fraud. But imagining that and seeing it in truth were two very different things. Now seeing her so broken was anything but pleasant.

It made him feel guilty. Again. And he did not like that feeling.

"I shouldn't have come here," she whispered. "I should not place my silly problems at your feet. I apologize."

She moved toward the door, but Jeremy caught her arm.

"No," he said, holding her steady. "You have been . . ."

He hesitated. He was going to lie, he was going to manipulate. Those things had never been hard for him before, but now. . .

No. He shook his head. He couldn't let Penelope steer him from his course. This was the perfect opportunity to continue with his plan.

"You have been a friend to me. The least I can do is be the same to you." He released her, and she stumbled a step out of his reach. "May I take you on one of my excursions?"

Penelope wrinkled her brow. "Right now?"

He nodded. "I think I may be able to show you something that will help you." He glanced at the clock on the mantel. "If we leave now, I'm certain of it."

She worried her lip for a moment, darkening the smooth, full flesh to a tantalizing deep red. Then she nodded. "Very well."

He smiled as he offered her his arm. He had never had such trust from a woman before.

And he had never betrayed that trust so fully.

But there was no getting around it. Not anymore.

"Where are we?" Penelope asked as she peered out the carriage window at the large, fashionable home that rose up before her.

"This is John and Arabella Valentine's Pleasure Palace," Jeremy explained with a smile.

Penelope looked at him, feeling her eyes go wide even when she wanted to appear unmoved. "*Pleasure Palace?*"

He nodded. "An exclusive club for the most particular of men . . . and women."

He reached into his pocket and withdrew a mask. "Here, you should wear this. There might be people inside who would recognize you. And you them."

Penelope stared at the mask. Instantly, her body grew wet at the sight. Memories roared back. Memories of her mystery lover spreading her wide. Memories of his tongue laving her flesh, his fingers breaching her in so many wicked ways.

"Penelope?"

She jerked back to the present with a blush and took the mask with shaking fingers. As she secured it around her face, she stared at Jeremy. He was hardly looking at her as the door to the carriage opened and he stepped out onto the drive. He extended a hand, which she stared at for a long moment before she allowed him to help her out of the vehicle.

She had come to Jeremy's home with every intention of confessing her activities the night before and pleading for his advice on how to proceed. But once she actually stood before him, staring up at the handsome face that had haunted her dreams and fantasies, she hadn't been able to confess that she had spent the entire night writhing in another man's arms. Nor could she admit that she hadn't allowed that man to actually make love to her, no matter how much she ached for that kind of intimate joining.

And she certainly couldn't reveal to Jeremy that while she surrendered to a mysterious man's touch, she secretly thought of *his* face.

What would he think of her if he knew the truth? After all, the more time she spent with Jeremy, the more she was beginning to think that perhaps he truly *was* changing.

The irony was that she was changing, too. If Jeremy was becoming a respectable gentleman, than she was becoming a wanton. Their roles were reversing. Did that mean that ultimately Jeremy would look on her with the same disdain that she had gifted upon him before they became truly acquainted?

The idea gave her an unpleasant shiver that she tried to stifle as Jeremy led her up the marble stairs and through the front door of the estate.

She straightened her spine. His feelings for her should make no difference whatsoever.

"Arabella!" Jeremy said as they entered the foyer.

Penelope tensed as a blond woman turned away from a well-dressed servant to look at them. Her face lit up as she started across the small hallway toward them. Penelope looked out of the corner of her eye at Jeremy. He was smiling genuinely, and who could blame him? The woman was a beauty. Her hair cascaded over her shoulders, sweeping over her full breasts, and her eyes were blue, but not pale like Penelope's. Dark and deep like sapphires.

"Kilgrath," the woman said with a laugh as she pressed a kiss to Jeremy's cheek. "We have not seen you in what seems like forever. Welcome. What are you doing here so early in the day?"

Jeremy motioned his head toward Penelope with an audacious wink. "I wanted my . . . *friend* to see your establishment."

Arabella turned her attention to Penelope. Again, she stiffened. Perhaps this woman would recognize her, despite the protective mask. Penelope was certain the purveyor of what amounted to a house of prostitution would not be a fan of hers, since she had spoken out against such places quite publicly in the past.

But if Arabella recognized her, she made no indication. Instead, she merely smiled. "Good afternoon, my dear. Welcome."

Penelope nodded without speaking, fearing that Arabella or one of the other people milling in the lobby would recognize her voice. Again, Arabella made no indication that Penelope was being rude or strange by remaining silent.

"Let me fetch Valentine before we discuss your pleasure. I'm sure he'd like to see you. He has missed playing cards with you in your absence." She pressed a hand to Jeremy's arm and slipped away.

"Missed taking my money, you mean," Jeremy called after her with a laugh that she echoed from a distance.

Penelope clung to his arm and whispered, "You are friendly with her?"

Jeremy glanced down at her with genuine surprise in his eyes.

"Arabella is impossible not to like. I dare you to spend more than ten minutes in her company and not feel a kinship to her. And her husband is a friend, as well."

"Her husband?" Penelope shook her head. "What did he do, pull her out of the ranks of his whores?"

Jeremy chuckled. "You really are completely unacquainted with the world you fight against. This is Arabella's place. John is half owner now, of course. But Arabella built this establishment herself. John came into her life long after she had an empire all her own."

As Arabella began to make her way back to them, her arm laced through a tall, handsome gentleman's with a stern face, Penelope stared. A *woman* had built this establishment? A woman had that kind of power? And clearly wealth, judging from the accoutrements of the home and garments of those around her.

"John," Jeremy said as he shook Arabella's husband's hand. "Good to see you."

"Yes." John Valentine glanced down at Penelope with a brief smile that made his serious face very handsome, indeed.

As the three of them briefly chatted, Penelope watched in awe. The Valentines were educated, well spoken, and so devoted to each other that it almost hit her like a wall.

In short, they were nothing like she expected, and once again all her thoughts and preconceptions were dashed like ships against a rocky shore.

"Now, on to business," Arabella said as Valentine bowed away. "What is it you desire, Kilgrath?"

Jeremy cast a quick side glance at Penelope before he leaned in close to Arabella and whispered something in her ear. Penelope was surprised when a harsh, hot blade of jealousy sluiced through her chest at the sight of Jeremy murmuring in the other woman's ear. And when Arabella smiled at him, knowing and sensual, she was ready to scratch the madame's eyes out.

"I think that can be arranged," Arabella said. "Come."

They followed her down a hallway and through a series of twisting corridors that led past room after room. Penelope blushed as she heard the occasional lusty cries or guttural grunts of pleasure from behind the doors, even though it was the middle of the day. To her ultimate shame, Penelope found herself not shocked by the sounds, but curious. What were those unseen people doing to pleasure each other?

Finally, Arabella led them to a room. It was small, tidy, but with a big bed in the center, its velvet coverlet dark and inviting. Penelope looked away as she released Jeremy's arm and paced into the room. What in the world did Jeremy have planned for her, alone in the bedroom of a house of ill repute?

"You'll want to examine the picture there," Arabella said softly as she motioned across the room. "Enjoy."

Then she slipped away and left them alone. Penelope turned toward Jeremy with a nervous shift. "This is not right. We ought not be alone together."

He moved toward her slowly. "Afraid I'll ravish you?"

She swallowed as her gaze moved, almost against her will, to the bed a second time. It was just far too easy to picture Jeremy's big body over hers, his mouth on her skin, his cock tunneling deeply inside her waiting, weeping slit.

"I assure you," he said softly. "If I wanted to do so, I could have easily managed that on my own, far more comfortable, bed. No, I brought you here to see something else entirely."

Penelope's breath was short as she managed to grind out, "What?"

He stepped to the picture above the fireplace that Arabella had indicated before she left them. It was a portrait of a woman from the waist up. Entirely commonplace, except that she was naked and holding her breasts, offering them up to some unseen lover. Penelope blushed as he maneuvered aside a camouflaged panel over the painted woman's eyes and motioned to Penelope to join him.

She stepped up, and noticed there was a small bench before the fireplace. With Jeremy's help she positioned herself so she could peer through the panel. She caught her breath in utter shock. The painting allowed her a perfect view of the next room. A place where she could see onto the opposite bed.

But the room wasn't empty. On the bed were a man and a woman. The man reclined on his back, his stiff cock already hard as a naked woman, her bare back to the painting, rubbed it in her palm. With every firm stroke, the man arched his hips and let out a low groan of pleasure.

Penelope jolted back and nearly fell off the bench.

"What . . . ?"

Jeremy placed a hand on her waist to steady her, and Penelope felt the touch through her clothing all the way to her skin.

"*Shhh,*" he said softly. "Just watch."

Although she wanted to turn away, to tell Jeremy no, to flee this place, Penelope was too drawn, too aroused by what she saw not to look into the other room again.

The naked woman's mouth was on her lover's aroused member now, just as the other woman Penelope had seen at the Cyprian ball. Her head bobbed up and down, dark hair dancing down her bare back as she lustily pleasured her lover. His hands flexed against the coverlet, fisting handfuls of fabric with every stroke of her lips.

Penelope watched in fascination at the way the man's face tensed and twisted as his pleasure grew. Again, she thought of her own lover. She hadn't done anything like this to him. She'd only allowed him to touch her. What would it feel like to draw him between her lips? Would he groan like that if she pleasured him?

"Turn around," the man ordered, his voice strained.

The woman looked up at him briefly, but then repositioned herself. Penelope strained to get a look at her, but her dark hair fell around her face in a curtain as she moved to all fours in front of the man.

He got up on his knees behind her and began to rub his hard erection against her, stroking lazily over her backside and down around to her pussy. Penelope held her breath, waiting, waiting for the moment when he drove inside.

And finally, the moment came. With a loud moan, he thrust his hips forward and disappeared into his paramour's welcoming, wet body. The woman's back arched, her hands gripped at the sheets and she cried out a curse that didn't often leave a woman's lips.

It was clear the two had been lovers before, because the man had no hesitation. He didn't explore, he simply took, slamming his body into hers with a fevered intensity that made his partner quake and quiver beneath him.

Penelope's mouth went dry as she watch them couple furiously. Her fingers curled around the wooden mantel edge and she leaned in until her nose almost touched the canvas of the portrait.

The man slid his hand up the woman's spine without losing a stroke in his powerful rhythm. Penelope watched as he tangled his fingers into her long hair and began to pull, arching her back up and turning her face.

Penelope stared as the woman's thick hair fell away from her face.

"Oh my God," she murmured, and this time not even Jeremy's steady touch could keep her from staggering off the bench and backing away from the shocking view. "That is-that is Lady Turncroft."

Jeremy stepped away from the scene and faced her. His face was unreadable. Stoic. "Yes."

Penelope swallowed. "That was not her husband."

"No."

She covered her mouth as she paced the room restlessly, still aroused by what she'd seen and shocked by *who* she had seen involved in such illicit activities.

"B-But she is one of the most respected women in Society," she stammered. "She runs a charity guild, for heaven's sake. She approached me at a ball not two weeks ago and whispered to me how supportive she was of my 'fight.'"

Jeremy arched a brow. "And yet here she is."

Penelope stared at him. "You knew she would be in that room." She folded her arms. "You knew she would be with that man."

"Or some man." He shrugged. "Or two."

Penelope's eyes went wide. "Two!"

"From time to time. She's a woman of certain appetites."

"Does she know that people can see her?" Penelope asked, clenching her hands behind her back. Even as she asked the questions, she still had a strange urge to look into the room again. To watch the end of the erotic scene. She fought to stay in place.

"She knows. Arabella does not give that room to anyone who doesn't like to be watched." Jeremy glanced toward the painting. "You would be surprised by how many requests there are for that room. And for this one. Seeing or being seen are popular fantasies."

Penelope swallowed at that thought but ignored his statement, at least for the time being. "But she doesn't wear a mask. Anyone in this room might recognize her as I did. Isn't she afraid of being called out for her shocking behavior?"

Jeremy shrugged. "There are rules to this club that offer its members a level of protection. Anyone who talks about what they see here is banned for life. And if that wasn't enough, the very essence of this place is protection in itself. After all, what would someone say if they wished to reveal her secret? They couldn't very well say, 'I was fucking my mistress while spying on someone and saw Lady Turncroft being taken from both ends by two strapping blokes.'"

Penelope shut her eyes. Jeremy's blunt terms should have put her off, but they didn't. Instead, her treacherous nipples grew hard beneath the soft fabric of her gown.

"I suppose they couldn't," she conceded, trying to catch her breath. "But why did you show me this?"

He moved toward her and she started. She didn't think she could take him touching her right now. She felt needy and hot and on the edge. Ready to beg for something from Jeremy that she couldn't demand. At least not without losing herself completely. She was already too close to doing that.

"You were so upset today, berating yourself for being a hypocrite," he said softly. "I wanted you to see that there are many women of Society who have secrets. Secrets far more shocking than any of yours could ever be."

Somehow that was cold comfort. After all, Jeremy wasn't aware of just how shocking her own secret was.

"You mean, you were trying to show me that my enemy might very well have my own face," she said softly.

He looked at her, clearly taken aback by that assessment. But he didn't deny her claim, merely inclined his head in silent agreement.

Fourteen

Penelope shivered, though the low fire had warmed her room to a more than comfortable level. No, it wasn't temperature that caused her tremor.

With a sigh, she sat down in one of the armchairs beside the fire. It was confusion that plagued her, nothing else. She had been feeling it since she and Jeremy went to Arabella and John Valentine's Pleasure Palace earlier in the day.

Over and over, the images she had spied upon played in her head.

"Penelope?"

With a start, Penelope looked over to her chamber door. Fiona stood in the entryway, staring at her with concern plain on her pretty features.

"Yes?" she asked, trying to keep her voice light.

Fiona stepped inside with hesitance. "If there is nothing else, I will retire to my chamber for the night."

Penelope smiled as kindly as she could when her mind was racing. It was almost midnight, and she knew her long night was only beginning. There would be little sleep for her tonight. Only more pleasure. More confusion.

"There is nothing else," she said as she waved her maid toward the door. "Thank you."

Fiona didn't back out of the room as Penelope expected. Instead she frowned. "Are you certain, my lady? No tea? Perhaps some warm milk to calm you? Or something to eat? You barely ate anything for supper tonight."

Penelope pushed to her feet with a shake of her head. "No, I'm fine." When the former courtesan didn't look any more convinced, Penelope crossed the room to her. "I truly am very well. Now, off to bed with you."

Fiona opened her mouth like she was going to say something, but then she shrugged and turned to the door. But before she stepped into the hallway, she said, "I am only concerned for you, Penelope. You have been . . . strange for the past few weeks. I know some of that has to do with Jeremy's frequent visits here and some of it likely has to do with your secret admirer. But I worry for you."

Then the young woman stepped from the room and shut the door behind her. Penelope sighed.

"I'm worried for me, as well," she murmured as she scrubbed a hand over her eyes.

"As am I."

Penelope spun around to face the rough, masculine voice that suddenly echoed from the window. Her heart staggered as she watched the dark shadow of her secret lover turn to latch the window behind him.

"I was almost caught when your maid came inside," he said softly. "Thank goodness she was too caught up in confessing her concerns about your well-being to notice me standing on the window ledge, waiting to utterly debauch you." He moved forward one long step. "You might want to lock that door, my lady."

Penelope backed up and found herself against the very door he had ordered her to lock. Her heart pounded wildly as he came closer, step by step, until she could smell the masculine scent of sandalwood combined with clean skin. A hint of pine and a hearty dash of lust.

Her knees went weak even as she tried to remain unmoved.

"Oh, please," she whispered, turning her face as he pressed one hand against the door next to her head. "I can't. I can't do this."

He chuckled, a low, feral sound that instantly turned her protests to moans that she bit back. Her body went wet as he trapped her in with his opposite arm, caging her.

"But you will," he said softly as he dipped his head down to nuzzle her throat. "You *need* this. I can practically taste it on your skin." His tongue darted out to sample her throat. "I smell it mixed with your perfume. So sweet."

He nuzzled lower, his lips dancing along the scalloped edge of her gown's neckline. Her breasts swelled, the nipples hardening with even this grazing, slight touch. She whimpered at her body's betrayal. Her mind was no better. All her protests were lost as sensation took over.

"If you didn't want me here," the stranger continued as his fingers dropped down to the little row of buttons along her bodice. He began to loosen them with deft fingers. "You would not have put a lamp so close to the window. Your fire would be a blazing light, not a low one. You may not want to admit it, even to yourself, but you were waiting for me tonight."

Penelope pursed her lips together, biting her tongue to keep from crying out when he peeled her gown away. God, he was right. She *had* been waiting for him. Waiting for this.

"So pretty," he purred as he thumbed the hard nipple that thrust against the thin fabric of her chemise.

Penelope's back arched against the door as pleasure's hot fingers tore through her in an out-of-control burst of sensation. She was vaguely aware of the stranger reaching around her and turning the key to lock her door. She lifted her hips to him helplessly, her wet body forcing her to behave in ways she had shunned so publicly and for so long.

He ignored her hips and kept his attention focused entirely on her breasts. As he continued to massage one aching mound, he pulled her chemise strap down and exposed the opposite breast. His hot lips latched around the nipple and he sucked, hard enough that Penelope jolted. Hard enough that the pleasure danced along the edge of pain, but didn't quite fall over.

Penelope stopped fighting her desires. She let her fingers come up to tangle in his hair. She tugged him closer, moaning as he laved her nipple, nipped at it with just the edge of his teeth, sucked her tender flesh until her knees trembled and her pussy pulsated wildly against emptiness.

He let out a low rumble of pleasure as he moved his mouth to her opposite breast. This time he lowered the chemise even slower, letting the soft fabric rasp across her sensitive skin while Penelope writhed helplessly against the door, her hands clenching at his hair, her back arching wantonly with every sinful touch.

He seemed to enjoy tormenting her as he cupped both breasts in his hands, lifting them, bringing the small mounds together so he could languidly lick one nipple, then repeat the touch on the other. Back and forth, little nips, gentle tugs and finally he stroked his hot tongue in the valley he had created between them.

Penelope's eyes went wide. She felt the wet stroke of his tongue between her legs as if he had repeated the action there.

"Please," she moaned, lifting her hips to him. "Please!"

He tilted her chin up so that their mouths almost touched. "Please what?" he murmured as he rubbed the rough stubble of his chin across her cheek.

She bit back a frustrated cry. She wanted to plead for him to fill her. To take her. She wanted to throw caution and her boundaries away and let him spread her legs wide and spear her with his cock. That was what she wanted and he knew it, the bastard. He *knew* he was testing her. He reveled in it.

But she couldn't. It was too much.

So instead of asking for what she craved, she let her hands unclench from his hair and glide down. She stroked her fingers over his chest, feeling hard muscle contract beneath the linen shirt he wore. Lower to the scratchy woolen waistband of his trousers.

And lower still until her palm cupped the hard length of him through layers of heavy fabric.

Now it was his turn to gasp in pleasure and surprise as his body jolted into hers, forcing her fingers to wrap around him.

"Don't start something you won't finish," he warned as he pushed into her again. This time his hard cock pushed through the cocoon of her fingers and pressed hard between her legs, nudging the fabric of her chemise against her clit and eliciting a yelp of pleasure from her lips.

Penelope hesitated. She had seen one way to bring a man pleasure without allowing him to breach her body. And she was so very curious about that forbidden act.

"Who says I won't finish?" she murmured, shocked by the husky, tempting tone to her voice. She sounded like a wanton, a courtesan, a woman of pleasure.

And she liked it.

Without pausing to consider that fact, she began to work on removing her faceless partner's shirt. It was hard to unhook each button in the dark, but she managed with shaking fingers. She caught her breath when she touched his bare skin. He was a very well-formed man, in every way. His skin was smooth, stretched over incredibly toned muscles and peppered with a light dash of curling hair. She clenched her fingers over his skin, loving how the muscles contracted with her touch.

He didn't feel like a pampered member of the Upper Ten Thousand. Was he a laborer of some kind? If he was, how in the world had he seen her, chosen her as his conquest?

Thoughts of Jeremy Vaughn again invaded her mind as she pushed the other man's shirt away to flutter to the floor. Jeremy had a fine body and *he* was a duke. A woman would have to be blind to miss how lean and athletic he was. So perhaps this man was of a similar ilk.

She shut her eyes, even in the dark. She had to stop thinking of Jeremy. Especially while she touched another man. Let another man touch her. It was just wrong.

As her fingers glided down bare flesh, her lover caught his breath. She smiled as she followed the trail of his chest hair and found the waistband of his trousers. She unfastened each hook with deliberate slowness, reveling in the way this man, who was obviously well versed in sex and pleasure, caught his breath. The way he leaned into her, as if to silently plea for more. The way he tensed as she hooked her thumbs around his pant waist and pushed the fabric away in a smooth motion.

Her palms traveled down his hips as the trousers fell away and both of them sucked in their breath. Penelope shivered. God, he was so hard everywhere. Like he was a granite statue, come to life to fulfill her every fantasy.

Every fantasy but one.

She shook away the thought and instead concentrated on touching him. She stroked the narrow expanse of his hips, her palms were tickled by the light curls on his hard thighs, and she stifled a nervous giggle as she let her fingers cup his backside.

"Remember what I said," he growled, and this time his voice was less than playful. "Don't start something you cannot finish, Penelope."

She stared into the darkness, frustrated by the fact that she could only make out a ghost of this man's features. She wanted to *see* her affect on him, not just hear it in his voice or feel it beneath her skin. She wanted to meet his eyes while she touched him.

But that was impossible. Foolish. This was all she could have. Just a lover in the shadows.

But while she had him, she intended to make full use of him. Without saying a word, she dropped to her knees. The discarded clothing was a perfect cushion as she slid her hands up his legs and captured the hard thrust of his erection in her fingers a second time. But this time there was no fabric between them. Nothing but his hot skin on hers.

"Penelope . . ." His voice was a warning, but behind it was a tremor of anticipation.

And that was too much to resist. Penelope leaned forward and brushed her cheek against him. His flesh was so hot, so hard. It jumped against her skin, twitching out of control. She just wanted . . . more. So she pushed aside her racing thoughts, cleared her mind of troubling images and allowed herself pleasure.

Given and taken.

Jeremy's knees buckled as Penelope brushed her lips back and forth across the exquisitely sensitive tip of his erect cock. Her breath was hot on his skin, her lips smooth and soft and just wet enough that he twitched with pleasure. Normally, he was in control. But at that moment, he was anything but. He wanted to drive into her mouth, he wanted to feel her tongue on him.

But more than that, he wanted to drag her up, pin her against the door with his weight, and plunge into her pussy. He wanted to have her, hard and hot and fast. Even though that went against his every plan.

She was the one who was supposed to beg. Not him.

But he was ready to do just that when she parted her lips and darted her tongue out with a light, teasing lick. Jeremy moaned and braced his arms on the door behind her.

The next lick wasn't teasing. She glided her mouth around the head of his cock and sucked, drawing him inside her inch by inch, massaging him with her tongue, giving him gentle nips with her teeth. She took him as far as she could, holding tight to the base of his cock with every stroke.

It was utter madness.

No woman should be this talented at an act she'd only seen twice. But damn, she was. A natural at giving intense pleasure. A wanton at heart.

Jeremy shuddered as she withdrew, rubbing her palm over the wet path her mouth created as she pulled away from him.

"Christ," he murmured, the word dragged from his mouth against his will as she sucked him back inside.

He tangled his fingers into her hair and felt her stiffen. She was thinking about what she'd watched earlier in the day. About seeing Lady Turncroft pleasuring her lover just as Penelope was doing now. Of the look of ecstasy on her face when that other man pulled her hair back.

Jeremy waited, his cock throbbing with pleasure, to see if Penelope would draw away. Perhaps even confess about what she'd seen. But after a brief few seconds, she returned to pleasuring him. If anything, her pace increased and he forgot all his plans for her. He forgot all the mixed up emotions she caused.

And he focused on pleasure.

Penelope smiled as her mysterious lover started to arch his hips against her mouth and the pressure of his fingers at the back of her hair increased. He was starting to lose control because of what she was doing. Her mouth, her tongue, her hands . . . they had the ability to make him moan. To make him stiffen. To make him come.

And she had never felt so powerful in her entire life.

She *liked* feeling his cock grow harder in her mouth. She *liked* the way his breath caught. It aroused her. She was so wet, so ready, and every stroke of her mouth over him made her own desire sharper and more defined. She was right on the edge of orgasm when her faceless lover let out a guttural grunt and suddenly pulled his cock from her lips.

In the dark, she heard him groan in pleasure and she knew what he had done. She felt an odd sense of disappointment that he hadn't found completion at her lips, though she realized it was a gentlemanly action to withdraw.

"You are a minx," he murmured as he caught her upper arms and pulled her to her feet. With the brush of his fingers he pulled her tangled chemise away, leaving her naked.

She sucked in her breath in shock. She had assumed that after he found his pleasure, he would leave. Her husband had never expressed any interest in her once he had his own release.

"What are you—?" she began.

He silenced her with a kiss that melted her bones. His tongue drove inside, stroking over hers with promise and passion that made her ache.

"Did you think I was finished?" he growled before he dropped his mouth for another rough, needy kiss. "Not at all. Now that the edge is off my own desire, I can concentrate solely on *you*."

Penelope's eyes went wide at that thought. So the night before his attention *hadn't* been solely on her? Dear God, he had made her weak. What in the world could he do when his own desire was slaked and her body was the only thing to distract him?

She didn't have to wait long to find out. He lifted her arms over her head with one big hand, pinning them to the door. Then he wedged a knee between her thighs and pushed them open. Penelope gasped as the hard muscle of his thigh flattened against the wet lips of her sex. The dull ache of desire immediately ratcheted up to a new level.

But behind it was an entirely different emotion. An anxious, needy fear. She was totally naked, totally at his mercy without the use of her hands to fend him off. And he was unclothed, as well. If he wanted to, he could take the one thing she had made him promise to leave be. He could have sex with her without asking her leave.

And the worst part was that if he lifted her up, if he filled her with his cock, she knew for certain that she wouldn't fight him. She would writhe and moan and come, despite herself.

"You promised," she protested weakly, pushing halfheartedly against his hands.

His body went perfectly still so that all she could feel was the hot brush of his breath against her cheek.

"Not to take you?" he panted. "And I shall not, as tempting as that is. I don't force women to do anything, Penelope. If someone else did so in the past, then he shall rot in hell."

Now she was the one who went perfectly still. She had only ever confessed the harsh reality of her marriage to one person: Jeremy Vaughn. And yet this mysterious man who didn't know her at all had guessed some of the truth. Her body, her reactions to him had betrayed her deepest, most painful secret.

"Penelope, I will only take what you have offered," he whispered. "Until you ask me for more."

His mouth found hers again, but there was nothing rough or forceful about his kiss. This time it was gentle. Reassuring. So soft and sweet and unexpected that it brought tears to Penelope's eyes. When was the last time she had felt tenderness? From any person, but especially from a man? She relaxed against him, forgetting her position, letting her mind go quiet and just *feeling* the soft pressure of his lips on hers.

When he drew away, she heard the quiet intake of his breath. She felt her own. This man had many plans for her, but that kiss hadn't been one of them.

And that made it even more special.

No longer afraid of having taken what she did not offer, Penelope surrendered to feeling. The knee that was pressed between her legs pushed up, higher and higher until her feet came off the ground and her sex was spread against his thigh.

"God, you are so wet. So ready," he murmured, more to himself than to her.

He moved his hand, lowering her trapped arms until they were wound around his neck. They were face to face now in the dark and he cupped her backside and dragged her forward. Sweet friction was the result. She bucked as her clit was rasped against his unyielding muscle, tickled by the little hairs along his legs.

He moved her again, guiding her until she was grinding down on his thigh of her own accord. Almost instantly, all her pent-up desire, all the heated pleasure she had been fighting for two days, bubbled forth. Overflowed.

She tilted her head back and let the wave wash over her. When his lips touched her throat, it send her over the edge. She bucked wildly, riding his thigh as tremor after tremor of pleasure rocked her. Her orgasm seemed to last an eternity, never easing, never slowing until she went weak against his sweat-slicked chest.

His arms came around her back and he held her as he slowly let her feet touch the ground. Unsteady, Penelope kept her own arms around his neck, clinging to him as little tremors occasionally continued to rack her sensitive body.

The stranger tilted his head and his mouth found hers. His tongue breached her lips and explored her mouth with lazy purpose and slow torment. The fire that Penelope had only just had extinguished immediately came back, and then doubled when her lover cupped her backside and pulled her against him.

"More?" she whispered, weak as he slowly guided her toward her bed.

"So much more," he promised as he placed her against the pillows.

She shivered as his big body covered hers, pressing her into the mattress, molding into every soft curve with unyielding hardness. She stared up at the blank outline of the man who was slowly changing her, yet whom she had never seen. Who was he? How had he found her? Why did he want her?

She wanted to ask those questions and more, but he didn't allow her time to think, let alone speak. His fingers began to move, dancing over her skin, teasing her and testing her. She arched up as his fingertips slipped over her nipples, her thoughts emptying from her mind like water from an overturned glass.

He glided down, touching every inch of exposed flesh until he cupped her sex, opening her with a few lazy strokes of his fingers and thumb. She strained up, offering herself to him like a wanton, waiting for him to breach her body with his fingers.

But he didn't.

"I want you, Penelope," he groaned, his voice low and husky in the dark.

She arched again, forcing the tip of his finger into her wet sheath. She bit back a cry as she panted, "Then touch me."

"I would rather drive inside of you," he whispered.

Penelope froze. Was he asking her . . . ?

"But you won't allow that," he said, before she could respond.

She wanted to be glad for that fact, but she wasn't. Part of her knew that if he had hesitated a moment more, she might have allowed him to make love to her. To fill her.

"So your mouth," he said, as he leaned up over her. He pressed his lips to hers and Penelope gasped as she felt the long, hard length of him against her belly. "I want your mouth on me again."

She pulled away. "Already?" she whispered. "I didn't think . . ."

With a blush, she broke off. What a foolish, naive girl she must sound like. Obviously *this* man could want her again in such a short time. Her husband had simply not been able to desire her after he spent himself.

"Penelope, I have been ready for you since a few moments after you made me come." He pressed his mouth to hers again. "You make me mad with desire. I can think of nothing else but you. But I want to give you pleasure. Will you trust me that we can each have our release, simultaneously?"

Penelope swallowed hard. "How?"

He shifted onto his back next to her. "Now, straddle me so that your mouth is near my cock. Let me taste you while you taste me."

She drew in her breath sharply. She had never heard of such a thing, but already her body throbbed with the anticipation of her mysterious lover's mouth against her. His talented tongue arousing her.

Carefully, she shifted into the position he had described. His cock was fully hard already as she leaned over him. When her hair brushed the sensitive head, he jolted beneath her. And when she took him in hand, guided him between her lips a second time, he let out a shuddering, pleasure-filled sigh that blew a gust of warm air against her exposed body.

And then his tongue speared into her. Penelope arched, and his cock popped free from her lips as she cried out in focused pleasure. She rubbed his erection as he licked her, swiping his tongue against every crevice, lapping at her juices like they were fine wine.

Her moans grew louder and more strangled as he added a long, thick finger to the torment. Slowly, he glided inside her clenching sheath, even as he continue to nip and lick at her clit.

Penelope fought to hold off the wave of pleasure, returning her focus to his cock. She covered him with her mouth, sliding her tongue over him with the same rhythm that he slid his finger in and out of her body. Her body was already starting to tremble, release loomed up like the shadows in the room. Penelope strained for it. Reached for it, but it remained out of reach.

Because she wanted more. She *wanted* this man to rise up behind her and fill her with his hard body. She *wanted* to be pressed into the mattress beneath his weight. She wanted to give him everything. Her body, her surrender.

Only when she pictured a man rearing up behind her, pressing her against the bed as he took her, the face on her faceless lover belonged to Jeremy.

With one thought of him, her body roared with pleasure. She shook as she continued to suck and slide her mouth over her mystery lover's body, she slammed her hips into his mouth as she moaned around his girth.

She felt his legs stiffen, and then he came. Penelope was surprised by the sudden eruption but didn't find it unpleasant. Her own pleasure was too keen for her to be disturbed by anything. With a final cry, she arched up, his cock falling from her mouth.

Penelope collapsed onto her lover's legs, panting as her body shivered a few more times. He leaned forward and gathered her up, moving her to lay beside him. Penelope didn't argue. She was too weak and boneless with pleasure. Too warm and satiated.

"It is growing late," he said softly as he pressed a kiss to her forehead. "I should go."

Penelope looked up at his shadowy face. "Very well."

He kissed her, and she tasted the earthy essence of her own pleasure on his lips. Immediately, her body responded at shocking speed. How could she want him again? He moved away and she heard him gathering up his clothing, dressing in the dark.

"Will I . . . ," she said, halting as heat filled her cheeks. Thank God he couldn't see her.

"What?"

"Will I see you again?" she asked softly.

There was a moment's hesitation. "Tomorrow night."

Relief flooded her. Troubling relief, considering how close she had come tonight to demanding he take her. She would have to be strong when he visited her again. Perhaps make the next time the last time.

A thought that troubled her.

"I will leave my window unlocked for you," she promised.

"Good night, Penelope," he said softly. "Dream of me."

Then the window clicked open and he was gone. Penelope rolled over to stare at the low coals of her fire. The ones that provided so little light that she didn't even know the man who had given her such pleasure.

She was already empty without him. Aching for his touch. And it seemed satisfaction wouldn't come from his fingers, his tongue. It only left her craving more. Craving the one thing she had sworn to stay away from.

And craving Jeremy, no matter how wrong that desire was.

Fifteen

Jeremy strummed his fingers along the arm of the wingback chair he was uncomfortably situated in. He gazed around Penelope's parlor with a frown. It was a fine room, very pretty with all the very best in furniture and accoutrements, although there was a cold quality to the decoration. It reflected the public persona that Penelope put on.

But it didn't reflect her true nature. The passionate nature that Jeremy had begun to unleash as her mystery lover. He clenched his fists. Being a faceless seducer had seemed like the perfect plan when he thought of it. And it had certainly worked. The anonymity of his disguise put Penelope at ease. It allowed her to unleash her desires, or *some* of her desires. But she still held back.

And Jeremy found that breaking her barriers, giving her secret pleasure, knowing that she was providing him fodder for blackmail and ruin was far less pleasurable than he had planned. In fact, it was downright frustrating.

Jeremy wanted to be inside of her body. He wanted to feel her arch beneath him as he entered her inch by inch. He wanted her to admit that she craved that as much as he did. And none of those desires had a damn thing to do with his plans. He wanted her to ask him to make love to her, not for blackmail, but for some other reason. Some troubling thing that he couldn't understand, let alone name.

He simply wanted her to want him.

The door behind him opened, and Jeremy rose to his feet as Penelope entered the room. He noted that she left the door open as she gave him a tired, weak smile of welcome. She looked haggard. Far more exhausted and confused than she had even the afternoon before.

After he left her last night, had she lain awake, tormenting herself? Or had she been up pacing her room out of unfulfilled desires of her own?

"Good afternoon, Penelope," he said, smiling as if he didn't notice her red eyes or the smudges beneath them. He could only hope she was too distracted to notice his own.

"Hello," she said softly, but didn't meet his gaze.

Interesting. Was she feeling guilty over what she had done in the darkness the night before? Or was she simply afraid he would see the truth? After all, Penelope didn't know that *he* was the man who made her cry out in the night. She simply thought of him as a friend.

A label that was troubling in more ways than one.

"Are you ready for today's excursion?" he asked, shaking off his troubling thoughts as he motioned to the door behind him.

Penelope looked at him for a long moment in silence. Then she paced past him and sat down in the chair across from the one he had recently occupied. She stared at her folded hands for so long that Jeremy couldn't help but step toward her in true concern.

"Penelope?"

She looked up at him with a weak shake of her head. "I realize you came all this way to escort me on one of your outings, and I do appreciate how much thought and time you've put into your . . . *education*. But, I am in no mood for it today."

He straightened up. "Have I done something to upset you?"

She shook her head immediately. "No, you have been nothing but kind to me, even when I didn't deserve it."

He winced. When she found out the truth about his deception, she was going to hate him. He shouldn't have cared, but he did.

"Do you wish for me to leave you in peace?" he asked and was surprised that a knot formed in his gut at the thought.

He had actually been looking forward to spending time with Penelope in the light. Being able to look at her, see her reactions to the sensual delights he exposed her to that day.

She pondered his question for a moment. "No. Would you stay?"

He stepped away from her, taken aback by that unexpected request. "Of course," he stammered as he retook his seat across from her.

They sat in silence until a maid arrived and deposited tea on a small table between them. After Penelope waved the girl away and began to pour, she spoke again.

"Do you think I am an utter hypocrite?"

Jeremy tensed. There it was. The question he had been waiting for her to ask. The one that could easily turn the tide in her so-called war against excess. He ought to tell her yes. To preach to her about her true nature. To use the trust she had developed in him against her.

But now that the moment was upon him and he was looking at Penelope's tired expression and broken eyes, he found his response far different.

"I don't know. A hypocrite is someone who says one thing, yet does another. Or keeps another in her heart or her soul. Someone who denies the truth of what she is in public." He shrugged as he took the cup she had poured for him. "And I could not begin to guess the truths you may or may not hide from others. Or even from yourself."

She stared at the steaming liquid in her cup and Jeremy saw the battle she was waging. He held his breath, waiting for her to confess that she had been indulging in dark passions with a man whose face she did not know.

But she didn't. Finally, she shook her head. "I suppose you are correct. But some would say that my excursions with you are proof of my hypocrisy. Some would want to use those times against me if they had a chance. To silence me."

Jeremy found himself strangely bothered by the fact that she did not confide in him about her secret lover. But it was foolish. After all, what would he say if she *did* confess? Would he reveal himself to her? Would he complete his plan as he had promised his friends?

"Jeremy?" she said softly. Then she shook her head with a blush so fierce that it darkened her cheeks to crimson red. "I mean, Your Grace."

He smiled. "In private, I see no harm in your calling me Jeremy. After all, I have long been impolite enough to call you Penelope, and you have been kind enough not to correct me."

She dipped her chin. "We are friends, aren't we? Friends might refer to each other by their given names and it wouldn't be improper. As long as we continue to use titles in front of others."

Jeremy frowned. There it was again. Her unbending resolve to remain proper, at least in public. To fight what she desired in the public eye.

"Yes, I suppose. As for what you said about others wishing to silence you, it is true, you *have* created enemies with your words. But if you know yourself, know your own heart, then what others say shouldn't matter to you."

She looked up at him, surprise in her expression. "Do *you* know yourself and your own heart?"

He shifted uncomfortably. He wasn't accustomed to talking about himself. His friends didn't require such openness, and his lovers had always known their place was only in his bed. He was very rarely pushed beyond the comfortable distance he chose to maintain.

"What do you mean?" he asked, mostly to stall for time.

She shrugged. "Your behavior used to be quite different. You were known for your excess, your sinful lusts." He thought he detected a very slight shiver when she said the word *lust*, but he couldn't be sure as she continued. "And now you claim to be changed. What made you the man you were before? And what has turned you to the man you now claim to be?"

Such direct questions. And now that she had asked them, he wasn't certain he truly knew the answers she sought. He was the man he was. He'd never paused to ask why. He'd never considered any other path.

Until now. Drinking tea with a woman he was lying to. *Now* he considered the truth of his life.

"I know *I* was shaped by my family," Penelope continued before he was forced to answer her pointed question.

He breathed a sigh of relief before he pressed her. "Your sister, you mean."

She nodded, and her cheeks pinkened again. "Yes, by Miranda and what I uncovered about her true nature. But Miranda's lies weren't my only influence. My parents had a great impact on my life."

Jeremy wasn't quite able to stifle a shiver at the thought of Penelope's mother, Dorthea Albright. The entire *ton* was aware of the overbearing woman, who seemed entirely oblivious to how her outrageous behavior actually hurt her younger daughters' chances in the marriage mart.

"I see from your expression that you know my mother," Penelope said with a slight smile that softened her haggard expression. "She is . . . difficult, I know. Growing up in the shadow of her moods, of her criticisms, of her drive for more and more and more . . . that certainly shaped me. I realized, quite young, that I would be expected to better our family's situation. So it wasn't only Miranda's behavior that drove me to marry to financial gain."

Jeremy found himself leaning in. Very few women were so frank. At least with him.

But then, he doubted Penelope would have been so frank with him in the past, before they were, as she put it, *friends*. A false friend he might be, but he found himself interested in what she had to say, nonetheless.

"What about your father?" he asked. "He must have had some influence on you."

"Oh, he did." Her voice was even softer, and a sadness entered her eyes. "He was a dear man in many respects. He loved me and my sisters, I truly believe that. He was kind in every way that my mother was harsh. But he lived in a world of excess."

Jeremy looked at her in question. "You mean—"

She interrupted. "No, not sensual excess." She frowned. "Not that I ever knew of. But he gambled, he raced, he could never quite get a handle on his vices, even when they began to ruin him, ruin our family. His selfish needs became more important than our comfort and even our survival."

Jeremy nodded. It made her quest against such selfish behavior all the more understandable. She had seen and felt the consequences of excessive behavior. First from her father, later from her sister.

"What about you?" she asked as she leaned back. "I know very little of your family. You must have been shaped by them."

Jeremy shifted, no more comfortable about talking about his family now than he had been when she first broached the subject. "I suppose that must be true, but I have never thought much about it."

Penelope frowned. "You have a brother, yes? Are you close?"

Jeremy straightened up. "Yes, well, no."

She let out a little laugh. "Which one is it?"

"Both." He smiled, despite the unpleasant subject. "Christopher used to be much like I am. Or was. He was wild. But then he fell in love, of all things. He got married." He frowned. "And I didn't know what to do. Or think. I resented him, I suppose."

"Because he was rejecting the life you still lead?" she asked softly.

Jeremy's gaze jerked up. Dear God, she had hit upon the very thing he'd been denying so long. Christopher had forced him to wonder if his life, which he had always enjoyed, was frivolous. Seeing his brother's newfound happiness and fidelity had altered Jeremy's view on his own existence.

"Yes, I suppose that is true," he admitted. "That was when I started to change."

He frowned. Except he hadn't changed. He'd simply fought harder to keep the life he had been living. And that fight included his agreement to destroy Penelope.

"What about your parents?" she pressed.

He frowned. "My father died four years ago."

"I'm sorry," she whispered.

He shook his head. "I wasn't."

She drew back, and he saw the surprise in her eyes. He felt it in himself. He'd never admitted that to anyone, even Christopher.

"We weren't close," he explained as he shoved to his feet and began to pace the small parlor. "He was never cruel, or even neglectful. He taught me many valuable life lessons and I always respected him. But there was something . . . missing. I never knew what it was until one day I saw him with his other family."

"His other family?"

He nodded. "He had a longtime mistress, and they had a son

and daughter together. I saw him with them once. He was an entirely different man." He thought of the way his father had tossed his young daughter in the air. The way he'd laughed. "Affectionate and loving."

Penelope rose and stepped toward him. "That must have been painful."

"I assume it must have been at some point to my mother. But by the time he died, they had a cool relationship. Now she travels. She seems very happy."

Not that he would know. Another revelation that shamed him.

Penelope shook her head. "I meant painful to you. To see him with another family. To see him give them love so easily, when it was not something he'd shared easily with you or your brother."

He shrugged. "Not painful. Just . . . strange. I never looked at him the same way again. I was his . . . family business in a way, as was my brother. We were a way to insure his legacy, but he left his passion and his emotion somewhere else."

"And that was what you decided you would do, as well," Penelope said.

Jeremy looked down at her. A parade of willing, wanton women briefly passed before his eyes. Women he had taken to his bed, but never any further. There were a few he had actually liked, but the moment any one of them grew too close or demanded more than he was willing to give, he pushed them aside.

Until Penelope.

"I suppose I did," he admitted softly.

"Wouldn't it be nice, though, if you could have both under one roof," she said with a wistful sigh. "A wife you loved *and* felt that passion for. A woman you could see as a partner, not just a business transaction?"

She looked so pretty, staring up at him, her face filled with naive hopes. Jeremy wished he could hold that image of her forever. Because eventually that naivety would be gone. He was sworn to crush it.

"Your crusade, again?" he asked with a soft chuckle.

"That was all I said, you know," she sighed. "The first day I spoke to my friends. All I said was that it wasn't fair that we were asked to sit at home while our husbands found love and passion elsewhere. That we deserved more thought and respect than that. And that the only way we would get it would be to demand it." She shook her head. "I must have hit a chord, for the entire thing escalated from that moment on. And now I am the one who is hissed at, stared at, the one who is supposed to lead some kind of uprising."

There was a wistful, longing quality to Penelope's voice, and for the first time Jeremy realized just how trying this quest of hers had been. She had been chosen, somehow, to be a voice for the voiceless. But she didn't relish the attention or the hatred that came with her position.

"You can stop this any time you like," he said softly. He took a step closer and their bodies almost touched. "It isn't fair that you should have to shoulder all of that responsibility."

Penelope's breath caught, a tiny hitch that seemed to echo like a shotgun blast though Jeremy's very soul. She stared up at him, her blue gaze slightly hazy, her tongue darting out to wet her lips. All the need he had felt for her in the dark of her bedroom swept over him, taking over his reason. Washing away his plans.

And when she looked at his mouth, Jeremy couldn't help it. He reached out, trembling fingers brushing her cheek. He cupped her chin, tilting her face up to his and reveling in the way she shuddered with desire. She wanted him to kiss her. *Him*, Jeremy. Not a faceless lover, not a secret admirer whom she could dismiss in the cold light of morning. *Him*.

And that made any desire he'd felt for her in the past a pale shadow of what boiled within him now. He forced himself to temper his feelings and slowly drew Penelope closer. Her body, so soft, brushed his, molded into his. And it felt so good.

She tilted her head back, lifting her lips in silent offering to him. Her eyes fluttered shut in anticipation. Jeremy leaned in, close enough that he was aware of the soft brush of her breath on his lips, close enough to smell the faint perfume of fresh roses on her skin.

Close enough that he felt her tremble.

But he didn't press his lips to hers. Because this kiss was different than any other. He had confessed some part of his soul to her, a part no one else had ever seen. And as he stared down at her, he knew that if he kissed her, it wouldn't stop there. It would only begin. He would be compelled first to touch her and then to have her.

And when it was over, everything would change.

He wasn't willing to allow that. With a shake of his head he did the most difficult thing he'd ever been forced to do and stepped away. Penelope's eyes came open and she stared at him. Her cheeks darkened with a hot blush, her eyes reflected hurt and embarrassment.

Jeremy felt an odd urge to comfort her, but he wouldn't allow it.

"I-I'm sorry," he murmured, his apology so very lame on his lips. "I'm sorry."

Then he backed out of the room and left Penelope alone. Knowing he had hurt her.

And knowing that deep down inside, by denying himself her kiss, he had hurt himself just as much. Even though allowing that emotion was a folly that would only make him weak.

Climbing into his carriage outside, Jeremy scrubbed a hand over his face. The situation was getting entirely out of hand. Penelope Norman had woven some kind of spell over him, but he couldn't . . . he *would not* allow that to continue. Tonight, he would come to her as her secret lover one last time. And before the night was over, he would end this madness.

Once and for all.

Sixteen

Penelope sat on her bed, staring with sightless eyes at the open window across the room. In a few scant moments, a man with no face would step over the threshold. He would reach for her and she wouldn't resist. He would seduce her and she would let herself be seduced.

He would want her.

And yet, she didn't feel much excitement about that fact tonight. Yes, she looked forward to the pleasure about to come. Her heart beat faster at the idea that her mystery lover would introduce her to more pleasures than ever before.

But she could not be fully immersed in the anticipation because of Jeremy Vaughn. Because of the almost kiss they shared just a few hours before, downstairs in her parlor.

Because he didn't want her.

Jeremy didn't want her. He had touched her, he'd drawn her

close, he'd let his breath mingle with hers, but then he had withdrawn without explanation. And his eyes, his hollow, horrified eyes had said everything his lips had not.

Penelope's stomach churned with emotion every time she thought of it.

She should have been happy, should have thanked him for his prudent response. If they had kissed, it would have been a terrible mistake. Jeremy's reputation, the friendship they had developed, the fact that she was still uncertain of his true motives, no matter how much trust she found herself putting in him, all those things precluded them from being together. Not to mention that she had been surrendering herself, almost completely, to another man for many nights.

And yet, she still longed for what might have been. She continued to wish that Jeremy had wanted her enough to touch his lips to hers, all the very good reasons to pull away be damned.

She sighed and flopped an arm over her face as she fell back against her pillows.

"Are you asleep?"

Penelope bolted to a seated position as she watched the shadowy figure step through her window. She stared at his silhouette as he snapped the latch shut behind him. *He* wanted her. All of her.

Without answering his question, she slipped down from the bed and crossed the room. She reached for him, feeling the edge of the mask he wore before she lifted her lips to his. He tasted of a faint mixture of fine port and minty freshness. And desire. Always desire.

She moaned as she arched against him, pulling him closer. He was already hard against her belly, evidence that he found her attractive. That he was willing to throw away caution to touch her.

And oh, how she needed that to erase Jeremy's expression. The humiliation of watching one of the most notorious rakes bolt from her sitting room like she was a wart-covered frog demanding his lips.

"Touch me," she murmured between kisses, clasping his hands and sliding them up her sides, across her belly and finally pressing them to her breasts.

"With pleasure," he growled.

And then he was backing her across the room, his hot mouth and hands roving over her body like he was a hungry man who had encountered a feast. She arched against him, loving how wanted she felt. How beautiful and erotic.

Her backside hit the edge of the high bed and he stopped. Penelope could hardly contain a groan of displeasure as his hands left her skin. But the groan turned to a gasp as she felt him tie a blindfold over her eyes.

"What?" she asked, reaching for the cloth.

He caught her wrist. "I want to see you," he whispered. "I *need* to see you, Penelope."

She hesitated. In the total darkness, their shadow coupling put them on equal ground. But blindfolded, he would have the upper hand and she would be forced to put her trust in him. She tensed at the thought. She didn't know his name, and yet he would be in the position to do anything he liked to her.

Her mind turned to Jeremy yet again. Her trust in him had

led to his humiliating rejection. To a wash of pain. But this man would not reject her.

"Very well," she whispered, dropping her hand away.

He breathed a sigh of relief, and she felt him move away, heard him adding logs to the fire and lighting candles around her room. Through the opaque cloth around her eyes, Penelope felt the light brighten.

She couldn't help but blush as her faceless lover moved to stand before her. He caught the thin straps of her night shift and glided them down her shoulders, letting the fabric pool at her feet and leaving her naked.

He sucked in a breath and Penelope lifted her chin so that he wouldn't recognize how difficult such exposure was for her. He had only looked at her in faint light before this. What if he didn't find her quite so alluring without darkness? What if he didn't want her after all?

"You are magnificent," he whispered.

The air left her lungs in a whoosh of relief, and Penelope blinked back unexpected stinging in her eyes at his assessment. How foolish was she that a stranger's admiration could make her proud? Or that a rake's rejection could make her weak?

She shook her head. No! No thoughts of Jeremy! She wouldn't let what had happened between them ruin this night. And she wouldn't let images of him enter her mind while this other man touched her. Not again.

She heard the gentle thump of something hitting the floor and stiffened. "What are you doing?" she asked, her voice sounding small and uncertain.

"Removing my mask," he admitted.

Penelope stepped forward and reached out her fingers. She found her lover's chest and sucked in a breath. He had removed more than just his mask. His bare skin greeted her palms, hot and smooth. She slid her hands up until she grazed his chin.

Slowly, gently, she touched his face. There was a hint of stubble on his defined cheeks. His lips were full, just as they felt when he pressed them to her body. She sighed as he darted his tongue out and teased her fingers.

Once again, Jeremy's image invaded her mind, and she pushed it away with violence. No. No. No.

"Are you all right?" her lover whispered.

She nodded. "Yes. Just . . . touch me."

He lifted her up to sit on the very edge of the high bed and she opened her legs shamelessly to let him step between them. The wiry hair on his chest tickled her thighs as he tilted his face up to capture her mouth. His tongue swirled around hers, thrust in rhythm, took and tenderly explored.

And she craved even more. When his hands touched her naked sides, she moaned into his mouth. When he cupped her breasts, she shivered with desire. It seemed like her weak body was utterly out of control. Her hips surged toward him, grinding against him in a wild rhythm. Her hands fisted in his hair, pulling his mouth to her skin. Her tongue danced and speared his when he kissed her. And she offered her breasts shamelessly when he dragged his lips down her body.

Being blindfolded, being in the dark when she knew he could see everything about her, was a wildly arousing experience. One she never would have said she wanted if she had been asked, but one she couldn't get enough of now that she was being pleasured.

The only thing that destroyed the perfection of it was that her mind kept wandering, taking her to places she didn't want to be. Making her think of Jeremy and the way his mouth had moved toward hers. Making her recall just how much she had wanted his skin on hers.

Her faceless lover tugged at her nipples with his mouth and her body jolted as pleasure ricocheted between her legs. She wrapped her calves around his broad back and writhed against him all the harder, but still her ache wasn't appeased.

He seemed to sense her need, for he dragged his hands away from her breasts and slid them down her stomach between their bodies. Urging her to lay back, he cupped her sex. She whimpered as a tremor of pleasure arced through her like summer lightning. He spread her open, and she heard him catch his breath.

"Lovely," he murmured as he ground his thumb against the hard ridge of her aroused clit and slipped one finger inside her clenching sheath.

Penelope arched, her hands fisting the coverlet as he drove into her body. She lifted her hips to meet his strokes, she clenched her inner muscles to prolong the pleasure, but it wasn't enough. She still felt empty, unfulfilled.

And she still wanted more.

"Y-Your mouth," she panted, not even caring that she was begging. "Please."

He didn't ask for clarification or question her demand. She felt his hot breath burn against her thigh almost instantly. His stare equally blistered her revealed flesh. Even with her eyes covered, she knew he was drinking in the sight of her naked body, finally revealed to him.

And then his tongue lapped over her exquisitely sensitive flesh. Penelope jolted at the contact and the cry that escaped her lips wasn't one she could have controlled if she were paid a thousand pounds to do so. This man had stripped away every polite nicety she had always prided herself in and left her a writhing, begging wanton.

And yet, she didn't care. She just wanted more.

He gave it to her. He speared his tongue inside, lapping up to suckle her clit until her head thrashed back and forth against the wrinkled coverlet. The pleasure had never been so intense, pulsing in time to her rapid heartbeat, building and building until it bordered on pain and she wanted to scream for release.

But it never came.

Frantic to feel the waves of pleasure, Penelope squeezed her eyes shut and let herself think of Jeremy, as she had so many other nights that this man touched her. She imagined *him* between her legs, caressing her thighs, stroking his tongue over her wet flesh, sucking and dragging pleasure from her.

The pleasure peaked a second time, but still she couldn't find release. Not even with her fantasies in overdrive.

There was only one thing that would give her what she craved. As she lay there, the stranger's wicked mouth working over her at a frantic pace, she knew exactly what she needed.

She needed to be taken. *Fucked*, as she had heard other men whisper when she walked by. Hard and fast. Slow and steady. She didn't care. She just wanted this man's cock inside of her body.

Now.

"Please," she moaned, heat flooding her already flushed cheeks. "Please. Take me."

The pressure of his mouth on her flesh was suddenly jolted away and Penelope groaned aloud in protest.

"What?" he panted, his voice thick with desire.

"You heard me," she gasped as she lifted her hips to him helplessly. "Give me what you've wanted. Join your body to mine. Take me."

Jeremy stared at Penelope in utter shock. Her blond hair was tangled around her flushed breasts, her legs splayed open to reveal the glistening mound of her sex, her back arching out of control. She looked nothing like the proper lady who shunned sensuality anymore and every inch the lustful hoyden.

Finally, Jeremy had broken down her last wall. She wanted him to put his cock in her. Claim her. The one thing he had desired more than any other since the first night he touched her. The final barrier to both breaking her will and blackmailing her.

He stroked his hard erection once as he maneuvered over her, driven to feel the heaven of her body lock around his in a wet, hot fist. He braced his arms on either side of her head and hesitated, taking a moment to look down at her.

Penelope arched, her body thrusting toward his. Half her face was hidden by the black satin blindfold that hid the truth from her. But her full lips were tense with anticipation, her cheeks flushed as she panted out breath after breath.

She was utter temptation. She was passion personified. He wanted her more than he'd ever wanted any woman he'd ever bedded.

And yet, he couldn't do it. Not this way.

That afternoon, he had pulled away from Penelope because she was too close. Tonight, he realized he had to pull away because she wasn't close enough.

He wanted to "take her," as she had asked him to do. But he didn't want to do it while she was blindfolded, unaware of his face, without knowing his name. He didn't want to be a pleasure she allowed in the night and denied in the light of day. A dirty secret that she never shared with anyone.

No, the surrender he wanted, he realized, was much deeper. And it had nothing to do with the promise he had made to his friends.

He wanted Penelope to look into his eyes as he glided inside of her body. He wanted her to whisper his name as he took her over the edge of pleasure. He wanted her to blush when she next saw him at a gathering, because she remembered the intensity of their joining.

He wanted her to know exactly what she was doing and whom she was doing it with.

It went against his every plan. It violated all his codes about keeping the women he bedded separate from the everyday life he led.

But that was what he wanted. And he wouldn't . . . *couldn't* settle for anything less.

Even though it meant getting up and leaving Penelope without taking her. Without feeling her body pulse around him. Even if it meant going home aching from being unfulfilled.

It served him right.

With effort, he pushed away from her and back to his feet

where he swept up his trousers and quickly put them back on. He didn't bother with the rest of his things, merely shoved them together in an awkward pile.

Penelope sat up, and the expression on her face was much the same as it had been earlier in the day when Jeremy denied her his kiss. Even though he couldn't see her eyes for the blindfold, he could tell she was embarrassed. Hurt.

"What . . . ?Why . . . ?" she whispered.

"I'm sorry, Penelope," he said softly as he moved for the window, repeating the refrain he had started in her parlor just a few hours before.

"You don't want me?" she said, her voice flat even though her mouth was still twisted with pain.

"I'm sorry," he repeated before he tossed his remaining clothing out the open window and stepped onto the ledge.

Once he was outside, he turned back. Penelope stood with her back to him. Her shoulders were hunched.

He fisted his hands at his sides. He had hurt her twice in one day. And he hated himself for it. He hated himself for letting anyone close enough that he had the power to hurt them.

He hated that the realization of how much pain she was in made his own chest ache.

Penelope stood in the silence a long time after her mysterious lover was gone before she reached up and removed the blindfold from her face. She stared at the cloth. It was a fine black handkerchief, but there were no initials stitched on the fabric to reveal her lover's identity.

With a frown, she dropped it onto the floor next to the pile of her nightgown. Perhaps it was best not to know. If the man was someone in her acquaintance, she couldn't bear seeing him and knowing he didn't want her anymore.

She sighed as she swept up her night shift and pulled it over her head. During the nights her mystery lover had joined her in her bed . . . and even before that when he was nothing more than a series of erotic words and descriptions in the letters he sent, Penelope had *liked* being wanted. She had liked being touched and told she was beautiful. She'd craved the power she had when she touched the faceless man in return.

And that reaction was more than an experiment. It was more than a study in passion so that she would know her "enemy," as Jeremy had said so many times. She had truly given in to her desires. Fully.

Only to be denied at the last moment.

She shook her head as she pulled a dressing gown from the armoire and draped the heavy robe over her shoulders. Images bombarded her, even as she fought to keep them at bay. They were memories of the many varied pleasures she had experienced. There were so many ways she had been touched and touched in return.

For the first time, she really understood why people would sacrifice so much to feel as she had felt. Both men and women. Even her sister's behavior began to make sense now that desire had become a driving force in her own life. Penelope thought about it day and night. It had compelled her to do things she had never thought she would.

And now she had lost it. Not once, but twice in one day. From two different men. And that loss hurt her. It cut like a knife down to the marrow of her soul.

She opened her door and moved into the hallway quietly. She wanted to find Fiona. To talk to her. Her maid had experienced pleasure in the past, and she had also been through great pain. Perhaps she could help Penelope clear her head. Remember all the very good reasons she had for avoiding such passion.

At the very least, Fiona would understand what she was going through, perhaps better than anyone else.

The house was still as Penelope moved through the hallways and up into the servant area. Most of the staff would be in bed by now, deep in dreams and completely unaware of their mistress's torment.

She stopped in front of Fiona's door and drew in a breath to calm herself. Quietly, she turned the handle and pushed the door open a fraction, ready to apologetically wake her maid.

Instead, she staggered back a step and reached a hand up to cover her lips. Fiona wasn't asleep. And she wasn't alone. No, the former courtesan was bent over her narrow bed, totally naked. Candlelight cascaded over her pale flesh. Next to her stood one of Penelope's footmen. He was stripped down to only his trousers and he was swatting Fiona across her backside with his bare hand.

Penelope swallowed her gasp and stared. Fiona didn't seem to mind the spanking, even though her backside was pink from the results of the slaps. In fact, she arched up with a lusty moan every time the young man made contact.

Too shocked to know what to do, Penelope spun around and

fled, the sounds of Fiona's cries of pleasure echoing in her ears as she flew down the stairs and all but ran back to her own chamber. She slammed the door and leaned back against the barrier, her breath short.

It felt like her whole world had been yanked off its axis and thrown into a different place. Penelope didn't know herself, she didn't know her body, she didn't even know her own beliefs anymore. Everything she had come to depend upon was different now.

When she discovered Fiona and heard the former courtesan's story, she had been certain that by offering the other woman a place on her staff, she had been saving Fiona. That her maid had desired to leave her life as a courtesan because she didn't enjoy it. But now . . . now Penelope didn't know anymore. Fiona had clearly been enjoying the shocking activities Penelope had just seen.

What did it all mean? Had Penelope been totally wrong? Had Fiona simply been unhappy with the *man* who was her protector, not the life she had been leading? And did her maid secretly wish she could return to that decadent life she lived before? To the erotic days and nights she had spent as the plaything of powerful men?

Penelope blinked at sudden tears as she threw herself onto her bed. She winced. The masculine, arousing scent of her secret lover still clung to the bedclothes. Tempting and taunting her.

She had no one to talk to. No one to share her confusion with. No one to give her council.

"Jeremy," she whispered, her own harsh voice startling her.

Could she go to him after his rejection? She had no other choice. Even if he didn't want her, he would at least understand. And she needed his friendship and guidance, at least one more time.

Perhaps for the last time.

Seventeen

Jeremy stared out the window at Worthington's Club, watching as droves of the *ton*'s elite wandered down the sidewalks, seeing and being seen in the fine summer weather. He frowned. They all looked so damn happy. So content and certain.

While he was twisted inside like a wrung-out handkerchief.

"Are you even listening?"

Jeremy turned to face Anthony Wharton. His friend was pacing around the private room, his face a dark, ugly red and his hands clenching in and out of fists at his sides. Jeremy arched a brow. He'd never seen his friend so angry before. It was clear it bothered the others, as well, for everyone in the room was staring at him.

"You have had more than enough time to finish this foolishness," Wharton railed. "And yet Lady Norman continues to be a problem. You have not properly humiliated her, and the mistresses and wives are still in an uproar caused by her ridiculous notions."

Jeremy pursed his lips and tried to remain calm. There was no way he could tell his friends that he was beginning to see Penelope's thoughts as less than foolish. Or that they had no one to blame but themselves if the various women in their lives were upset.

Dunfield chuckled, but it was clear he was only trying to lighten the mood in the room. "Great God, Wharton, is it worth all this bluster?"

"Shut your mouth, Dunfield," Wharton snapped, spinning on the Earl with a scowl. "You haven't suffered at all from this woman's tongue. I'm the one who lost my mistress, and I still haven't found the little bitch."

Jeremy stared. He hadn't been aware that Wharton was continuing to look for Fiona, despite her rejection of him. His language and his demeanor made that revelation troubling. It certainly didn't encourage Jeremy to share the fact that Fiona was now Penelope's servant.

"Let it go," he advised as he lit a cigar and tried to feign nonchalance. "Why would you want a woman who didn't want you?"

He flinched at his own choice of words. He had rejected Penelope the night before. Did she believe he didn't want her? That she was undesirable when the utter opposite was true. She was *too* tempting.

"I would wager my best mount that Penelope Norman knows something about it," Wharton said with a scowl. "And if you aren't going to take care of her, Kilgrath, then you'll leave me no choice but to do it myself."

Jeremy flicked his still burning cigar onto the floor and advanced on Wharton in three long steps. Before his friend could react, Jeremy caught him by the throat and slammed him against the nearest table. Wharton gasped for breath as Jeremy leaned over him, his face mere inches from his friend's.

"That is enough, Wharton," he growled, fighting hard to temper his rage. "Perhaps you are only blowing off your frustration, but you will cease your tongue's flapping before you lose it. No one will bother Lady Norman. I am taking care of the situation, and I don't want to hear anything else about it. Am I making myself clear?"

Wharton shoved him away and rubbed his red throat. "Perfectly," he said, his voice hoarse.

His friend straightened up from the table and strode from the room without so much as a word for any of the remaining men. The Earl of Dunfield got up from his lazy seat on the settee and sighed.

"Well, he'll need to complain about this to someone. I'll go after him."

The Marquis of Chartsfield clamored to his feet with a side glance for Jeremy. "I'll go, too."

Jeremy watched the two men follow Wharton out with a frown. How had it come to this? These were his best friends, and now they were fighting like schoolboys. And all because Jeremy hadn't kept one promise. He might claim he had, but it was a lie.

He'd had plenty of opportunities to resolve the situation with Penelope. He could have revealed her, blackmailed her, crushed her spirit over and over. Yet, he hadn't. But Wharton's reaction, his veiled threats against Penelope had struck a chord in Jeremy, a protective reaction that he hadn't expected any more than his shocked friends.

He looked up to find the remaining Nevers, Ryan Crawford and Viscount John Lockwood, staring at him.

"Want to discuss it?" Lockwood asked as he leaned back in his seat with an appraising look for Jeremy.

Jeremy hesitated. How could he discuss something he couldn't even fully explain to himself? He shook his head. "Not particularly."

The door to the private room opened, and a footman dressed in the club's fine livery appeared. "I beg your pardon, gentlemen. Lord Kilgrath, you have received a message. Your servants forwarded it from your home."

Jeremy stepped forward and took the letter that was propped onto a silver platter. Waving the man off, he turned the missive over to look at the seal. An ornate N. His heart lodged in his throat as he broke the seal and read the contents.

It was from Penelope. Her hand had been shaking when she wrote that she had to see him and would be arriving at his home at two that afternoon. He glanced at the grandfather clock across the room. It was one now.

"I must go," he said, folding the papers into his pocket.

"Ah, there he is!" Ryan Crawford crowed.

"There who is?" Jeremy asked with a scowl at the younger man's elation. "What are you going on about?"

"We've all been wondering where the wolf went," Crawford explained. "Since you began your pursuit of Lady Norman, he has been hidden. But I just saw a flicker of him in your eyes. It must be a woman who wrote to you. Happy hunting, my friend."

As Lockwood joined Crawford in chuckling, Jeremy shook his head and exited the room. He certainly didn't feel like a wolf when he thought of meeting with Penelope. Not after everything that had happened the previous day.

He felt like something. But not a predator.

Penelope paced around the quiet back parlor in Jeremy's home. Her hands shook and felt sweaty as she clenched them behind her back and tried to find some semblance of calm. She failed miserably. Her mind was spinning and her stomach did flip-flops as she awaited Jeremy's appearance and prayed he wouldn't appear chagrined when he saw her there.

The door to the parlor opened, and Jeremy stepped inside. She stared at him, examining his face for any adverse reaction to her presence. But there was none. In fact, he hardly reacted at all. Her heart sank.

"Is everything well?" Jeremy asked as he moved into the room and motioned her to a chair. "I worried when I received your missive."

Penelope fought a blush of pleasure. It had been a long time since someone worried about her.

"I'm sorry, I didn't mean to trouble you," she said. "I am . . . well enough. I just needed . . ."

She broke off. Oh, it was so hard to explain this to him. She was going to sound silly. Fragile. Wanton.

"Needed?" he pressed, his voice soft as he looked at her with encouragement.

"I just needed to talk to you." She shook her head at her own folly. "It seems you are the one I have been turning to as of late. Perhaps too much."

He frowned. "I'm glad you came. I actually had a question for you."

Penelope slowly sank into the chair he had indicated and looked up at him with wide eyes. A question? She couldn't read his expression at all, almost like he'd purposefully blanked his emotions away. Dear God, did he already know about her behavior? Her shocking conduct?

"What is it?" she asked, her voice cracking.

"Fiona," he said as he took his own seat. "Why did she run away from Wharton?"

Penelope felt her face fall. That was the last question she had expected, and while she was relieved that Jeremy hadn't discovered her activities from some other source, she was now in an odd position. Jeremy was Anthony Wharton's closest friend and confidante. Could she truly trust him with Fiona's secret?

But then again, she was willing to trust him with her own. Perhaps he would understand her better if he knew what drove her.

She cleared her throat uncomfortably. "Your friend," she began, locking eyes with him. "He was abusive to her."

Jeremy sucked in a breath.

"He beat her quite badly before I met her. I noticed the bruises beneath her makeup one night when we bumped into each other at the opera. We talked, and one thing led to another. I offered a place on my staff, and Fiona took it to escape Wharton's abuse. And I thought to escape the life of a courtesan." She frowned as she thought of Fiona's shocking behavior the night before. "But now I don't know. Perhaps I was a fool to think Fiona wanted to be 'saved.'"

Jeremy scrubbed a hand over his face, and his ashen countenance drew Penelope's thoughts from her own confusing troubles. He looked physically sick as he stared at the floor with unseeing eyes.

"How could I have not known?" he murmured, almost more to himself than to her. "Was I so blind, so selfish, that I couldn't . . . or didn't want to see?"

Penelope's lips parted in surprise. "You berate *yourself* for Wharton's behavior?"

He glanced up at her as if he had momentarily forgotten her presence there. "I was with them many times. I should have seen, should have guessed. But I was too interested in only myself to notice."

She got to her feet with a shake of her head. "It is not your fault, Jeremy. Fiona told me many times that she hid what was happening from the world. No one knew."

"He seemed so angry," he muttered, again to himself. "I thought he was just blustering, but . . ." He stopped and glanced up at her with wide eyes. "You stay away from him, Penelope."

She sucked in a breath at the concern she saw on his face. He was pale and almost shaking as he rose to his feet.

"Jeremy—"

"Just stay clear of him." He paced toward the door. "I need to speak to him. I need to make sure he won't . . . do anything."

Penelope leapt forward as Jeremy approached his parlor door. He was so distracted by the realization of his friend's true nature, so upset that it appeared he was ready to leave her without hearing her true reasons for coming that afternoon. And she might not ever have another chance to tell him.

"Wait, please," she said, hurrying to catch his arm. "Jeremy, I need your help. I need your council. I have nowhere else to turn."

He stared at her fingers, curled around his arm, and then his gaze moved to her face. Suddenly there was a powerful flame of heat in his eyes. Desire. She was sure of it. It caught her off guard.

He had rejected her! He didn't want her . . . did he?

"You need me?" he said with a tilt of his head.

She swallowed, recognizing the double meaning of his question. She chose to ignore it. "Yes."

"What is it?" he asked.

She closed her eyes. Heat flooded her cheeks, but she forced her nervousness aside and let the words flow in a burst. "I told you about the man who was secretly writing to me. The one whom I met with that night at the ball. But I never told you the rest. He has been coming to me ever since, Jeremy. And I have been allowing him . . . liberties."

She opened her eyes to judge his reaction and found that Jeremy was staring at her. But he didn't seem horrified or upset or even surprised. He just . . . *stared*. Like he couldn't believe she would confess such a thing.

"You have been letting him make love to you, you mean?" he asked blandly.

She shook her head as she released his arm and moved away. "No. Other things, but never that." The words were hard to say, but they were also freeing. As if saying them out loud made them lose their constrictive power over her. "I somehow thought that I could distance myself if I didn't let him actually make love to me. That I could remain only logical and use what happened between us in my fight against sensual excess, as you suggested."

He moved toward her one step. "But it didn't work?"

"No." She sighed. "As hard as I tried, I was still moved by everything we did. More than I should have been. I'm so confused, Jeremy. I fought so hard against such things. I told myself I could live without passion, without pleasure. But now I understand why so many people lose themselves in lust. I did. I even went so far as to beg this man to take what I originally withheld, but he . . . he didn't want me."

There was a moment's silence. "He is an idiot."

She shook her head. "No, he isn't. Perhaps he only sensed what a fraud I was. That I thought of . . . of someone else while he touched me."

She covered her mouth the moment the words escaped her lips. She hadn't meant to admit to that. Slowly, she let her gaze move up to Jeremy's. He was staring at her, and for the first time strong emotion lined his face. His face had darkened, and the fire in his eyes was no longer lust but anger.

"Who?" he growled, moving toward her again.

She shook her head. She couldn't confess that. Not for anything in the world. It was too much. Too hard.

"Who?" he repeated, and this time he said it louder. "Who did you think of while he touched you?"

Her breath was coming faster now, and tears stung her eyes.

"You," she whispered. "I thought about you."

Jeremy stopped advancing on Penelope as shock flooded him. He'd thought he understood every working of Penelope's mind and body. He'd thought he could almost read her thoughts when he touched her. But he'd never known that while her "stranger" touched her, it was his own face that had danced before her eyes.

Her emotions were raw and real. And she had been so brave to confess them when she already believed he had rejected her. Certainly, he had never been so daring or lain so much of himself on the line.

Without thinking, he caught her arms and yanked her against him. His lips came down and covered hers, and he devoured her mouth like he had been longing to do since the moment he entered the room. She was stiff in his arms for a moment, just a fraction of time while surprise shook her. But then her hands jerked up to his hair, and she returned his kiss with a fire and passion that was deeper and richer than any time he had come to her as the stranger.

Together, they staggered back toward the settee and fell against the cushions. Without breaking the kiss, Jeremy found the scooped neckline of her pretty blue gown and slipped his fingers beneath, nudging fabric aside until he found her rapidly hardening nipple beneath. She arched toward his hand with a little cry and sucked his tongue harder.

He didn't ask her leave, and she didn't resist as he tugged at buttons and pushed away layers of cloth to bear her breasts entirely. In fact, she helped him by shimmying out of the way as he pushed her dress and chemise around her waist.

His head dipped down and he caught the distended nipple, suckling her until her pulse quickened and she cried out softly. Her fingers tangled in his hair and she tugged him closer, urging him to take more, to explore more. To taste her and have her in the blaring afternoon light of the parlor.

Penelope didn't stop to analyze or question what was happening. She just *felt*. Felt Jeremy's hands on her skin. Felt the pressure of his growing erection move against her thigh. Felt the way his panting breaths caressed her breasts.

He wanted her. She wanted him. And there was no way in hell she was going to stop this from happening. She pushed at his jacket, tossing it behind the settee carelessly and then she went to work on his shirt, tearing at buttons until she had revealed a muscular, tanned expanse of flesh. Slipping her hands beneath she shuddered at the smooth, hot skin she found there.

He felt so good. She wanted him to press her into the cushions. She wanted him to slide his erection deep into her body. And she wouldn't be satisfied until he had.

She tugged and they fell back, his mouth finding hers a second time. His fingers began to smooth her skirts up, higher and higher, closer and closer to her core until she almost couldn't hear anything else for the rush of blood to her ears.

And then he touched her. Lightly. Slowly. His fingers caressed the wet lips of her sex, and she shivered with a delight and anticipation more powerful than any she'd felt before. Because she knew that these touches would lead to an intimate joining. And because this time, the man who touched her was Jeremy.

He growled his dissatisfaction as her gown slid down over her legs again. With a tug, he pulled it and her chemise over her hips in one smooth motion. She arched up to allow him to pull her gown away, leaving her only in her stockings and slippers.

She moved to drop her hips back onto the settee, but he didn't let her. Instead, he cupped her backside, keeping her arched as he spread her legs with his shoulders.

Penelope watched as Jeremy cupped her thighs with his warm hands and looked down at her. Heat flooded her cheeks. Her faceless lover had looked at her like this, but she hadn't been forced to watch. But with Jeremy, she saw every strain in his jaw, every sparkle in his eyes, every parting of his lips.

Then he lifted his gaze and snagged hers.

"So beautiful, Penelope," he whispered before he bent his head and touched his lips to her sex.

She gripped at the settee cushions with a cry of pleasure. But it was also one of frustration. She had been tasted before. She had found release at the touch of a man's fingers, his lips. What she wanted was a far deeper connection. A joining of two bodies.

She wanted to be had. Held. Pleasured even as she gave pleasure in return.

"Please," she panted as he swirled his tongue around the hard nub of her clit. "No more torment."

He jerked his head up and looked at her. Then he nodded. Pushing to his feet he shed what remained of his shirt and then kicked his boots away before he wrenched open the fastens of his trousers. Penelope sat up to lean against her elbows as the woolen fabric fell around his ankles. She sucked in a breath.

In all her midnight gropings of her secret lover, she had never been able to see his body clearly. But Jeremy stood before her, utterly naked and completely unabashed. He was hard and toned and proud as the sunlight warmed his skin. He was perfect.

Broad shoulders tapered down to an athletic, narrow waist. He had strong legs, ones that didn't require the ridiculous padding that some gentlemen still wore to make them look bigger. And where his upper and lower body met, his strong, hard cock curled up against his stomach.

She leaned forward, shifting to her knees on the settee as she reached for him. Taking him in hand, she shivered against her will. He was so hot. So hard. She couldn't help leaning forward and darting her tongue out to trace the rigid vein along the underside of his erection. To swirl her tongue around the sensitive head and lap up the little droplet of moisture that she found there.

Jeremy dipped his head back with a strangled moan. "I thought we weren't tormenting anymore," he growled as he caught her shoulders and lowered her back onto the settee.

Her legs came open as he settled between them, and her pulse began to race out of control as he positioned himself against her. She felt the hard tip of him probing her wet, soft entrance, and she stiffened as she prepared for the invasion she hadn't experienced for over a year. The last time she felt it, it hadn't been particularly pleasant.

"I won't hurt you," Jeremy said softly.

Penelope looked into his eyes in shock. Could he read her nervousness so clearly? Was that how close they had become in such a short time? She nodded.

"I trust you."

He flinched a little at that statement, but then he leaned closer and pressed a soft kiss to her lips. "Look into my eyes, Penelope," he ordered. "Don't look away."

Penelope hesitated. She was ready to surrender her whole body to this man. To let him claim her in an ancient and elemental way. And yet the idea of looking into his eyes seemed almost too intimate. But she finally lifted her gaze to his and held, losing herself in heated green depths.

As he stared at her, he slowly thrust forward, pressing inside her wet and ready body inch by inch. Penelope clutched at his arms as her channel stretched to accommodate him, but she never let her stare falter even as the pleasure mounted to a new and powerful height.

This was what she had been missing all those nights with her faceless admirer. This feeling of joining. Of completion. But she had a strong feeling, as Jeremy seated himself fully in her body, that even if her lover had taken her like this, it wouldn't have been as powerful. Because she knew Jeremy. She had longed for Jeremy.

She loved Jeremy.

Penelope blinked, and her gaze darted away from his at that strong, stark realization. Love him? Was that possible? They had come together in an intense, personal relationship over the past few weeks, but *could* she love him? A man who had lived a life entirely opposite to hers? A man she still didn't fully understand? A man who could hurt her so very easily if he tried?

"Penelope," he said on a groan. "Look at me, sweetheart. Look at me."

She forced herself to stare into his eyes. He began to thrust, so very gently, holding her gaze with a focused intensity that made the joining all the better. In his stare she saw so many things. Tangled emotions, hidden heartbreaks, and a gentleness that he rarely showed the world.

And she knew that loving him wasn't something she could argue away or pretend hadn't happened.

All she could do was surrender to the inevitable.

She clutched his arms and began to lift her hips to meet his shallow strokes. On each one, his pelvis ground against her sensitive clit, and the waves of pleasure built almost immediately. He held her stare evenly as he took and took, building the speed of his thrusts, increasing their depth until Penelope could no longer hold back the overwhelming tide of pleasure. It washed over her as she cried out and dug her nails into his skin. But she never looked away from him. She took advantage of the light, of the intense closeness of their faces, and she watched every flicker of pleasure, every twitch of his strong jaw.

She knew he was going to lose control a moment before he actually did. And the knowledge that she had driven him over the edge catapulted her into another strong, unexpected orgasm. They arched together, their moans mingling as he stiffened and she felt the heated warmth of his essence flood her.

Jeremy dropped his head, and their foreheads touched gently. Their breath mingled and slowed into one seamless rhythm. And she felt his rapid pulse gradually slow to match her own.

Only when the calm was complete did he tilt his head to the side and kiss her. So gentle, so sweet. She tasted herself on his mouth. Tasted the remnants of desire and her body rippled around his.

He chuckled as he rolled to the side and held her against his chest. "You'll have to give me a moment, Penelope."

Penelope smiled as she placed her hand against his chest. She could feel the steady beat of his heart and it comforted her. As did his warm, strong arms around her. Something had happened here. Something more than sex. Something more than the realization that she loved him.

They had made a connection. And although she knew nothing of Jeremy's heart, he seemed to be in no hurry to dismiss her. In fact, he pulled her closer.

"Next time, I want to savor you," he murmured against her ear.

She shivered at the promise in his tone. "Next time, eh?"

"Yes." He pressed a kiss to her neck, and Penelope tingled. "I plan on spending an eternity simply touching your skin. And then another tasting you all over."

She smiled again, but then she stopped. Why did those words seem so familiar?

"I want to take you, Penelope. Hard and fast. Slow and easy," he continued.

She sat up suddenly and stared down at him. She had heard

those words before. No, not heard them. Read them. Both his statements were familiar because she had memorized them from her secret lover's erotic letters to her.

Her eyes widened.

"Did you go through my things?" she asked, her voice cracking with the sheer impact of what she was starting to understand.

He shook his head as a look of confusion crossed his face. "Of course not, Penelope. Why would you ask me that?"

She got to her feet. "If you didn't go through my things and read my letters, then how would you . . ."

She stopped as she watched Jeremy's face twist with emotion. And suddenly the puzzle slipped into place. He knew what her letters had said because-because *he* had written them.

For weeks, Penelope had thought she had two men in her life. But now, staring down at his guilt-stricken and horrified face, she realized she'd been wrong. There was only one man.

And he had been playing her for an utter fool from the very beginning.

Eighteen

"How could you? How could you do this to me?" Penelope asked, her voice no more than a broken whisper as she began snatching up her discarded clothing from the floor around the settee.

Jeremy jumped to his feet and tried to catch her arm, but she staggered away from him with a cry that mimicked that of a wounded animal.

"No! Don't you touch me." She stared at him, holding her chemise up to her chest as a flimsy shield. "Is it true? Am I correct?"

For a moment, Jeremy pondered feigning ignorance, but he quickly dismissed that tactic. If there was one thing he knew more than any other, it was that Penelope was no fool. If he denied what she already knew to be true, it would only make matters worse. Instead, he bent and grabbed his trousers. Stepping into them, he took a long breath before he answered the question.

"Yes," he admitted softly. "I was the man who wrote you those letters. I was the one who visited you by night."

Penelope's face crumpled, pain and anger twisted her mouth until her lips were painfully thin. But she said nothing. She only stared at him.

He almost would have preferred she react. Scream. Swear. Anything but that pointed, penetrating gaze that cut more deeply than any poisonous or pointed words could have.

"Why?" she finally asked.

He dipped his chin. If there was any time for honesty, this was it. "You were causing problems for so many of the men in my acquaintance with your crusade. And I . . ." He hesitated. He did not relish this, for he was certain it would only serve to hurt and anger Penelope all the more.

"What?" she asked, harsh and low. "What did you do?"

He released his breath in a shuddering sigh. "I drew the short straw and was asked to deal with you."

Penelope's nostrils flared, but that was her only outward reaction to what he'd said. Silently, she pulled her wrinkled chemise over her head and gathered up her dress. With shaking fingers, she slipped the buttons into place.

"Penelope," he whispered.

"Please don't say anything else," she all but growled. "I understand completely."

"No, you don't," he countered, moving toward her.

She backed away in three hurried steps. "You lost a draw and were forced to 'deal' with me, what else is there to understand?" She shook her head. "What were you planning to do? Seduce me then blackmail me? Or perhaps reveal me to everyone as nothing better than a whore? Or did you think that your seduction would be so life altering that I would simply cease my endless chatter and thank God that I was asked to your bed?"

Jeremy wanted to deny her angry, pointed words, but the truth was that he *had* considered all those possibilities. One or all of them had been a part of his original plan. Only, as he came to know Penelope, those tactics had slipped away. Leaving only desire for her, and deeper feelings than a mere physical attraction.

None of which he could say when she was staring at him like he was some kind of inhuman bastard.

She moved on him when he was silent for a moment, coming toward him slowly. Her entire body was trembling by the time she came to a stop before him. Jeremy looked down at her. God, how he wanted to touch her. To draw her into his arms. To apologize. To explain—but there was no explanation. There were no words to take back what he had done. To remove the bitter pain from her eyes.

Tears welled in Penelope's eyes, making the blue even darker. Then she reeled back and slapped him hard enough that his cheek stung.

"That is for what you did to me. Not in the dark, Jeremy. Not as the faceless lover. Not even for today when you made love to me . . . or perhaps we should call it 'fucking,' since there was nothing loving about it, only manipulation." Her voice shook as hard as her hands as she turned on her heel and headed for the door. "It's for betraying my friendship."

Then she was gone, slamming the door behind her and leaving Jeremy alone in the middle of the parlor. Voiceless. And for a man who was rarely at a loss for words, that was a powerful thing.

Quietly, he crossed to the poorboy and poured himself a stiff drink in a tall glass. He downed the alcohol in two long swigs, shutting his eyes as he heard the crunch of rocks under Penelope's carriage wheels.

She was gone. And he had done nothing to stop her. Not that he *could* have done anything. He couldn't deny any of her charges when each and every one of them was true. He certainly couldn't make a plea for forgiveness that he didn't deserve.

She thought him to be the lowest person in her acquaintance. And the fact was, she was entirely correct in her assessment.

Penelope paced restlessly around Miranda and Ethan's ornate sitting room. Why had she come here? Here to her estranged sister's of all places.

She sighed as she stopped to straighten her tangled hair in the mirror above the mantel. Her chest tightened at the sight of her disheveled appearance. Memories of how she had come to look so wretched slapped her as hard as she had slapped Jeremy.

With a sigh, she gave up trying to fix herself. She had come here because she had nowhere else to go. No one else to talk to.

Miranda was the only one who could possibly understand. And knowing her sister, she would offer more friendship and comfort than Penelope deserved.

At least, she *hoped* her sister would be more forgiving than she herself had been. Now when she thought of how cold, how angry she had been at Miranda, how long she'd held a grudge, Penelope was ashamed.

The door to the parlor opened, and she spun around to face her sister. She was ready to launch herself into Miranda's arms but stopped herself when her sister entered on the strong arm of her husband, Ethan Hamon, Earl of Rothschild. Penelope blushed as Ethan cast a quick glance over her and then shot his wife a brief look.

Penelope had never liked the Earl, even before she knew what he'd done to her sister. In her youth, she had thought him to be cold, distant, and domineering. And now she simply felt terribly awkward around him.

"Penelope," Miranda said with a wide smile as she released Ethan's arm and crossed the room to her.

Penelope sensed that her sister wanted to embrace her, but Miranda held back. Her heart ached. It was her own fault that Miranda hesitated. After all, she had denied her sister so many damn times as she held a prim little grudge over Miranda's head.

"Welcome to our home," Miranda said with a little smile.

"Yes," Ethan said as he entered the room and shut the door quietly behind him. "We are so very pleased you've finally come to call on us."

Penelope shot him a look. Was he being facetious? Certainly, Ethan couldn't want her here, not after everything she'd said and done in regard to him. But when she met his dark eyes, she found nothing but . . . kindness there. Unexpected and utterly genuine, as far as she could tell.

"Th-thank you," she stammered, uncertain of how to proceed. "I-I'm sorry it's taken me so long to call. It was wrong of me."

Miranda stared at her for a long moment, and Penelope saw the sparkling hint of tears in the blue eyes that looked so much like her own.

"You never have to apologize to me," Miranda whispered, her voice shaking with emotion. "You are here now and that is all that matters."

Ethan smiled at the two of them. "I merely came to greet you, Penelope. But I have, er, something to attend to. I hope you'll join us for supper."

Miranda smiled as her husband bowed out of the room, leaving them alone. "He doesn't have anything to do. He just wanted us to be able to talk."

Penelope nodded. "I suspected as much."

Her sister's smile fell a fraction, and she motioned to the settee in front of the merry fire. "Come, sit down. I can see in your eyes and by your appearance that something has happened. It is the only reason I can think of that you would come to me. Why don't you tell me what it is and perhaps I can help you. Is it Mama?"

Penelope moved toward the settee, but she didn't sit down. Instead, she covered her eyes and let the tears she had been holding back for so long . . . it seemed like forever . . . begin to fall.

"Oh, Miranda. I have made such an utter muck of everything!"

Miranda made a soft sound of distress and then Penelope was in her arms. They sat down together, and she buried her face into her older sister's neck and simply sobbed. Miranda held tight, not speaking, not offering any comfort other than her warm embrace and her gentle, calming presence.

Once Penelope's tears had eased, her sister drew back and wiped her tears with the back of her hand. "Tell me."

Drawing a shuddering breath, Penelope began to choke out the entire sordid story.

★ ★ ★

An hour later, Miranda had a drink in her hand and she let out a low whistle.

"Good heavens, you do know how to put yourself into a mess."

Penelope nodded as she sipped her own strong shot of whiskey that Miranda had nicked from Ethan's private collection about halfway through Penelope's tale. The burning heat of the liquor calmed her at least a little, though it didn't numb her emotions, no matter how much she wished for it.

"I have been so utterly hideous, Miranda. Especially to you. I judged you so harshly for what you did to protect our family. I stole so much time from myself. And here I ended up doing something even more shocking, and not for half of your good reasons." She reached out and touched her sister's hand. "I am so very sorry, Miranda."

Miranda sat down on the edge of the settee beside her, shaking her head. "Dearest, when you saw Ethan and I together, it frightened and upset you. You felt betrayed and confused by my actions, as well as my later explanations. I never blamed you for that. I only wish I could have helped you before now. Counseled you."

Penelope barked out a humorless laugh. "I needed your counsel. Perhaps if I had turned to you from the very beginning, I wouldn't have been such a naive little fool when it came to Jeremy and my 'secret lover.'" Penelope dipped her head as more bitter tears threatened. "He must have been laughing at me all along."

Miranda set her drink aside with an incredulous expression. "From everything you told me about your encounter this afternoon, I somehow doubt that Kilgrath has been laughing. It sounds to me like he has been just as confused as you have been."

"Oh no, he was so utterly in control." Penelope downed the remainder of her drink. She thought of Ethan's expression when he confessed all he had done to her. He had been so calm, so strong . . . so handsome.

God, she was hopeless, even now.

"Was he?" Miranda asked. "If he was truly in control, why didn't he simply reveal you that night at the ball when he first touched you? Or later, after you spent a night together? Why didn't he blackmail you, as he originally planned."

Penelope frowned. She had been so angry when she realized what Jeremy had done and why, she hadn't stopped to think of those questions.

"He certainly had enough ammunition against me to end my crusade," she admitted slowly. "I gave him more than enough with my wanton behavior."

Miranda shook her head. "Stop! Never berate yourself for what you felt. You have every right to experience desire. And pleasure. And to want more than empty loneliness. Those things are never wrong. Sometimes what people do in the pursuit of them is wrong, but the feelings, the needs, aren't."

Penelope sighed as she covered her face with her hands. "Oh, I'm so very, very confused."

"I know," her sister whispered. "I understand completely."

Penelope peeked at her sister from between her fingers, but before she could pursue Miranda's cryptic comment any further, the door opened and Ethan reappeared. He looked at Miranda, and it seemed like a world of communication passed between them in just that glance.

He crossed the room, and Miranda got to her feet to let him sit down beside Penelope. She lowered her hands and looked at him. He met her stare with an even and kind one of his own before he reached out and took both her hands.

"Penelope," he said softly. "Who do I have to kill for making you look so forlorn?"

Penelope laughed, the first one that felt real in weeks. His smile was her reward, and she couldn't help but notice just how ridiculously handsome a man Ethan was. She had forgotten that in the years she'd made him into a monster in her head. What else had she overlooked with her blind prejudice?

"No one," she said, squeezing his hands. "I'm afraid all of this is of my own doing."

Miranda smiled as she pressed a hand against her husband's shoulder and looked down at Penelope. "I'm not certain I agree with your assessment, but we shall leave that be for a while. The question remains, what shall you do?"

Penelope looked at the easy way Miranda and Ethan were a team. There was a unity there that she had never accepted. They were a good match. Anyone could see it after five minutes in their company. Yet Penelope knew that good match had come out of something so questionable.

Did that mean that there was hope for her? If Miranda was correct, and she had somehow moved Jeremy with the same intensity he moved her, could they mend the lies between them? Could she find some kind of sincerity hidden in the layers of manipulation that brought them together?

More to the point, did she want to?

She covered her face again. "I don't know."

It was Ethan who answered. "You don't have to know right now. Just stay for supper. Stay as long as you like. And we'll help you work something out."

Penelope nodded. "Let me write a note to my staff to tell them I'll be out for the evening."

As Ethan moved to summon a servant, Penelope sighed. As comforting as it was to be in the company of her sister again, she had no illusions that she'd find any kind of solution to her problems today. Or tomorrow. Or perhaps ever.

The pain in her heart felt too deep to overcome.

The dark was no comfort to Jeremy, nor was the ridiculously expensive scotch he was downing not in sips, but great gulps. It might as well have been water for all his enjoyment.

But then, perhaps he didn't deserve enjoyment. Or even the numbing effect of the alcohol. Not after what he'd done.

No, he wasn't even trying to convince himself he wasn't in the wrong anymore. He'd tried that for the first half hour after Penelope left him with only a stinging slap and even more painful words of well-deserved censure.

He'd fought to remember that at any time during their arrangements, whether as himself or her faceless stranger, she could have refused him. That she could have said no. He had desperately tried to reclaim that icy cold cloak of distance he once kept around him. But it was impossible. It no longer fit.

Penelope had changed him too much in the short time they'd spent together. Now everything was wrong, and he had no idea how to fix it.

"Lord Kilgrath?"

Jeremy didn't even bother to look over his shoulder at the servant who had breeched his lonely sanctuary. "No interruptions, please. I'm in no mood for company."

"Even mine?"

He turned at that. Christopher stood in the doorway beside a footman. And his brother looked worried.

"Of course, you are welcome," Jeremy said on a sigh.

As the servant left, Christopher closed the door behind him and crossed the room to the poorboy. He held up the rapidly emptying scotch bottle with a lifted eyebrow.

"At least when you wreck yourself, you choose the best," his brother mused. "May I join you?"

"In wrecking myself?" Jeremy asked as he took another swig of his drink. "By all means."

His brother poured just a splash of liquor into a glass and quietly swirled the liquid as he stared at Jeremy. "I came here because Anthony Wharton visited me this afternoon, complaining about some kind of falling out the two of you had. But I somehow doubt the look on your face has anything to do with that."

Jeremy pursed his lips. "Right now I couldn't care less what Wharton thinks. He isn't the man I thought he was." He stared past his brother at the fire. "Neither am I."

"Why don't you tell me what's going on?" Christopher said as he motioned to the chairs before the picture window.

Jeremy nodded as he took one of the seats. He leaned his elbows over his knees and quietly, calmly recited everything he had done. It felt like confession, but there was little penance or absolution his brother could offer. And judging from the shocked expression on Christopher's face, he didn't plan to give any.

"And then she slapped me and left," Jeremy concluded, and downed the last few droplets in his glass.

Christopher shook his head. "Well, judging by what you've told me, I think getting a slap on the face is better than she could have done. A knee to the balls sounds more fitting."

"Thank you," Jeremy said, his voice dry as he glared at his brother.

"Honestly, this is not a courtesan or a philandering married woman, Jeremy," his brother said. "Penelope Norman is a *lady*. And as silly as you thought her crusade was, you must have known what you were planning was wrong."

"Absolutely," Jeremy said. "But I didn't care. Actually, that seems to be the tale of my life, doesn't it? I have always done exactly what I wished, without thinking of the consequences to anyone else. I have been an utter bastard my entire life."

Christopher shook his head. "Come now! That isn't true."

"Isn't it?" Jeremy pushed to his feet and pulled a hand through his hair. "Do you realize, I don't even know where Mother is? I haven't *read* any of her letters. When you married, I resented you. Not for finding love, not for being happy . . . but because your marrying made *my* life less interesting. Christ, I could hardly remember Hannah's name the first month you were married."

Christopher frowned, but didn't interrupt him.

"I have never bothered to think of anyone else . . . ever. So, I certainly didn't think about Penelope. At least, not at first. And now I've hurt her beyond measure. She considered me a friend, and I betrayed her in every way imaginable."

"And you hate yourself for it," his brother said quietly.

Jeremy hesitated. Admitting that meant admitting to something much deeper. But he couldn't deny it. Not to his brother. Not to himself.

"Yes," he said, getting to his feet and pouring another drink. But this time, he didn't take a sip.

"You are in love with her."

It wasn't a question. Christopher made the statement with an even expression. Jeremy froze. He'd known his feelings for Penelope had changed in the time he spent with her. And not only the time in her bedroom, where he realized she was a passionate lover.

No, it was the time spent when she knew his face that really mattered. He'd realized she was intelligent, empathetic, and even funny. Over the weeks, he'd come to crave seeing her. Talking to her. Just being in her presence and watching her reaction to the broadening of her world.

He'd even confessed some of his deepest secrets to her and never once regretted it.

So the idea that he loved her . . . fit. It was terrifying and thrilling all at once. And it made his betrayal all the more devastating.

"It doesn't matter," he choked out. "I have ruined everything."

Christopher got out of his chair quickly enough that it rocked back. "What the hell is the matter with you? Are you my older brother or have you been overtaken by some mysterious force? I have never known you to surrender so willingly. And this is the most important fight of your life. If you love her, if you truly want to be with her, then you will go to her. You will do every-thing in your power to make her see that you *have* changed. That you would give up anything if it meant loving her."

Jeremy swallowed hard and set his drink down. "Is that what you did?"

"Yes," Christopher admitted. "And I have never regretted it." He motioned to the door. "Go. Now. Or you *will* be sorry for the rest of your life."

Jeremy straightened his shoulders and gave his brother a half grin. "I refuse to have regrets. Even if I have to fight for the rest of my life, I *will* win."

"I will wait here all day, but I will see your mistress," Jeremy said half an hour later as he stood in the foyer of Penelope's home, glaring at the servant who blocked his way to the woman he loved. "I know she is here."

"Actually, she isn't," Fiona said as she slowly descended the stairs. Her arms were folded across her chest, and there was a light of fire and protectiveness in her eyes that made Jeremy bite back a sigh. He'd vowed he would fight for Penelope. It seemed he would be forced to do so just to see her.

"Then where is she?" he asked, meeting the former courtesan's eyes with steel in his own.

Fiona motioned to the parlor with a cold stare. "Why don't we speak of this privately?"

"Very well." He followed her into the room. "Tell me where Penelope is."

Fiona slammed the door shut and glared at him. "I don't know what you did to her. I received a note from her not half an hour ago saying she would not be home. But the hand was very shaky. I have long suspected you were playing some kind of game with her, pretending to be reformed, but for what purpose? What did you do to her?"

"I lied to her," he snapped back. "And I played her for a fool."

Fiona shook her head. "You have no shame, Jeremy Vaughn."

He bit back a humorless laugh. "There is where you are wrong. All I have left is my shame. I hate myself for what I have done, more than even you can imagine."

Fiona drew back, her anger turning to surprise at his candor. "Hate yourself? You?"

He nodded. "Yes. For a great many things." He stepped closer. "Fi, why didn't you ever tell me what Wharton did to you?"

The color drained from Fiona's face so rapidly that Jeremy held out a hand to steady her.

"What?" she asked, her voice a mere cracking whisper.

He tilted his head. "You know what I said. I could have helped you."

Fiona barked out a laugh. "Please. You wouldn't have cared. Wharton is one of your best friends, and I was little more than a whore in your eyes. No one would have stopped him."

Jeremy shook his head. There were many things he questioned about the life he had lead so far, but this was not one of them.

"I would have cared, Fiona. And I would have done everything in my power to stop him. Everything."

"Perhaps you would have," Fiona said softly. "Perhaps I didn't think I deserved anything better until Penelope intervened. She told me I was owed more. That I was better than the life I lead. But I . . ."

She stopped and Jeremy watched as she paced away restlessly.

"Fiona, we have both been deceiving Penelope. I certainly don't compare what you've withheld from her with what I did. But a lie is a lie. You need to tell her the truth now. You don't really want to be a lady's maid, do you?"

Fiona hesitated for a long moment before she shrugged. "No. I don't. But I did my best to do so for her. Because she was so good to me." She turned back and stared at him. "What would *you* be for her, Jeremy?"

He sighed. "I would be a better man. But I can't make anything I've done to her right if I can't find her."

The former courtesan paced away to the window, pondering his words. Finally, she turned. "She is at her sister's. At Lord Rothschild's estate here in London. Do not make me regret telling you that."

Jeremy spun on his heel and headed for the door. "I will do my best, Fiona. Good night."

"And good luck," Fiona called behind him.

Nineteen

"You have barely eaten a bite," Miranda said quietly. "Is there nothing I can offer to tempt you?"

Penelope looked up from her supper with a start. She hadn't even been paying attention to her surroundings, let along thinking about food.

"I'm sorry," she said with a sigh. "It all looks wonderful. I just . . . can't concentrate."

"I'm going to break his arms," Ethan muttered as he took a sip of wine. "I swear to all that is holy."

Miranda arched a brow at her husband. "Come now, my dear. I don't think Penelope wants the man to be incapacitated, as lovely a thought as that is. And don't forget, you have made your own mistakes in life. As have we all."

Ethan shrugged. "I suppose that is true. But he had best not darken this door at present."

As the very words left his lips, a servant came into the room. "I apologize, my lord, but the Duke of Kilgrath has arrived and refuses to leave without an audience with Lady Norman."

All the blood drained from Penelope's face as she slowly pushed to her feet. "Jeremy is here?" she said, grasping the edge of the table for purchase.

Miranda jumped up and put an arm around her waist. "You do not have to see him. Ethan can handle him."

Penelope blinked. Her vision was swimming and she felt completely off-kilter. She had expected Jeremy to make some kind of appearance at some point, but not so soon. And not *here*!

The idea of seeing him was both tempting and terrifying. Despite all his lies and betrayals, her blood quickened at the thought of him. It was a desperate, visceral reaction that she wished she could quell with all her being, yet she couldn't.

Her terror was just as powerful. She wasn't certain she could face Jeremy without breaking down. Without admitting things she didn't want him to know. Without making a fool of herself yet again.

"Yes, let me deal with him," Ethan said, throwing his napkin on the table and shoving to his feet.

Penelope looked from her sister to Ethan and then gave a jerky nod. But as Ethan turned to go to the foyer, she said, "Wait."

Her brother-in-law turned back with a frown. "Yes?"

"Don't . . . ," she hesitated, " . . . hurt him. Promise me."

Ethan chuckled. "Very well. I promise not to do anything that will cause permanent damage."

As he left the room, Penelope turned to her sister. "I'm a coward, I know."

Miranda shook her head. "No. You are hurt. And when you are ready, then you will see him."

Penelope shivered as Miranda led her to a back servant's door so they could go upstairs undetected. Yes. She would see Jeremy eventually. But for now, she wasn't ready to face the possibility that only guilt drove him to her, nothing more.

Jeremy surged to his feet as the door to the parlor he had been shoved into opened. But instead of Penelope's face, it was Ethan Hamon, Earl of Rothschild who stepped in. Jeremy moved toward him with a scowl.

"I want to see Penelope."

Rothschild folded his arms, one dark brow rising with slow and dangerous intent. "I don't give a damn what you want. What you *want* got you into this mess. Now sit down before I seat you, myself."

Normally, Jeremy wouldn't have let a threat like that stand, but he could see that Rothschild had no intention of letting him see Penelope. So he returned to his seat and sank down.

"She won't see me?" he asked, trying to measure his tone.

Ethan took a chair across from his. "No."

The word was so small, yet it packed the power of a fist to his gut. Jeremy swallowed against a constricted throat.

"So this is over."

Saying the words out loud made him sick. He had never deserved Penelope, yet he had somehow earned her trust and obtained the precious gift of her caring. But he'd lost them both because of his own stupidity.

Ethan shrugged. "Right now Penelope is very hurt." He glared at Jeremy. *"Very hurt."*

Jeremy flinched as Rothschild continued, "However, I would never presume to guess the mind of a woman in such an emotional state. If it were me, I would simply give Penelope space."

Jeremy opened his mouth, but Rothschild shook his head. "Take it from a man who has been almost as big an ass as you are. Give. Her. Space."

Scrubbing a hand over his face, Jeremy paced to the window. He had never been a man to wait, to be patient. He was about action, not reaction. And he feared that at this point, nothing would help his cause.

"Space won't make a difference," he groaned. "What I did was . . . it was . . ."

"Unforgiveable?" Rothschild offered blandly.

Jeremy's stomach turned. "Perhaps."

"Horrible. Wretched. Asinine," the other man continued.

"Thank you," Jeremy interrupted with a scowl. "I understand your point."

He returned his attention to the gardens outside. Everything he had done since the first night he approached Penelope ran through his mind like a dream. From the ugly lies to the sweet responsiveness of her body. From the way her hands shook when she realized what he had done to the sound of her sighs as she slipped into sleep. All the memories, the good and the wretched, were the most important of his life.

So he would wait. God knew, she was worth waiting for. But

while he did so, he had to act. He had to do something to prove he was a changed man. Truly, this time. Not like the lies he had told her.

And there was only one thing he could think of that would begin to set things right.

He turned to face Ethan. "I need your help."

Rothschild paused. "You are in love with her, aren't you?"

Jeremy nodded. "Yes."

The other man sighed. "Very well. What do you need?"

Penelope rested her head against the back of the bench in Miranda's beautiful rose garden.

"I'm in love with him, you know," she said softly. Admitting it out loud was far less difficult than she thought it would be.

Miranda laughed. "Of course you are. Otherwise, you wouldn't be so upset."

Penelope stared at her sister. "You don't think I'm a complete idiot for loving him even after hearing everything he did? All the lies he told?"

"Of course not," Miranda said, taking her hand. "I, for one, believe that even the worst of circumstances can work out for the best in the end. Some women meet a handsome gentleman in a crowded ballroom, are courted very properly, fall in love and marry their prince charming. I know quite a few who did just that. But sometimes our princes are disguised as utter rogues, and we fall into the bedroom before we ever meet in the ballroom."

"Like you did," Penelope said.

Her sister nodded. "Perhaps Ethan and I did everything backward. But the fact is that our journey was what it was. We might not have fallen in love, or at least we would have found our road much harder, had we been proper and correct. Ethan, especially, would have had a difficult time allowing himself to court in that fashion. And Jeremy is very much like Ethan used to be."

Penelope laughed, but she didn't feel very amused. "Funny how I censured the man so completely and then fell in love with a person with an equally hideous reputation."

Miranda shrugged. "Rakes make good husbands. Especially when they fall in love."

"I said I loved him. I have no idea of his heart." Penelope plucked at a rose petal absently.

"I overheard him with Ethan before they left," Miranda said.

Penelope straightened up. "You did? How?"

Her sister shrugged with a mischievous smile. "When I went downstairs to call for tea, I eavesdropped. And if it makes you feel any better, the man sounded utterly miserable."

Penelope clenched her hands together. "His coming here does give me some hope. But how can I trust anything he ever says again? I believed him when he behaved like my friend, or when he pretended to be the secret lover in the dark. But those things were an illusion. So how will I ever know what is real?"

"Are you sure they were an illusion?" her sister asked.

Penelope pondered that. Jeremy had wanted her. That she knew was real. As for his friendship . . . well, that wasn't as clear.

Jeremy had been trying to manipulate her by taking her on his "tour," however the moments they'd shared during their time together were another story. He had confessed some painful parts of his past to her. Things she imagined were not readily shared.

And, after all, he hadn't used her confessions, her desires, against her, as he had planned.

"I don't know anymore."

Miranda touched her hand gently. "Jeremy will come back. Perhaps not today. But I don't think he's the kind of man who will simply let you go. Allow him to come to you. Let him speak. Look into his eyes. He won't be able to hide the truth from you if you do."

"And when I have the truth?" Penelope asked. "What do I do then?"

"Only you can decide that," her sister said. "But dear God, Penelope, don't throw love away. If it is there, then take it. No one deserves it more."

Penelope got to her feet. "I have much to think about."

"You do," her sister agreed. "So go home and think. I will be here if you need me."

"I know." Penelope hugged her, hard. "You have always been here for me. I was just too stubborn to take your love."

Miranda smiled sadly as she linked her arm through Penelope's. "Just don't be too stubborn to take his."

The Worthington Club was crowded as Jeremy and Ethan made their way to the private room in the back. As they entered the room, Jeremy drew in a harsh breath. This was not something he relished, but it had to be done.

For a variety of reasons.

Wharton was alone in the room, smoking a cigar, and he turned as the two men walked through the door.

"Didn't expect to see you again after your little scene a few days ago," he growled. "And what are you doing here, Rothschild? Decided to join the Nevers, have you?"

Rothschild chuckled, but it wasn't a friendly sound. "Not exactly."

"We've come here to speak to you about Fiona," Jeremy said through clenched teeth.

His friend lifted his gaze slowly, and the muscle in his cheek twitched. "What about the little whore?"

"Watch yourself," Rothschild said softly.

Jeremy stepped forward. "I know what you did to her while she was under your 'protection,' Wharton."

"What did I do?" his friend said, almost innocently. "You mean bring her in line when she acted up? That was my bloody right, what do you care?"

Jeremy reached out and caught his friend by the cravat. With a twist, he yanked him forward, nearly cutting off his air. Wharton's cigar fell to the floor, and Jeremy ground it out with his heel.

"Listen to me, you bastard," Jeremy said softly. "There are things a gentleman does and does not do. Beating a woman is one of the things in the latter column. Only a weak, small-pricked ass raises his hand to someone who cannot defend herself."

Wharton was turning purple, so Jeremy let him go. His friend hit the ground, bouncing back a bit as he gasped for air for a second time in as many days. He glared up at Jeremy.

"What, so now you are noble?" he hissed. "You aren't a saint, Kilgrath. And if I remember correctly, neither are you, Rothschild. Kilgrath, you've been planning to blackmail that shrew Penelope Norman by fucking her. And Rothschild, everyone has guessed that you made your wife a whore before you married—"

He didn't get to finish the sentence before Rothschild stepped forward and kicked the man as hard as he could in the ribs without even flinching. He crouched down next to Wharton as the other man gasped for air.

"Another word about my wife and we'll be dealing with pistols tomorrow morning. And I am an excellent shot."

Wharton paled and clutched his ribs silently.

Ethan stood back up and motioned Jeremy forward with a tight smile. Jeremy yanked Wharton up, taking some small pleasure in the groan of utter pain that escaped his friend's lips.

"Wharton, you are the third son of an earl. You have some prestige and some power, but it is nothing compared to what Rothschild and I wield. I think you know that I could destroy you, as could he, without much more than a raised finger." He smoothed Wharton's jacket with a thin smile. "So here is how your life is going to be from this moment on. You will *never* look at Fiona Clifton again. You will never speak to her. You'll certainly never threaten her, or you will suffer greater than any cowardly thing you ever did to her."

Wharton nodded slowly.

"As for Penelope, you will forget your ever heard her name. If you breathe a word about the bargain we made to stop her, if you do anything yourself to silence her, I will do things to you that will make you wish I had killed you." Jeremy smiled thinly. "Do you understand?"

"Yes," Wharton said. All the blood was gone from his cheeks, and he shook like a leaf.

Jeremy released him. "As for us, we are not friends. We will never be friends again. You are no longer welcome in this club."

"You can't stop me from—" Wharton began.

"Yes, I can," Jeremy interrupted. "And I will. Now get out. And if I ever hear that you have lain a finger on another woman again, the brimstone of hell will seem pleasant."

Wharton backed toward the door, then turned and ran from the room. Jeremy watched him go with a frown. Now it was finished. The life he had once known was over. And the future was hazy.

Ethan clapped a hand on his shoulder. "Look, your friend left some of his fine cigars. Care for one?"

Jeremy laughed as he looked at the box Wharton had left behind. "Yes."

Ethan handed one to him and smiled as he lit his own. "You may not be a total loss, after all, Kilgrath."

"Really?" Jeremy said as he let the flame dance over the end of the cigar. "I feel like a loss. Or at a loss, at the very least."

"Well, what you did tonight, it makes the past fade a little," Ethan said as he sat down in one of the plush leather chairs.

Jeremy shook his head. "Tell Penelope that." He stopped. "No. Don't tell her."

Ethan cocked his head in surprise. "No?"

"No." He sighed. "I don't deserve any consideration she isn't willing to give me herself. What I did tonight was right. I don't want it to be a mere show to make her speak to me. You were right when you said she needed time. I have taken everything else from her. The least I can do is allow her that."

Ethan smiled. "Sit down. We'll have a few drinks and play some cards. If you get me drunk enough, I'll even tell you how badly I made a muck of things with Penelope's sister. And how she loved me anyway."

"Why not?" Jeremy said with a faint smile. "It isn't as if I have anywhere else to be."

Penelope smiled at Fiona. Her lady's maid—*former* lady's maid—was wiping away tears.

"So you don't hate me?" Fiona said with a sniffle.

Penelope shook her head. "Of course not. I only wish you had told me you didn't want to change your life, just the man you were with."

Fiona wiped her eyes. "I wanted to live up to what you believed of me. That I was worth more."

A wave of shame washed over Penelope. She shook her head. "Oh, Fiona, you are worth more than Wharton, but I never meant to make you believe I thought less of you because of your profession. I was a foolish, stupid girl."

Fiona squeezed her hand. "No, Penelope. You were never foolish or stupid. You have been nothing but good to me, and I shall never forget that."

"Be happy," Penelope said as they released each other. "And come to see me often."

Fiona drew back in surprise. "Really?"

"Of course. You are my friend. That will never change."

Fiona smiled sadly as the door to the parlor opened.

"My lady," her butler said, nodding. "A gentleman has arrived to see you."

Penelope's heart leapt.

"A Lord Rothschild, my lady," her servant finished.

Fiona and Penelope exchanged a glance, and she saw that the other woman had read her thoughts, her hopes that it was Jeremy.

"I will go upstairs and begin my packing," Fiona said with a smile.

Penelope nodded. "Send Lord Rothschild in," she ordered her servant.

She got to her feet as Ethan entered. He smiled as Fiona left, then turned his dark eyes on Penelope. "I'm sorry to call so late."

Penelope smiled. "It isn't too late. Please, sit down."

He settled into one of her chairs, dwarfing the small piece, and looked at her. Penelope shifted uncomfortably under his piercing gaze. Even though she no longer felt animosity toward the man, she didn't yet feel close to him and wasn't certain how to deal with him.

"I have just left your Jeremy," he said quietly.

Penelope tensed. "And he sent you to bear me a message?" She held her breath as she waited for Ethan's response.

"No."

Her breath left her lungs in a disappointed rush. "I see."

Her brother-in-law smiled gently. "No, I don't think you do. Kilgrath has decided that he deserves no consideration from you. That after so many weeks of manipulation, you must be left alone to make your own decisions when it comes to him and your forgiveness."

Penelope looked at him in shock. "O-oh," she stammered.

"But even though I admire his determination," Ethan said. "I also think that you can better make up your mind if you understand what he did tonight."

"What did he do?" she asked, breathless as she imagined all the endless possibilities, both for good and for ill.

"Do you know his friends? I believe they call themselves the Nevers," Ethan asked.

She nodded, a bitter taste filling her mouth. "I know none of them well, but I do know of them. I believe they were the reason Jeremy began pursuing me in the first place. They wanted me silenced."

"Then you know he feels a great loyalty and friendship with them, especially with the one called Wharton."

She bit her lip. Wharton who had abused Fiona. Jeremy had tormented himself over that fact when she confessed it. "Yes."

"Tonight, Kilgrath made it very clear to Wharton that his days of hurting women are over." Ethan looked at her evenly. "If your friend has been concerned for her continued safety, I think she need not be anymore. Wharton wouldn't dare defy Kilgrath after his threats."

Penelope gasped. "He threatened his friend?"

"Yes, and in the process, Kilgrath severed his ties to the man. And he may have damaged all his relationships with his Nevers."

Now Penelope surged to her feet. "No!"

"He sacrificed something he held dear, his friendships." Ethan smiled.

"Because he wished to regain my good graces?" she asked. "Is it another manipulation?"

"No." Ethan rose with her and stepped toward her. "In fact, he told me not to reveal to you what he had done for fear you would take it as such. He did it only because it was the correct thing to do. I believe he convinced you once that he had changed, although he hadn't."

She nodded, and the bitter taste in her mouth doubled.

Ethan touched her hand. "I think now he wants to truly change, to show you by his actions that he is worthy of your love, even if he never gains it."

Penelope blinked, as sudden tears had flooded her eyes. "But can he change? Truly change? Is it possible for such a man to become a new person?"

"For love I think it is." Ethan backed toward the door. "After all, my dear, I changed for a very similar reason."

As her brother-in-law stood in the doorway to her parlor, Penelope stared at him. He was correct, he *had* changed. Ethan had become a different man, all for the love of her sister. The two of them had taken a chance on love, and the dividends they received were great.

But could she take a similar risk?

"Thank you, Ethan," she whispered, following him into the foyer. "Not just for coming to me tonight and telling me about Jeremy's actions, but for loving my sister."

His handsome face softened. "My dear, both were and are my greatest pleasure." He pressed a brief kiss to her hand. "Good night."

Penelope watched him depart and then slowly made her way upstairs. Her mind turned furiously on everything that had happened, on every fear and hope that burned in her feverish mind.

Tonight she would get no sleep. There would be no lover to distract her. All she would have were her thoughts. And by daybreak, she hoped she could sort them all out and decide, once and for all, what she should do.

Twenty

Jeremy sat at his desk, afternoon sunlight dancing its way across the papers in front of him. He lifted the sheet and read another of his mother's letters. He'd been reading them for a few hours, starting back to ones she'd written months ago and moving forward to the last one that had landed on his desk just a few days before.

It was shocking to see how much he'd missed when he was so utterly involved in himself. And how little he'd known his mother. He found her to be witty, interesting and wellversed in many things after all her ports of travel. Jeremy was bound and determined to write to her this afternoon. Not his usual scrawled, meaningless note that mentioned nothing about anything of import.

Something that actually told her he was attentive to her.

He lifted his gaze from her neatly written words. It was odd to suddenly examine one's own life. But he had been doing just that since . . . well, since Penelope came into his life. And through her eyes he'd recognized just how selfish and pointless it had been. *He* had been.

But when he approached her, Penelope had believed he was capable of change. She had cautiously allowed him to become her friend, to become her lover, because she thought that somewhere deep inside of him, there was a better man.

So perhaps now, if he actually *became* that better man, he could win her love back. Or at least endeavor to deserve it.

"Your Grace, a letter has arrived for you," a servant said from the door.

Jeremy lifted his gaze to the man and motioned him inside. He took the letter from the servant's silver tray and motioned him to go. He stared at the handwriting. Even, neat, he did not recognize it.

When he turned it over, the seal on the back was blank. There was no outward identification to say who the writer was. Wrinkling his brow, he broke the seal and unfolded the pages.

Your Grace:

Long have I imagined what it would be like if you were here with me. Not as a mystery lover whose face I cannot see, but in the light. With no lies between us. With no darkness to blind us. Tonight I will put a candle in my window for you, Jeremy. Come to me at midnight if you desire something more than the lies we have shared in the past.

Jeremy read the letter three times before he set it down in shock. It was unsigned, but he knew it was from Penelope. Hope like nothing he had ever known made its way through him. She was offering him a chance. She was reaching out to him.

He got to his feet and rushed to the hallway. He had much to do if he intended to prove to her that her tenuous faith would be rewarded with truth and love.

Penelope stood in front of her roaring fire and smoothed her dress absently. Everything was prepared, well, everything but herself. She was nervous and anxious and uncertain. What if Jeremy didn't show up? What if he came and thought they would simply fall into bed?

No, she couldn't think about that. As tempting as it was, that was not her plan tonight.

To distract herself from her nervousness, Penelope looked around the room. It had never been so bright. Her fire was high and warm, lamps were lit and candles had been placed all around, including one that flickered in the window. A beacon to bring Jeremy home.

There was hardly a shadow in the room. Tonight, whatever happened would happen in the light. Which was a rather terrifying thought. But Penelope straightened her shoulders and called upon all her strength. She didn't want to live with questions or regrets, so this was her only choice.

She heard the window click behind her and turned slowly to watch Jeremy climb in over the ledge. Like her, he was wearing his finest clothing. Dark evening clothes with a silver waistcoat and an impeccably tied cravat. She looked down at herself with a smile, she too had donned her best. A blue gown sewn through with silver that matched his waistcoat perfectly.

Penelope decided to take it as a sign and moved toward him.

"It seems as though we had a similar idea," she said with a shaky motion toward her outfit.

Jeremy didn't smile, just let his eyes move over her. She blushed under the heated scrutiny, but forced herself not to look away.

"You have seen the very worst of me," he finally said softly, meeting her stare. "I thought the least I owed you was my best."

"Will you sit with me?" she asked, motioning to the chairs beside the fire.

She didn't miss how his gaze moved to the bed briefly, but he followed her to the sitting area without comment. They settled in, and she poured him a glass of her finest port, as well as wine for herself. He set the drink aside without touching it and looked at her.

"I am glad you invited me here tonight, though I was surprised," he said. "Especially after you would not see me yesterday."

She blushed. "I was so upset and confused. I couldn't face you."

"I understand." His chin dipped down. "I am sorry for all the pain I caused you. For every lie I told you."

Penelope drew in a breath. She had never seen Jeremy look so . . . forlorn. It was a revelation, but was it real? Or just another manipulation?

"I have a hard time having faith," she whispered. "I *want* to believe that you are sorry. That this isn't just some lie you are telling in order to bend me to your will. But I keep thinking of all the other things you said. The untruths."

He nodded as he fingered the stem of his glass. "I understand that, Penelope. I violated your trust. I know that it may take a long time to regain it. Perhaps I never will. But I want to try. And I will change, I will show you how I've changed."

She straightened up. "Changed? How do you mean?"

He frowned. "I have severed ties with the Nevers."

She gasped. "So Ethan was right? Your harsh words with Wharton ended all your friendships?"

He lifted his gaze and shook his head. "I see that your brother-in-law has spoken to you, despite my request that he not repeat what I had done."

"He did," Penelope admitted. "But I'm glad he broke your silence."

Jeremy shook his head, and she sensed his frustration. "But I did not confront Wharton as some kind of manipulate to you. I did it because I do not believe a man should raise a hand to a woman. No one should be forced to another's will and punished with violence if she will not bend. No matter what you think you know of me, I hope you know that."

Penelope nodded immediately. Once she hadn't been so certain, but she now knew this man before her better.

"I do."

A flash of relief softened Jeremy's expression. "After my encounter, I wrote a letter to the others, explaining that I could no longer be a part of the group. I'm sure I will remain friends with some of the men. But I do not want to associate myself with their reputation anymore."

Penelope tilted her head. "How long have you been friends with those men?"

He hesitated, and she saw a hint of pain around his eyes. "Most of my life, my lady."

"And you gave those friendships up, just for the hope that I might someday see you have truly changed and forgive you?"

He met her eyes. His were so dark that she could lose herself in them. And sad. Almost unbearably sad. It was the first time she had ever seen Jeremy reveal his inner feelings so plainly.

"I do not want your forgiveness, Penelope," he said, his voice as rough as he had always made it as her secret lover. "I *need* it. And I will do anything to earn it. And your love."

Penelope rose to her feet and looked down at him. He did not rise, but he did hold her stare. "Do you want my love, Jeremy?"

He nodded. "More than anything. I love you, Penelope Norman."

Penelope staggered back a step, biting a cry of surprise off before it could leave her lips. Slowly, Jeremy got to his feet, but he did not advance on her.

"You don't have to believe that now," he said. "But you should know that I intend to prove it to you. Every day. For the rest of my life. And one day, I aspire to deserve your love in return."

Penelope swallowed. Jeremy had just laid out all her hopes, her dreams in front of her. Spread them out in offering. But he didn't demand she take them. He simply showed her that they were there for her when she was ready.

She looked into his eyes. For the first time since she met him, there was nothing hidden there. His emotions, the dark and the noble, were as bright and clear as the light that flooded her bedchamber.

Her hands trembled as she moved toward him. He stiffened,

but did not reach for her. Did not draw her into his embrace and force her to his will. As she fisted her fingers around his jacket lapels, he merely sucked in a ragged breath and stared down at her in waiting.

"Let us aspire to deserve each other's love," she whispered. "Because I do love you, Jeremy. I love you with all my heart. And I know I have done things that were foolhardy and silly. I have been bitter and angry with the world. I don't want to be those things anymore. And with you, I am not."

She lifted up on her tiptoes, coming in for the kiss she had been craving since the moment he came through her window. "Will you take a chance on a future with me?"

His arms finally came around her waist and Jeremy pulled her to his chest. Their bodies molded, and his mouth came down toward hers.

"It isn't a chance, Penelope. It's a guarantee." He pressed his lips to hers, drawing her even closer as their mouths merged with passion and love.

"A guarantee of happiness," he whispered before he kissed her again. "And pleasure." He cupped the back of her neck and glided his lips to her throat. "And reckless abandon for the rest of our lives."

Penelope drew back and looked up into the eyes of the man she loved. "I will take that guarantee, Your Grace. But I think we should seal the bargain with a kiss."

Jeremy smiled as he began to back her toward her bed. "Where shall I begin, my lady? I would like to seal the bargain more than once tonight."

Jess Michaels

JESS MICHAELS always flips through every romance she buys in search of "the good stuff," so it makes perfect sense that she writes erotic romance where she gets to turn up the heat on that good stuff and let it boil. She loves alpha males, long-haired cats (and short-haired ones), the last breath right before a passionate kiss, and the color purple (not the movie, though, that's excellent, too, the actual color). She firmly believes that Cadbury Creme Eggs should be available all year round and not count against any diet.

Jess loves to hear from readers. You can find her online at _www.jessmichaels.com._